The Ticking Tenure Clock

The Ticking Tenure Clock

An Academic Novel

Blaire French

State University of New York Press

Cover painting, "Fayerweather Hall," by Richard Crozier.
Reprinted by permission of Richard Crozier.

Production by Ruth Fisher
Marketing by Dana E. Yanulavich

Published by
State University of New York Press, Albany

© 1998 State University of New York

For information, address the State University of New York Press,
State University Plaza, Albany, NY 12246

Library of Congress Cataloging-in-Publication Data

French, Blaire Atherton.
  The ticking tenure clock : an academic novel / Blaire French.
      p.   cm.
  ISBN 0-7914-3935-6 (HC : acid free).
  I. Title
PS3556.R397T5   1998
813′.54—dc21   98-13323
                                                    CIP

10   9   8   7   6   5   4   3   2

To Jim

Do you hear that ticking? No, you wouldn't, I suppose. It's sort of an internal thing, like my biological clock, only I hit the permanent snooze button on *that* thing a long time ago. I'm referring instead to the sound of the seconds vanishing on my tenure clock. It started up when Patrick Henry University in Albemarle, Virginia, hired me to teach political science six years ago. What happens at the end of six years is that the senior members in my department vote on whether they think I show great promise as a scholar. If the answer is yes, I win a lifetime membership, all expenses paid, as a university professor. If the answer is no, I receive my walking papers with a one-year deadline for clearing out.

I should know very soon whether I walk or dance. My department is meeting now to make its decision.

My name is Damocles.

No, that's not true—it's Lydia Martin. Speaking as a political scientist, I'd describe myself as white, single, thirty-three, and with a history of voting as an independent. I have no religious convictions to speak of, although in times of great duress I've been known to reconsider my options.

Like now.

I haven't always been worried. In fact, up until just about a year ago, I'd have told you I fell into the shoo-in category. But that was before the Great Sea Change.

I remember the day exactly, a dreary Thursday in mid-November. On that particular afternoon I was studying my little desk calendar, contemplating a weekend of skiing over Thanksgiving break. I was thinking something low-budget, like one of those resorts in West Virginia. I'd have to take a chance on the weather, but it was West Virginia or nothing. Unlike most of my students, I couldn't afford a trip to Stowe or Banff where there was sure to be snow, real or otherwise. In one of my classes a few days earlier, I had overheard someone saying he wasn't going anywhere for the break. I perked up, thinking at last I had found an undergraduate whose standard of living was not higher than my own. That was until I heard him add that he would, however, be spending Christmas vacation with his family in the French Alps.

That's nice, his friend answered.

I sighed and put down my calendar. Someday, I told myself, you, too, will be staking out a spot in the lift line at Mont Blanc. Someday, when you've made it—when you're a whale.

Just then there was a knock on my door.

"Lydia? Are you in there? It's me, Pam."

I got up to open the door. "Come on in," I said. "Have a seat."

I wasn't surprised to see her. Pam usually stopped by at least once a week to talk. She and I were the only two women out of a total of thirty-five faculty members in the political science department. Pam automatically assumed that we therefore had a special bond. I didn't necessarily feel it. After all, she had just been hired and was going through the usual first-year drowning ritual. Her area was Western European politics and mine was American government—so there was little overlap of interest there. But, by my calculation, there was also no threat. Pam was harmless, you could see that in the way she always offered to help. Every time I passed her office, there was a line of students waiting to talk to her. Already she had approached the chairman about coordinating courses with other departments and bringing in guest speakers. He barely managed to contain his glee as he handed over the first few administrative tasks. Here was another sucker in the hatching.

As for looks, Pam was pretty in a nonobvious way. She had medium brown hair of medium length and was neither tall nor short, fat nor thin. She wore suits of jackets and matching skirts, those uniforms of professional women everywhere. I wore them, too, but managed to avoid the coordinated scarves and pins Pam favored. Plus, I was taller and leaner, and could get away with more stylish cuts and lengths. I kept my auburn hair trendily short, my face makeup-free, and cultivated the air of someone who would know the best Thai restaurant in town, if there were any. But Pam had something I didn't have—a warmth of expression in her medium brown eyes that practically screamed I AM A CARING PERSON at you.

If I had those eyes, I thought, I'd wear dark glasses.

At that moment, however, she looked unusually frazzled.

"Have you heard the news?" she asked, breathless.

"No," I said. "What news?"

She gave a quick glance outside and then closed the door.

"You had better sit," she said, and I did. She pulled a chair up to my desk.

"What is it?" I asked. "Did somebody die?"

She nodded. "Sort of. Word has just gone out. Walter Kravitz went down."

"Walter? Walter went down?"

"Yes. Can you believe it? He didn't even make it out of the department."

I sat back, stunned. No, I couldn't believe it. Walter Kravitz had been denied tenure, and denied at the lowest level of review. He had not even had the opportunity to be swatted down by the dreaded dean's committee, which could and often did overturn a department's favorable recommendation.

"But ... but why? He had a book, and at least three articles." Even as I spoke, my eyes scanned the bookcase against the wall and picked out the white dust jacket almost immediately: *When Tyrants Speak: The Manipulation of Language Within Totalitarian Regimes*. It had come out last April, a few weeks before the publication of my own book, and we had exchanged copies as a way of congratulating each other. At the time I remembered thinking how alike we were, two confident minnows knocking on the gates of cetacean paradise.

"I know. But get this. They said one book wasn't enough, not any more."

They. *They*, of course, were the whales, the tenured members in the department, all of associate or full professor rank. The older whales, the ones above the sixty-year mark, had come up in the profession in a different era with different standards. Thirty years ago, just *having* a Ph.D. had been sufficient to see you through the tenure door in some places, Patrick Henry University included. But in the intervening years competition for teaching positions everywhere had grown by leaps and bounds, so naturally qualification standards had shot up, too. And now, Pam was telling me, a new level had been set: One book is no longer enough.

"How can they do this?" I asked.

"It's completely unfair," she said. "Walter's book is good, or at least I heard it got decent reviews. And he's published a bunch of articles. Sure, maybe he isn't working on something right this second, but come on! His wife just had another baby, after all. That makes three kids, right? Now he has to find another job by next year. Do you know how tough it is these days to get a political theory position? What in the world is he going to do?"

But right at that moment I wasn't thinking about Walter. I was thinking about me. What was *I* going to do? What was going to happen to *me*?

I'd only published one book, too. It was called *Bringing in the Green: Profit as Incentive in the Environmentalist Movement*. It showed how amidst the environmental zealots there are a good number of savvy businesspeople. Specifically I did a study of the folks who years ago helped write the tax breaks and incentives for windmills and solar energy panels, and then subsequently went into the alternative fuel business themselves. They ended up turning sunbeams into a cash crop, and reaped a hefty profit.

The book got good reviews. The *American Political Science Review* called it the best book on interest-group politics to be published that year. The *Journal of Politics* said it was a "must read" for organizational theorists. Even *The Wall Street Journal* included it in one of its book review roundups, saying, "*Bringing in the Green* shows that some environmentalists *do* live in glass houses."

My mail picked up. I received an invitation to present a paper at the yearly American Political Science Association convention. A think tank in Washington, D.C., asked me to participate in one of their panel discussions. (A televised broadcast of the session aired at 2 A.M. on C-Span. I taped it and sent a copy to my parents.) After a few months, I even got a royalty check. All in all, to my mind it was beginning to look distinctly like whale mail.

Except of course for the letters from those readers who hated the book. And there were quite a few. They thought *Bringing in the Green* was an attack on the noblest cause in the world, and that I was an oily tool of Imperialist Petroleum, Inc. I responded to everyone, telling them I never meant to insult the environmental movement. What I really wanted to say was, Read a book, any book, on organizations and you'll find that even in the most ideologically righteous groups there lurks the dreaded profit motive. It can take different forms, such as a desire for personal perks, power, and—yes—money. But it is always there, in someone somewhere within the fold. Count on it.

To paraphrase one of my heroes, James Madison, if men were angels, we wouldn't need Earth Day. At least the entrepreneurs in my study really *did* clean up while they cleaned up. Surely, I thought, that must count for something.

Looking back, at the time I must have radiated an invisible sensory field of tenurability. Some of my colleagues, the ones junior to myself, began asking me to read snippets of their works-in-progress and sought my advice on which publishers they should contact. For the first time I felt the gentle nips and tugs of minnow lips on my own minnow tail.

I have to admit, I liked it. I dispensed my opinion freely and in a variety of postures—leaning jauntily against the door frame of my office or with one hand cradling a glass of wine at a dinner party. The more I spoke, the more acutely I detected signs of nascent spout formation. So this is it, I thought. Transmogrification is under way.

Or so I believed until Pam walked in and delivered her little bombshell.

"This is terrible, just terrible," I said.

"Isn't it?" Pam sighed and shook her head. "I guess the vote was taken yesterday and that's when Walter found out. I knocked on his office door a little while ago to tell him how sorry I am but he wasn't in. I don't want to call his home—I don't really know his wife and it must be hard enough on her right now without having to talk to strangers about this. You know her, don't you?"

"Shelly? Yes, of course."

"Well, if you call, please say I'm thinking of them and that if there's anything I can do, anything at all, they only have to ask."

"Okay. Sure," I said.

She got up. "Well, I have to go prepare for class, so I'll let you get back to whatever it was you were doing before I barged in. Seems as if you're always working. I guess you won't have much to worry about when *your* turn comes next fall. Talk about someone who's got a million irons in the fire. . . . See you."

"See you," I said, and answered her farewell wave with a weak fluttering of my own fingers. As soon as the door closed I sat forward, head in my hands.

"Damn!" I said. A million irons in the fire! All I had going at the moment were a few spinoff articles from the book, hardly the stuff of impressive new research. What was I going to do?

I squinted back at the cardboard calendar. November. I had nine months to write a book, or at least something that someone could possibly say could be a book at some future time.

Nine months.

Just like having a baby, I thought. Easy. No problem. I can do this.

Before my eyes, my skiing weekend took flight. It was clear I'd be spending the Thanksgiving break in the library. Gone was West Virginia, wiped clean off the map. But it was a small sacrifice to make in the scheme of things—so long as I got to keep Mont Blanc.

T he next morning, I received a message via E-mail from my department chairman, Tom Shepherd. He had called an urgent meeting with the assistant professors to discuss "recent departmental actions."

In addition to Pam, Walter, and myself, there were four other untenured faculty members: Victor Garshin, the department's expert on Eastern Europe, whose wire-rimmed glasses failed to conceal a chronic blink; constitutional law scholar Felix Wright, the only one of us who could afford tailored suits and a fifty-dollar haircut; Danny Yamashita, a second-generation Japanese-American who taught Asian politics and had to be the very first male professor at Patrick Henry to sport an earring; and the department's most active jock, Karl Willis, whose area covered political economy.

Not counting Walter (and who could count him now?), Victor and I were the most senior of the juniors. We had been hired the same year, which meant we also had the same tenure clock and were due to come up together before the department. You might think our situation would be grounds for dispensing mutual support and understanding, but such was not the case. Victor had problems that sympathy couldn't solve, like a first book that had gotten only mediocre reviews and a publisher who was late sending his second book to press. For months he'd been asking everybody if he should try another publisher, and the longer he debated, the less he could afford to pull out. With the passage of time his tics grew progressively worse, and by the beginning of that fall semester he'd picked up a new habit of pulling on his tie. It had begun to look like the pressure was literally choking him to death, and I avoided him as much as possible.

Plus, I suspected that being around me provoked these nervous attacks. The department party line was that two people in two different subfields were not in competition with each other for tenure. The truth of the matter, however, was that budget constraints at Patrick Henry limited the number of professors who could be given permanent positions. Comparisons were inevitable, and at the time there seemed to be no question who the department would choose if one of us had to be sacrificed. *My* book, after all, had made something of a splash.

The meeting was set for ten o'clock. I arrived at the chairman's office a few minutes before the appointed hour to find all the other assistants—save Walter, of course—already waiting.

"Hi, everyone," I said.

Victor nodded, blinking hard, and then continued his conversation with Danny.

"How's it going?" Karl asked me. His athletic good looks always made our conversations a pleasure. Today, however, I noticed a few lines around his eyes and mouth showing through the tennis tan. I guessed he hadn't had that great a night's sleep either.

"Okay," I said. "And you?"

He glanced around the group. "I think I'm still in shock. You know, about Walter."

"We all are," Felix said. His closely shaven babyface cheeks were as smooth as ever. I got a whiff of his cologne. It smelled nice, whatever it was. "Who would have thought he'd go down?"

"Has anyone spoken with him yet?" Pam asked.

I shook my head. So did Karl and Felix.

Just then Tom Shepherd opened his door. He was the department's only Virginia native, as well as its sole breeder of champion foxhounds. He himself had something of a pedigree, coming from old Albemarle stock. What always amazed me was how he managed to combine the progressive political views of a liberal academic with the habits of his class. The result was a chairman who tolerated male jewelry while remaining a member in good standing of the Melilot Country Club (once all white, now only ninety-nine percent so).

He tilted his head down to look at us through the top half of his bi-focals, a shock of light brown hair falling over his forehead.

"Good, you're all here," he said in his exaggerated drawl. No other Virginian I'd ever met had such a strong accent, and I suspected Tom cultivated his for effect. "Come in and let's get started. I'm afraid there aren't enough chairs for everyone, but this shouldn't take too long."

We filed inside. I declined a seat and leaned against the wall. Tom sat at his desk and waited until we were settled before he began.

"This is a busy time for all of us, so I'll get right to the point," he said. "By now I'm sure you've heard that Walter Kravitz has been denied tenure. Needless to say, the department is sorry to lose him."

We shuffled our feet and mumbled something like yes, sure, of course.

So much for Walter.

"As sad as the situation is for our colleague, however, I think it's important to understand *why* he failed to win the support of the department. It's crucial that none of you makes the same mistake."

There was no mumbling this time, only obedient nods.

His gaze wandered over the group. "The problem with Walter was that he waited too long to finish his book. He should have gotten it out last year, and left himself some time to begin work on another project. As it stood, it appeared as though Walter had written his book for the *sole purpose of getting tenure*."

He paused, letting the words hang in the air. We looked at each other. And? So? Wasn't that what he was supposed to do?

"I want each of you to think about your own situation. You should examine your rate of progress with an eye to avoiding the tenure rush."

The tenure *rush*? Did anyone truly think that Walter had twiddled his thumbs for four years and then suddenly dashed off a book to make himself look good? Surely Tom had to be kidding.

But then again, maybe not. Tom wouldn't really know much about such things. He himself had written only one book, and that was many years ago. It was a textbook on southern state politics, a compendium of rules and procedures with some historical perspective thrown in. In the 1960s it was required reading throughout several southern state university systems in political science courses. With the help of graduate students, Tom kept it updated with revised editions every few years. Eventually other books had come along to crowd him out of his niche, but that was long after he had achieved full professor status.

Never mind that such a book would never meet the current definition of original research. No, Tom was not the least bit self-conscious as he dismissed Walter with a wag of his finger and a tsk, tsk, tsk! In fact, he seemed rather proud that Walter had not succeeded in pulling the wool over anyone's eyes. Just one book? Who did Walter think he was fooling!

"So. That's all I wanted to say. I know it's frightening when a colleague is denied tenure, but it is within the power of each and every one of you to protect yourself from the same fate. And I have confidence that you will. Any questions?"

"I have one," Danny said. "What does this mean for renewal?" he asked. "Have the standards changed for that, too?"

Renewal occurred in an assistant professor's third year of teaching. It was like a mini-review of one's progress, and had always been a perfunctory departmental exercise. Everyone knew that Danny was up for a decision that semester.

Tom gave him a sharp look. "The standards haven't exactly *changed*," he said. "To receive tenure, it's always been imperative that a person show great promise as a scholar. All we want to see now is a little more proof of that potential. As for renewal, I suppose you could say that you would be much better off if you had your first book almost done. Of course we won't expect it to *be* finished. That would be asking too much. But it should be close. Does that answer your question?"

Danny nodded. A slight sheen glistened his brow.

"Anyone else?" Tom asked, looking around. He made it sound like a challenge.

"Yes," Felix said. He put up his hand like a schoolboy, and then dropped it. "Are you saying that the department now expects us to have two books *out* by tenure time?"

"Not necessarily," Tom said.

Victor cleared his throat. "What about one book and a completed manuscript? Is that good enough?"

"It might be, but there's always the question of the quality of the work, now isn't there?" Tom said. There was no mistaking the irritation in his voice. He appeared to catch himself and tried for a smile. "Look, people. The point is simple. The department wants to tenure those who are truly committed to the academic enterprise. No resting on laurels. You can't come out with a single solitary book, dust off your hands, and say 'Okay, I'm done now.' We expect to see some demonstration of ongoing, dynamic, and *fruitful* scholarship in your particular field. Clear enough?"

No one spoke.

"Good," he said, and glanced at his watch. "In that case, I'll let you go. I've got a meeting with the dean in five minutes. If I don't see you, have a good Thanksgiving."

We left the office and spilled out into the hall. We didn't say anything right away—not until we'd moved a discreet distance from Tom's door.

"Can you believe that?" Pam began in a hushed voice.

Felix shook his head. "We have no choice *but* to believe it. We have *prima facie* evidence: Walter."

"Jesus!" Karl said. "As if we didn't have enough pressure on us already. Don't they realize that?"

"Oh, relax. It's not so bad," Victor said.

"Easy for you to say," Danny said. "You've *got* a second book, or at least you will have soon."

Victor waved away his worry. "There's no need to panic. Come on. Surely if I can do it, you can, too," he said.

This was a new tone for him, brimming with a Buck Up! brand of encouragement. I recognized it because it used to be *my* tone. It occurred to me that perhaps more than the publication requirements had changed. The balance between Victor and myself was also shifting.

"We haven't heard from you, Lydia," Felix said. "What's your assessment of the situation?"

I shrugged. I wasn't about to give up the high ground of indifference to Victor, of all people. "Oh, I suppose we'll just have to put the pedal to the floor on our current projects, that's all. I was counting on the summer to finish up my next book, but if I have to have it done earlier, so be it."

The lie won me the admiring looks I'd grown to know and love from Felix, Karl, Danny, and Pam. From Victor I got a blink and a tug, which was all I was really after anyway.

Less than an hour later I was lecturing in front of one hundred and twenty-five undergraduate students. I was not at my best, but it could have been as much the fault of the subject matter as my distracted discourse. I mean, it's hard to make a description of the separation-of-powers system fascinating. But it didn't really matter. Whatever I said I could always count on seeing one hundred and twenty-five pens scribbling notes in one hundred and twenty-five notebooks. Fascination is not important for students— getting a good grade on the exam is, as any professor who has ever tried handing out a C will attest.

Of course, my graduate student teaching assistants were the ones who battled on the front line with the students over their grades. I was only called upon to serve as a court of last appeal. Invariably I backed up my teaching assistants—not, however, out of any sense of solidarity with them. No, the reason I sided with my assistants was because almost all the protesting students presented the same argument. They believed that since they *needed* a good grade, they should *have* one. If I pointed out that they had failed to answer a question on the exam or to make the necessary point in their paper, they responded, "But I'm trying to get into law school," or, "But I have to pass this course to graduate."

Then you should have studied, I always tell them. They look at me like that was just about the cruellest thing they'd ever heard.

When my lecture was over there were the usual three or four students who came up to ask questions. They were brown-nosing, but I didn't mind. Five minutes a day of intellectual exchange with undergraduates was just about right. Then I headed back to my office through the noon-hour crush in the corridors.

I was looking forward to a quiet lunch at my desk, more for the purpose of digesting the morning's developments than my chicken salad sandwich. But as I turned the last corner I saw Pam waiting in front of my office. Beside her stood one of the department's graduate students, Tony Donatello.

"Hi," she said. "Do you have a minute?"

"Sure," I said, unlocking my door. "Come on in. How are you, Tony?"

Tony had been in a couple of my seminars in the past few years, and I liked him because he was both hard-working and smart. He had a dark Mediterranean look, with a smile that must have won him quite a few dates. On this day, however, I saw no trace of it.

"Good, thanks, Professor Martin."

"So, what's up?" I asked when we were all seated.

Pam looked at Tony while he intently studied the linoleum tiles. His leg jiggled up and down like a steam piston.

Pam turned her warm brown eyes back to me. "Lydia, we have a problem."

Whoa, I wanted to say. Who's "we"?

Instead I tilted my head in a politely inquisitive manner. "Oh?"

"Yes," she said. "You see, Tony here is in sort of a fix. He needs a new director for his dissertation. I told him I thought you'd be the perfect person."

"Me?" I looked back at Tony, but he was still memorizing the speckle pattern beneath his feet. "But surely for his first reader he should have someone more established. I don't even have tenure yet." I paused. "What's your topic, Tony?"

Tony raised his head to answer. His leg jiggled even faster. "Nonvoters. I want to research how many nonvoters in the last presidential election *chose* not to vote instead of simply having been hampered from voting by circumstances."

"How do you plan to do this research?" I asked.

"Through polling."

I sat back. "Professor Tanner's the one you should be asking, not me. Electoral studies are his bread and butter. Plus, he's got the big name and all kinds of money. Polls are expensive to conduct, really expensive. And Professor Tanner has a polling center already set up and fully funded. Of course I'd be pleased to serve as your second reader, but clearly you'd be much better off working with him as your first."

Tony didn't say anything. Instead his gaze sank back to the floor.

Pam sat up straighter. "Uh, Lydia, I'm afraid that isn't an option. Bill had originally agreed to direct Tony's dissertation, but recently they've had a significant difference of opinion. Tony needs to find someone else to help him."

Double whoa. Tony was on the outs with Bill Tanner? I felt like crossing my fingers against the evil eye or throwing salt over my shoulder. This was not good.

Bill Tanner was the senior American government scholar. His territory of expertise was vast, covering the presidency, political parties, and the nominating process in campaigns and elections. Everyone also acknowledged him to be thoroughly knowledgeable about interest groups, and thus eminently qualified to pass judgment on me.

All indications were that Bill was willing to abide a colleague who studied fringe groups—as long as that colleague was herself peripheral. Peripheral here meant someone whom the local television stations did not interview for comments on the upcoming national election, and to whom *USA Today* reporters did not turn when they needed some analysis of the current political climate.

No, when the media called, it was Bill Tanner who answered. He himself had made this particular point clear to me one day when my name had popped up on page A13 of the local newspaper. A journalist for the *Albemarle Register* had called the political science department the day before, asking to talk to someone about lobbyists in Washington. Being the only professor the secretary could get hold of at the time, I had the honor. All the reporter wanted was a quote to fill out his story, so I gave him one: "A good lobbyist knows Congress, in the biblical sense."

Granted, when I read it in the paper the next day it did look like a fairly flippant thing to say. But I figured, who's going to see this? I was not only below the fold, I was nudging up against the classifieds.

I failed to take into account the magnified effect of a single ripple within the wide sea. When I checked my mail in the department office that afternoon, there was a note from Bill asking to see me.

Bill was young by full-professor standards—only forty-eight. Of all the whales he had the highest profile, and definitely fell within the national heavyweight division. Often you'd see him striding down the hall, a carry-on-size suitcase in hand, hurrying to the airport to catch a plane. Sometimes he was off to give a lecture at another university (for a $1,000 honorarium, plus expenses), or to participate in a three-day conference at a yacht club in Newport Beach (sponsored by a private think tank), or to tour Europe giving talks for the United States Information Agency (paid for by you and me). Or sometimes you'd see him striding without a suitcase, hurrying downtown to the local TV station to hook up by satellite with Dan or Peter or Tom (as in Rather, Jennings, and Brokaw). He'd even appeared on the *Jim Lehrer Newshour* a few times, and said "Jim" in a way that made you think he and Lehrer had actually met.

He had the perfect look for television, combining a boyish smile with a distinguished touch of gray at the temples. He also had bright icy blue eyes, which had shot up at me when he saw me at the door with his note in my hand.

"Come in, Lydia! Come in! Please, have a seat."

"I don't want to interrupt," I said, easing myself down into the chair across from his desk. "You look busy."

"Oh, I'm going over the results of last week's CBS/*New York Times* polling data. You know, just checking the pulse."

I smiled. "Is the patient still alive?"

He gave me only half a smile in return. "I know you're trying to be clever. But surely as a political scientist you would not wish to suggest that the voting public is moribund?"

My smile vanished. "No, no, not at all. It was just a joke. I really didn't mean anything by it."

He sat back and pursed his lips. "Of course. But it does sound a tad cynical. That's why I asked you to drop by. I saw your quote today in the *Albemarle Register*."

"Oh," I said.

"Yes. All in all, I was happy to see that the paper has begun to take some notice of the fresh faces around here. The junior members of this department are a terrific resource."

He paused, and I said nothing. With one finger he smoothed an eyebrow.

"But I did find your statement to be in somewhat question-able taste, especially coming from a scholar like yourself."

I straightened. "Well, I didn't mean much by it. I was only trying to give a new spin on the old word 'bedfellows,' and certainly in the case of Congress and lobbyists the description fits."

"So you say, so you say," Bill said, and rocked back in his chair. "But let me ask you this. When you cover Congress in your Introduction to American Government course, is that what you tell your students, that senators and representatives are in bed with special interest groups?"

"Uh, no, not in so many words," I answered, my grip on the armrests tightening.

"What do you tell them, then? In so many words."

I took a couple of deep breaths and fought down the impulse to hyperventilate. "Let's see. I tell them that a lobbyist serves vari-ous functions, often providing members of Congress with informa-tion they would never have time to find on their own. Senators and representatives quickly learn which lobbyists give them the full story on an issue, and any lobbyist who gives misleading information once seldom gets the chance to do it again. In addition, lobbyists usually only try to influence those politicians whom they feel are already predisposed to listen to them. The successful lobbyists match their special interests to the particular member's own interests."

He nodded. "Now that's a much more illuminating—and dignified—description of the relationship. I think, as part of our jobs as political scientists, it is important that we show our respect for the institutions of government, whether our forum is the class-room or the local newspaper. Do you understand what I'm saying?"

I nodded. "Yes, Bill. I think I do."

He flashed me the boyish smile. "Good. Don't get me wrong—I know how tough it can be when the phone rings and there's some reporter on the line who expects you to come up with on-the-spot analysis. It takes some practice to know how to handle that sort of thing. My advice to you is, next time just pass them over to me. If I'm not here, you can tell them to call the department main office and leave a number with the secretary. I always return calls. Always."

"I'll be sure to do that," I said. I waited a moment in case there was more, but he didn't say anything. "Well," I said, smiling, and reached for my purse. "I guess I'd better be on my way to class."

"I'm glad you stopped in, Lydia, and I hope you really do understand. As a member of the faculty, what you say matters. Our department needs a fine scholar such as yourself, and I don't want anything to diminish the high esteem people have for you. We really think a lot of you around here, Lydia."

"Thanks. I appreciate that." I rose. "Goodbye, Bill."

"Take care, Lydia."

I started walking and didn't stop until I'd reached my office and closed the door behind me. My heart felt as big as a basketball thudding against my chest. I didn't need neon lights or ten-foot-high letters, or, for that matter, a pair of icy-blue daggers—I had gotten the message.

Thereafter, whenever I saw Bill he always said, "Keep up the good work." I assumed he was congratulating me on keeping out of the papers. And out of his way.

Which I did, gladly.

I admit it seems awfully weak to accept without protest such patronizing and condescending treatment. But I had long ago decided to live by something I called the Roll Over Rule. It went like this: My mission was to get tenure, and until I got it I would roll over in all conflict with whales. I was willing to endure six years of submissiveness in return for a lifetime of freedom.

And, after hearing of Tony Donatello's predicament that day in my office, it was clear to me that Tony had not even learned the rudimentary gestures of self-protection necessary to survive life as a graduate student. I cleared my throat.

"Really, Pam, I don't think I'm the right choice for a first reader. Tony needs someone who is thoroughly familiar with the nonvoting data, and that's Bill. I don't know what the problem is, but maybe if Tony talks to Professor Tanner they can straighten out their differences."

"*No.*"

I turned back to Tony, surprised at his tone. His gaze once again met mine, but this time his eyes were blazing.

"*No,*" he repeated. "I will never work with him, ever! He's already stolen one idea from me. I won't let him steal any more."

"That's a very serious allegation, Tony," I said. "I'm sure you don't really mean to suggest—"

"Yes, he does, Lydia," Pam said.

"Pam—" I gave her what I hoped was a warning look. There was an unwritten law that junior faculty did not criticize anyone senior in front of graduate students, the idea being that eventually the senior person will hear about it.

"Tell her the story, Tony."

"Last semester I took his seminar on public opinion," he began. "We were supposed to do some original research—you know, conduct our own poll and analyze the information ourselves. We had unlimited access to the polling center and all the data banks there. The other students chose to do pretty big projects, polling state-wide. But I decided to do something with the students here at the university. I wanted to study their attitudes toward the political parties, and whether they felt any connection to them and why or why not. So I did a survey. The results were pretty interesting."

I don't want to hear this, I thought.

"I mean, they weren't revolutionary or anything," he went on. "They confirmed the trend you see reported everywhere for the same age group. You know, the students have a more conservative outlook generally than the last generation and they don't have much attachment to the parties. But there were some unexpected twists, small but significant, that showed where parties could make some effective appeals. I wrote up my analysis as if I were a consultant, first giving advice to the Democrats and then to the Republicans. Tanner really liked it. He gave me an A."

"Sounds like you did a good job," I said.

"Yeah, well, some of the other students thought I should try and get it published or something, but Tanner said no. He said the scope of the poll was too small to mean all that much. So come the end of the semester last May, I put the paper away and forgot about it."

He paused and then continued.

"Well, I went to the American Political Science Association convention in D.C. this past August, just before school began. Tanner was presenting a paper for one of the panels, so I thought, what the heck, I'll go hear him. Did you go to that panel?"

I shook my head.

"His presentation was called 'The Campus Vote: New Toeholds for Political Parties.' It was my paper. He presented *my* paper."

I shook my head again. "Tony, wait just a second. Are you telling me that Professor Tanner lifted your paper word for word?"

"Well, no, not word for word, but he took my idea, he used the same survey methods, and he came to the same conclusions."

"And you talked to him about this?"

"Yes, afterward. I confronted him as soon as the panel was over."

"What did he say?"

"He told me that I was exaggerating the similarities, that his ideas and mine were close but not identical. Plus, he implied that I had originally gotten *my* idea from his lectures anyway."

"And you'd used his computer lab data banks," I added.

Tony stopped and gave me a look. "You don't believe me," he said.

"I believe that *you* believe that Professor Tanner may have built on a few of your ideas—"

"*Built* on?" Tony cried. "Professor Martin, this guy ripped me off!"

"Look," I said, "I'm sure you're reading a lot more into this than is there. Professor Tanner is a top-notch political scientist, not the sort of person who steals ideas from students."

"Forget it," Tony said, getting to his feet. "Just forget the whole thing, okay?" He strode toward the door and slammed it behind him.

"Tony—" Pam said, but he was gone. She sighed and rubbed her forehead before looking back at me. "You don't believe him?" she asked.

"Do you?"

She grimaced. "I don't know. When I was a graduate student I heard all sorts of stories about professors who used students to do their research and then never gave them credit for the work. Still, it is pretty hard to imagine Bill doing such a thing. But I also know Tony. He wouldn't make something like this up."

"Pam, you know how graduate students are—they're desperate to believe that they'll amount to something someday. And if you can convince yourself that a professor got an important idea from you, well, then that's a sort of self-validation."

"I suppose you're right. But that still leaves Tony. What's he going to do? Bill won't work with him, he's made that clear."

"I still think my suggestion is the best," I said. "Let him make up with Bill. Or at least try. Otherwise, Tony doesn't have a prayer. Even if he manages to find someone else to direct his dissertation, he'll never get a job anywhere if Bill is against him."

"So that means you won't do it?" she said.

"I just don't think I'm the right one," I said, trying to sound as though I'd truly considered touching him with something less than a ten-foot pole.

"Okay," Pam said, getting up. "Thanks anyway. I guess that leaves Hamilton."

"Hamilton Farrell? Are you kidding? His graduate students never finish. He's had some writing and rewriting their dissertations for five and six years."

"Well, who else is there?"

"Surely anybody but Farrell. If Tony goes in with him he'll never see daylight."

"Then tell me what other choices Tony has," Pam said. "Hamilton's about the only person in the department left whose area has anything to do with Tony's thesis. Tony has to work with *somebody*."

This was true. Besides, what did I care who Tony hooked up with, so long as it wasn't me?

"Well, maybe Farrell won't be so bad. You never know. But you better tell Tony not to go around accusing Tanner of having stolen his paper. Tony could get himself in a lot of trouble that way."

"I'm going to try to find him now," she said, and walked to the door. "Oh, before I forget—Karl's having a get-together Saturday night. He asked me to tell you."

"Great," I said. "What time?"

"Seven. See you later, Lydia."

"Take it easy, Pam—"

She closed the door behind her.

I sighed and reached for my brown bag. I felt badly for Tony, I really did. But what was I supposed to do? Antagonize Bill Tanner before I'd even had a chance to win him over? Tom Shepherd had put me on the Financial Aid Committee for the next semester. It was an assignment I had requested precisely because Tanner had already been appointed committee chair. It was my one big chance to show him just how peripheral I could be.

When I *had* tenure. . . . Then I could take on Tonys galore.

I pulled some journals out of my satchel to read while eating my sandwich. Not even chicken salad could stand in the way of my toils. There had to be an idea out there somewhere, something I could really sink my teeth into.

I took another bite and read on.

3

The rain had started sometime in the afternoon on Saturday as a cold drizzle. By the time I pulled up in front of Karl's townhouse, it had turned into a downpour.

"Come in!" Emily, Karl's wife, held the door open as I dashed up the walkway.

"It's really coming down," I said, somewhat breathless. "You should see the flooding on the roads. The storm drains are backing up everywhere—they're all clogged with leaves."

She closed the door and the roar of the rain muted. "Here, let me take your umbrella and coat."

"I'm afraid they're both dripping wet," I said, handing them over.

"You're worried about the carpeting?" She laughed. "That's the nice thing about living in faculty housing. You can't do any damage to the place that hasn't already been done."

I didn't know Emily very well. She and Karl had only arrived in Albemarle the year before, the picture of the bright young couple. She was a small person, with pale freckled skin and short curly red hair. I figured she was in her late twenties, like Karl. The last time we'd talked was at the start-of-the-semester cocktail party, held every September. I remembered she worked as an editor for a law professor's research center and was hoping in a few years to go to law school herself.

"How's everything going?" I asked. "How's work?"

"Okay. I just finished a big project today, so I'm definitely in the mood to celebrate."

"Congratulations," I said.

"Thanks. But I'm not so sure it was wise to spend all day going over page proofs," she said, leading the way to the living room. "Karl wound up fixing dinner."

"That's right, so let's not hear any complaints," Karl called out. "Hey, Lydia. You're late. Do you want some wine?"

"Yes, thanks," I said. I nodded to the other guests seated about the room. It was the usual group: Victor and his wife, Julia; Felix and his wife, Gwen; and Danny and Pam.

"We were discussing that little lecture from our beloved chairman a few days ago," Karl said as he handed me a balloon glass brimming with red wine.

"I just said that Felix came home that day with the most awful migraine," Gwen said. She wore her dark brown hair in a ponytail, which emphasized her moonshaped face. Her eyes had a slight droop at the edges, making her look sad even when she smiled. She was a real estate agent by profession, and I assumed she was a good one. Felix's wardrobe hadn't been bought with an assistant professor's salary. "He went right to bed. Honey, how long did you sleep? It was something like twelve hours straight."

"I escaped into the arms of Morpheus," Felix said. "It seemed the most sensible thing to do."

"Thought you could dream up a book?" Karl asked. The joke was more than a little cruel, given that we all knew Felix had only published articles. He'd been through the renewal process last year, and at that time had received a stern warning about his progress in relation to the *old* standards.

"I still don't understand what you're talking about," Julia said. As she spoke she pushed back a curtain of straight black hair. I had heard somewhere that she used to study ballet—she certainly had the build for it. She was what my mother would have called a long drink of water. "What exactly did Tom Shepherd say that has you all so worked up?"

"Oh, come on, Julia—I told you," Victor said.

She turned her gray-eyed gaze on him. "Told me what?"

"That the stakes for tenure have been raised," he said. "Shepherd laid out the new requirements in a meeting the day after we found out about Walter. I know I told you."

"Well, what are they?"

"Two books," Pam said.

"Although one book out and another close on the way is good enough," Victor said.

Julia looked at him. "And what do you have?"

"Jesus Christ," he said. "You're my wife! How could you not know?"

She gave him a tight-lipped smile. "Gee! I guess taking care of our kids all day every day must have done something to my concentration. I can't always remember the really important things, like the latest entry on your vita."

"Oh, you think that's so trivial?" He pushed his glasses back up his nose and started to blink. "Really? Well, see how you feel if I *don't* get tenure. Then you can tell me how little my publications matter."

The rest of us exchanged glances. Victor and Julia's bickering was nothing new. They had moved to Albemarle from Berkeley, California, where Victor had gotten his Ph.D., and now had two very small children. Julia had never quite reconciled herself to being exiled to the East Coast or to the hand-to-mouth existence of an assistant professor with a family and no second wage-earner.

"Here's a good idea," Julia said. "If you're denied tenure, I'll go get a job and you can stay at home. Then you can run around after the kids while I eat your cooking and wear the clothes you've washed. But *I'll* be the only one with a license to bitch and moan. How does that sound?"

"Let's not talk about this now, okay?" Victor said.

"Whatever you say, *honey*," she said. I saw Gwen frown. Julia waved her empty glass. "I'm ready for a refill."

Victor took a big gulp of his own drink and pulled at the knot in his tie.

For a moment we said nothing and shifted awkwardly in our seats. Then Danny broke the silence.

"I still think it's all bullshit," he said.

"What is?" I asked.

"That the standard for tenure has been raised," he said. "If Walter hadn't made so many enemies he'd have sailed through, second book or no second book."

"You think Walter has enemies?" Pam asked.

"Sure. God, are you kidding? The full professors in the department hate him. Don't you remember that flap a couple of years ago?"

"I wasn't around then, remember?" she said.

"But you must know about the stunt Walter pulled."

"What stunt?" Karl said.

"I can't believe no one ever told you the story," Danny said. "I had just started teaching, so it must have been three years ago. Walter kept complaining that his salary was too low, but Shepherd told him that his pay was in line with all the other assistant professors. Of course, there was no way of proving or disproving this since no one ever talks about his salary around here."

This was true. Not even Pam and I had ever compared notes.

Danny went on. "So Walter declared that he was going to take a little trip to Richmond. Since Patrick Henry is a state institution, everyone's salary is a matter of public record. With a little digging you can get all the information. Walter told me later that he did indeed find that what Shepherd had said was true—the assistants as a group were getting lousy pay. But he also looked up all the salaries of the full professors and found some pretty impressive differences. Some of these guys were pulling down seventy, eighty, even over a hundred thousand dollars, and others were making forty-five, fifty thousand tops. So Walter decided to have some fun. He turned the figures over to the student newspaper—anonymously, of course, but everyone knew it was him—and it published everything."

"Wow," Karl said.

"I remember when that story came out," I said. "For a while you couldn't get into Shepherd's office, there was so much traffic from the fulls, with the guys at the bottom of the scale demanding to know why so-and-so was making twice as much as they were. Shepherd almost resigned the chairmanship. It was really wild."

"Yeah, but it was also really dumb," Felix said. "Walter should have known he was buying himself nothing but trouble."

"So that's the reason Walter went down?" Gwen asked. She made a face. "Forget research and books and footnotes. Getting tenure depends on how many people you tick off, that's all."

"But you'd have to say Walter's an extreme case," Danny said. "He managed to tick off many *important* people—like, everybody who had a vote on his case. Usually someone in Walter's position has both enemies and supporters, and the two sides tend to cancel each other out."

"When someone has only enemies, then the old boys start throwing around catchphrases like 'uncollegial behavior' or 'not a team player,'" Victor said. "You could win the Nobel prize and still not get tenure."

"Thank goodness you won't have that problem," Julia drawled. "Winning the Nobel prize, I mean."

"So, what are you saying, Danny?" Pam asked. "Do you really think this talk about needing a second book was just an excuse to get Walter?"

Danny nodded.

"You're probably right," Felix said. "But even if it did start as an excuse it's now precedent—*stare decis*, Patrick Henry style. You heard what Shepherd said when you asked him about renewal. The stakes have been raised for real."

"I disagree," Danny said. "There's no more precedent here than there is in a modern Supreme Court decision. Once Walter's case is over and done with, you won't hear any more about a second book, I guarantee it."

"What about it, Lydia?" Pam asked. "Should we be worried?"

"I don't know," I said. "Maybe Walter's an aberration, but what if he isn't? Does anyone want to take that chance?"

"Well, then I guess this means I'll be sleeping less," Karl said, and sighed. "I don't know where else to cut corners to get more work done."

"It's true," Emily said. "Karl practically lives in his office as it is. It's worse than when he was writing his dissertation."

"You should do what I did," Felix said. "I applied for one of those grants for assistant professors—the university gives you a whole semester off with pay. I'm taking mine this spring to get a running start on a book. You aren't eligible to apply for it yet, though," he told Karl. "The earliest you can take it is in your fourth year."

"You got one of those grants?" Victor asked. "I applied and was turned down flat."

"What did you expect, Victor?" Julia asked. "When has this university ever done anything for you? Or any of you?" she said, looking around. "They pay you a pittance and expect you to be grateful you were ever hired. It's ridiculous the way the department treats its junior faculty members. You're closed out of all the important meetings, so you haven't a clue about what's really going on. And when you *do* get a clue, it comes in a whisper, a rumor that you pass on to one another behind closed doors. In California—"

"Oh, no," Victor groaned. "Not again."

She paused to glare at him and then went on. "In *California* everyone in the department had a vote—on hiring, on salary, on tenure. Even on promotions. People talked to each other. Not like here, where a sort of medieval secrecy rules. It's really depressing, you know?" She drained her wine, and held out her glass for more. "God, I wish we'd never left."

"You make it sound as though *you're* the one who's being mistreated," Victor said. "If I can take it, why should it bother you?"

"It bothers me that you *can* take it," she said. "That all of you take it. If you stood up for yourselves every once in a blue moon maybe Shepherd and the rest of them would treat you with a little more respect."

"Yeah," Danny said. "Just like Walter. Is that what you mean?"

She shot him a look. "At least he showed he had balls."

"Okay, kiddies!" Karl said, and stood up. "What do you say to some food? I think the chicken is just about done. Get ready for the house specialty—Albemarle Poulet."

"Albemarle Poulet?" Gwen asked. "What's that?"

"Just a little something I made up," Karl said. We followed him to the table. "Remember, I spent my junior-year-abroad in Lyon, the culinary capital of France."

"How could we possibly forget?" Julia muttered. "You only mention it every time we come over."

Emily hastily broke in. "Now, where would everyone like to sit?"

No one said anything, but you could read the same expression on everyone's face: As far away from Julia Garshin as possible.

Danny was seated to my right. I watched him push pieces of overdone cutlets around his plate before he finally noticed my more skillful maneuvers. Droopy green beans provide excellent cover, I long ago discovered.

"What an interesting flavor," Gwen said slowly. "I don't think I've ever had anything quite like it."

"I use lots of mustard and garlic," Karl said. "That's the trick."

"Tasty!" Pam said, squinting hard as she chewed.

"Outstanding!" Danny said as, with a flick of his fork, his whole portion disappeared into a bank of mashed potatoes. Even I was impressed.

Once we had safely progressed to the salad course, Danny turned to me.

"So," he said in a low voice, "I understand you took a pass on directing Tony Donatello's dissertation."

I sneaked a glance at Pam. She was at the other end of the table, talking with Julia. "Yes," I said. "You know about Tony?"

"Yup. Pam came to me yesterday for some advice. She told me you had declined the privilege of being on his dissertation committee."

"That's not true," I said, bristling. "I said I'd be happy to serve as a second or third reader. But I'm not well suited to be his first. Nonvoting is not my area."

"Hey, I understand. You don't think I would take him on if I were in your shoes, do you?" He paused. "You and I both know who's best qualified to direct that dissertation."

"Did Pam tell you Tony's story about Bill Tanner?" I asked.

"From beginning to end."

"What do you think?"

"That everyone should stay away from Tony Donatello. Especially Pam. Tanner's not going to like it if he sees her taking Tony under her wing."

Ah, I thought. A fellow votary of the Roll Over Rule. I reached for my wine and sipped it.

"Do you think Tanner ripped off Tony's idea?" I asked.

Danny shrugged. "I don't know. And to tell you the truth, I don't care. Nobody should mess with Tanner. At least no one who doesn't have tenure."

"Is that what you told Pam?"

"You bet. And I gave her some advice for Tony, too."

"Which was?"

"That he should either keep his mouth shut or transfer to another university," he said.

I set down my glass and didn't say anything.

"Pam didn't like that advice, either, but I'm telling you those are the kid's only options. And if you're Pam's friend, you'll urge her to back off, same as I did. She can't afford Tanner's kind of trouble."

I nodded. "I will," I said.

"Hey," Emily said. "What are you two whispering about?"

"Sorry," I said. All other conversations had stopped and I saw we had the table's complete attention. "Still talking shop."

She shook her head. "It's Saturday night, time to kick back and relax. Instead you sit around discussing the department. Don't you ever get sick of it?"

"She's right," Pam said. "It's not healthy."

"I don't know," Gwen said. "I think it's a little like group therapy."

"By the way, has anyone spoken with Walter yet?" Pam asked.

"I've been meaning to call," Danny said.

"Me, too," I said.

"I told Karl we should have invited him and Shelly tonight," Emily said. "We would have normally, but Karl thought it would be too awkward for them."

"For them?" Julia asked. "Or for you?"

"What about you, Felix?" Victor said. "Your office is right next to his. Have you seen him?"

"No," Felix said. "I should have called, too. But I just don't know what to say to the guy."

"How about, 'I'm sorry'?" Julia said.

Victor turned to her. "And I suppose you were on the phone the minute you heard he went down, offering your condolences!"

"No," Julia said. "I wasn't. I thought all his friends would be."

"What's going to happen to his graduate students?" Pam asked. "He has a huge following, you know."

"The same thing that always happens in these cases," Victor said. "They'll find someone else to work with."

"In other words, once he's gone, this place won't skip a beat," Julia said. "Everybody's replaceable."

"So, what are his chances out there?" Emily asked.

"On the job market?" Felix gave a grim laugh. "It's bad for everyone, but political theory is the worst of all the fields to be looking in. How many universities do you suppose need an expert in the philosophy of language?"

"What will he do if he doesn't find another position?" Gwen asked.

Karl picked up the bottle of wine, and poured refills. "If he's smart, he'll go to law school. An ear for linguistic manipulation would serve him well there." He lifted his glass for a toast, and everyone followed suit. "Here's to the academic life—nasty, brutish, and, for some of us, all too short."

We drank.

"So," Felix said, setting down his glass. "Let's move on to a more cheerful subject. Lydia, tell us about this new book you're working on."

"You're writing another book?" Emily asked.

"Disgusting, isn't it," Karl said to her. "The woman never quits."

Victor reached for the knot of his tie.

"Are you doing something more with the environmental movement?" Danny asked.

I cleared my throat. "Well, sort of. I've got a few articles I'm about to submit to journals that play out themes I wasn't able to fully develop in my book."

Danny frowned. "Articles?"

Around the table I could see the disqualification light flashing in my colleagues' brains: Doesn't count. Doesn't count.

"I thought you said you started a new book," Felix said.

"Well, not yet," I said. "Not exactly." I shifted in my seat. "I've got some ideas, though."

"You haven't even started your research and you expect to have something finished by the end of next summer?" he asked.

"Sure," I said, and then added, too defensively, "Don't you think I can do it?"

He arched his brows. "I guess so."

"What?" I said to the others. "Why are you looking at me like that?" I tried to laugh. "By the end of the summer I'll *have* a book."

From across the table Pam gave me her most sympathetic smile. "We know you will."

Julia made a short snorting noise. "Yeah, right. *Sure* she will. There, you see, Victor? Come next fall, she's going to get screwed just like Walter." She held out her glass. "May I please have more wine?"

No one moved. I stared at my plate, my face burning with a fierce flush.

She poured it for herself. "Ah, what the hell," she murmured, and then sat back. "It doesn't really matter. Sooner or later we all get screwed."

I didn't stay for dessert. I said I had a headache, which was true, and I sure as hell didn't have any more appetite. It wasn't until I'd said my farewells and the door behind me had closed that I realized I'd left behind my umbrella. At that moment the choice was a drenching or a reentrance. I made my dash to the car. Back in my own townhouse, I flicked on the TV and then towelled my hair. A rerun of *Bewitched* was playing. I didn't bother changing the channel. Anything was better than staring back at the faces of my colleagues in my mind, and reading the disbelief in every one of them.

In over-large, easy-to-read print, thank you very much.

I lay down on the couch and watched as Samantha wriggled her nose and made everything all right. If only it were that easy, I thought. Darren was a fool not to let her just rip loose.

"Sam, don't *do* that!" he said.

Oh, shut up, you stupid jerk, Sam says. Can't you see that poor woman out there? You may not need magic spells, but she sure does. This one's for her.

And she wriggles her nose.

I awoke the next morning on the couch, the TV still on. For a moment I wondered, did someone really come to rescue me from Julia Garshin's drunken prophecy?

But then I realized no, of course not. It was only a dream. On the screen Richard Simmons was leading a group of obese women in jumping jacks to the tune of "It's My Party (I'll Cry If I Want To)." I quickly clicked it off and sat up.

I looked down at my rumpled clothes. My stockings were shot, but I didn't care. As Julia so helpfully pointed out, everything's replaceable.

Outside a steady rain continued to fall. On the walk leading up to my door lay the Sunday paper wrapped in plastic. I grabbed my raincoat, held it up as a canopy over my head, and dashed out in my ripped stockings, *sans* shoes.

I had just stooped to grab the paper when I heard, "Lydia!"

Even without turning around there was no mistaking that voice, trained as it had been over years and years to reach from the blackboard to the far corners of a high school classroom.

I straightened and returned the greeting.

"Good morning, Frances," I said.

Frances Taylor was my neighbor. We'd lived side by side for over three years, and I'd managed to keep our acquaintance on a Hi, Nice to see you, Bye! level, despite all efforts on her part to proceed further. She was dressed in a yellow mackintosh and boots with an oversized umbrella, looking like a bespectacled and withered Christopher Robin. She gave me a good look up and down.

"What in the world are you doing out in this wet without shoes?" she demanded.

"Just getting the paper," I said, and raised one soggy foot and then the other to give them each a good shake. The rain was cold.

"I've just been for my walk," she said. "I love it when it rains on Sundays—everyone stays indoors."

Good for you, I wanted to say. Now let me get the hell inside.

"Must be nice," I said.

"They say it's going to rain off and on all week, right through the Thanksgiving holiday," she said. "You'd better call ahead if you're still planning on skiing this weekend. They aren't predicting any snow south of New England."

"Really?" I said. My feet were freezing. I flexed my toes to make sure I could still feel them. "Well, it doesn't really matter. It turns out I have to stay here anyway. I've got some unexpected work."

The words were out of my mouth before I could catch them. At once I knew I had made an enormous mistake.

"You'll be here for Thanksgiving? Wonderful! You can share my turkey then."

"Oh, Frances—how sweet! But I'm afraid I've already accepted an invitation. Thank you, though, very very much."

"Oh," she said, and the corners of her thin lips drooped. I couldn't tell if she knew I was lying. "Next year, then."

"Right. Thanks again!"

I headed for my door and waved before disappearing inside. That was close, I thought.

I threw the paper on the counter and went back into my bedroom to change.

4

True to the forecast, the next day, Monday, it continued to rain. I parked my car in its assigned parking lot and made my usual fifteen-minute hike to Russell Hall. There were buses, it was true, but on ordinary days they were crowded and on rainy days they were packed. In wet weather you always found yourself crammed against a student's soaked knapsack or wound up standing in a pool of water from closed dripping umbrellas. I preferred to make my way on foot, except when it snowed.

The senior faculty, of course, had their own parking lot. It was located directly outside the back entrance to Russell and entailed no more than a hop, skip, and jump from car seat to office. No, you never saw a whale scraping mud off his shoe or staring down at stains on his pants in the wake of a hydroplaning car. All they had to do was shuffle-step a second on the doormat and they were home free.

I cut through this parking lot on my way in. Through the rivulets dribbling off the rim of my new umbrella I gazed at the sleek shiny machines—the Volvos and Mercedes and the more recently acquired four-wheel-drive vehicles, rugged enough to negotiate the climb to a ski condo in the mountains or traverse the gravel lanes of thoroughbred country.

For a moment I paused. Would my Honda Civic ever rub hubcaps with this fleet? Only a week ago a parking slot had seemed assured. Now, as my confidence slipped, it, too, was receding, moving farther and farther to the outer reaches of campus satellite parking, behind the football stadium and beyond.

Once through the doors of Russell, I shook out my umbrella and raincoat. Holding these articles at arm's length before me, I carried them and my briefcase up the stairs to the third floor. With every step my shoes squished. Behind me, all the way to my office, I left a wet smeary trail.

The phone rang while I was rubbing my feet in a vain effort to warm them before putting on a pair of dry shoes.

"Hello?" I said.

"Hello, Professor Martin?" came a young perky female voice. "This is Kimberly Adams. I'm in your 101 class?"

"Yes?"

"Well, um, I was wondering if you'd be giving back the quizzes today."

"No. Those will be returned Wednesday," I said. "The teaching assistants won't be finished grading them until then."

"Oh." There was a pause. "I was sorta hoping to know my grade before vacation."

"Well, you will. On Wednesday."

"Yeah. Okay. Thanks." And she hung up.

I put the phone down and gritted my teeth. Kimberly Undergraduate was obviously planning to be absent the day before the break, along with seventy-five percent of her classmates. It peeved me to get up every year the Wednesday before Thanksgiving and lecture to a virtually empty room.

With a sigh I pulled out my notes for class that day. The topic was the presidential selection process. I planned to give the usual historical overview, from the founders' original plan as spelled out in the Constitution, through the rise of political parties with Martin Van Buren, to the attack on parties by the Progressives and Woodrow Wilson, and winding up with the current emphasis on candidate-centered politics in primaries. In an election year I could always count on a lot of interest in the subject, but such was not the case this semester. I would have to rely on my own enthralling descriptions of dark horse candidates, Super Tuesday, and the caucus system.

Lots of luck, I told myself.

I sat forward and put my head in my hands. Who knows? I thought. Two years from now I might not be facing this problem.

Now just hold on a minute, a voice inside me said. You've got to get some perspective on this tenure business. You're still the person who wrote *Bringing in the Green*, which, by all objective accounts, is a good solid piece of scholarship. In fact, the voice went on, I bet if you marched into Tom Shepherd's office right now and asked about your chances for promotion, he'd tell you it was ridiculous to worry.

My hand moved to the phone and punched in the department office extension. After two rings, Tom Shepherd's secretary answered.

"Hello, Roberta?" I said. "This is Lydia. Any chance that Professor Shepherd can see me today?"

"Hmmmm, let me look at his appointment book," she said, and paused. "How long do you need?"

"Not long. Ten minutes, max."

"How about at eleven forty-five?"

"Can we make it just before noon? I've got a class that runs until then."

"Noon it is," she said.

"Thanks, Roberta."

"You're welcome. Bye."

I hung up and went back to my notes.

When the time came for me to step up to the lecture podium, there were already noticeably fewer than one hundred and twenty-five present, but no matter. Pens were all at the ready, poised over notebooks and an open blank page. Tabula rasa.

I began.

More than a few students paused before joining their comrades in taking notes. At the time I believed it was the zest with which I delivered myself or the rapid succession of ideas that arrested them.

But afterwards, as I was freshening up in the Women's Room for my meeting with Shepherd, I caught sight of something in the mirror. It was a large brown stain the shape of a banana covering one half of my blouse. I stared at it in disbelief. Where in the world had that come from?

For the answer, I needed only to lift the shoulder strap of my leather briefcase. It was still damp. I dabbed at it with a white paper towel. The dye rubbed off in a dull brown stain.

I closed my eyes and pressed hard at my temples.

Minnow Redux.

A little before noon I presented myself to Roberta wearing a bright red cardigan sweater that in no way matched my peach blouse.

Roberta, a middle-aged black woman, stared at me for only a moment. "I'll let Professor Shepherd know you're here," she said, and picked up her phone.

Tom didn't seem to notice anything amiss. He opened his door and ushered me inside with a gracious smile.

"Why, Lydia, good to see you, good to see you," he twanged as he closed the door. "Have a seat."

He motioned to a chair, which I took, and then edged back to sit behind his desk.

"So," he said. He gave a quick glance at his watch and then took off his glasses. "What can I do for you?"

I clutched the red sweater close about me with both hands.

"Well, I thought I'd just touch base with you about a few things," I began. "You know I come up for tenure next fall."

He nodded. "Yes. I know that."

"I guess I was wondering if maybe the department's decision on Walter had any particular bearing on my case that I should be aware of."

His eyebrows shot up. "Surely you're not worried!" he said.

"Well, no—it's just that—"

"Why, Lydia." He paused, then shook his head as he smiled and clucked at me. "I can't imagine why you would give what happened to Walter a second thought."

See, I told you so, the voice inside me said. I let out a deep breath I didn't know I was holding.

I smiled and blushed. "It *is* pretty silly, me coming in here and troubling you like this. But I suppose I needed to hear *you* say it."

"Everybody requires some reassurance now and again," Tom said. "Especially after something so distressing as seeing a colleague fail to get tenure. But you really shouldn't compare your situation to Walter's. We're all looking forward to your promotion," he said.

The grip on my sweater relaxed.

Tom went on. "Indeed, your tenure review will be this department's opportunity to show just what we expect from our junior faculty, in a positive way. Walter, sad to say, could only provide a negative demonstration."

I cleared my throat and sat forward. "Really? How's that?"

"Well, obviously Walter didn't have the proper motivation to produce scholarship. He wrote that one book, published a few articles, and then that was it! There was nothing in his file to indicate an ongoing engagement or any serious attempt to pursue another project. All he had was a statement of purpose for something else down the road, and even that had nothing substantial to back it up—no data, no preliminary research, nothing. I tell you all this in confidence, of course. Assistant professors aren't supposed to know what's in each other's files."

I nodded dumbly.

"But now in your case . . . !" He spread his hands wide. "When did your book come out?"

"Last April."

"Well!" he beamed. "You'll have had a whole extra year— and then some—to get another project under way before your tenure review. We'll expect much more from you than we did from Walter. And I know we won't be disappointed! You're a hard worker, Lydia, I've observed that. And you're well liked by your senior colleagues. That's important—don't let anyone tell you differently. So you've got a lot going for you already. All you have to do is, come next fall, show us you have what it takes to be a true scholar."

"In other words," I said, keeping my voice as even as possible, "I should have another book."

"Ideally, yes," Tom said. He cocked his head. "That doesn't pose a problem for you, does it? You *are* at work on a new project, aren't you?"

"Of course!" I said. "Absolutely."

The smile broadened. "Good. You know, with all these budget cuts, the dean is looking to chop anywhere he can. It's getting harder and harder to promote assistant professors. But you'll be proof that those who deserve tenure do get it."

"Yes. I hope so," I said.

"I know so." He put on his glasses and peered at me from above the bifocal line. "Now. Was there anything else?"

"No," I said, and rose. "Thanks for your time."

"That's what I'm here for," he said, and got up to open the door. "Have a good Thanksgiving."

"Thanks," I said. "You, too."

And I walked out, my cardigan hanging wide open. There wasn't any point in trying to hide the stain. I knew then and there I was permanently marked, like Cain.

That evening I didn't even pretend to read. I couldn't. My mind was frozen, transfixed by the vision of my fate.

We'll be expecting much more from you than we did from Walter.

Much more.

I flipped on the TV, began a methodical cruise through the channels, and came upon Robert Stack ominously introducing yet another episode of *Unsolved Mysteries*. It looked promising.

And apropos. After all, I had my own little mystery to solve now, such as where I'd wind up, once I was fired from Patrick Henry.

Wherever it is, I thought, it had better have cable.

The next day the rain stopped, and by the time my graduate seminar rolled around the sky had cleared. Sunlight did nothing to improve my mood, however. That morning I had come upon Karl, Danny, and Felix huddled in the hallway outside the main office, having an intense debate. As soon as they saw me they stopped talking and gave me ridiculously fake smiles.

"Hi!" Karl said. "How's it going?" Saturday night and Julia's guerilla attack on me at his house had obviously never happened.

"Great," I said, and folded my arms across my chest. "What's up?"

"Oh, nothing," Felix said. "Just arguing, as usual."

"About what?" I asked, preparing to weigh in as I normally did with an opinion on current events.

There was a brief exchange of glances.

"Over whether there's an unofficial mandate to cut back on the size of the departments," Danny said. "Shepherd just put out a memo on E-mail. The dean's announced that there's a hiring freeze for all senior appointments throughout the university. No one gets to come in with tenure."

"You're kidding," I said. "What about the chaired position in American political thought?" A chair was the equivalent of a full professorship but with even more perks, like every third semester off and a slush fund for research expenses. "The search committee was just about to start bringing people in for interviews."

"Gone," Danny said, "along with the chair in Russian politics. Those lines are to be filled only at the assistant professor level."

"Wow," I said.

"Yeah, well, it was bound to happen," Felix said. "The state is facing a huge deficit this year and you can be sure those guys in the Virginia legislature look at Patrick Henry as the perfect place to trim some fat. Our salaries are in their hands, remember."

"Or at least our pay raises," Karl said, "which I hear will be zero again for all state employees next year."

"Yes, but you wait and see," Felix said. "I guarantee you that if this department has the chance to bring a big-name scholar in, someone with lots of prestige, the chairman can find the money. When it comes right down to it, the cash is there."

"Which leads me back to my point about what's really going on," Danny said. "I think the dean is using the general budget cuts in the university to get more power over the hiring decisions in each department. Pretty soon he and his elite select committee will be making *all* the hiring decisions. He already uses his veto to pick who gets tenure."

"You're crazy," Karl said. "The last thing the dean wants to do is get involved at the lower levels. He's just giving the department heads a signal: Cut positions where you can, when you can. And that means at all points of review, at the renewal as well as tenure stages. Then once they've reduced the number of regular appointments, they can fill in the gaps year to year with assorted adjunct professors. The university saves a hell of a lot of money going that route."

"That's not very good news," I said.

"I know," Karl said. "Not for any of us assistants."

"Yeah," Felix said. "Ultimately we're all in the same boat."

Yes, but some of our boats were going to sink sooner than others. I knew better than to believe any talk of solidarity. If I went down, no one was going to want to get caught in my backwash.

"Well, I guess I'd better go read the evil tidings for myself," I said.

"See you," they said. "Have a good Thanksgiving."

"The same to you guys."

And I turned to go. I heard their silence behind me as I made my way to the main office. When I reached the entrance, and was well out of earshot, they started their minnow murmurs.

Without me.

No doubt, about me. And Victor, of course. Now more than ever it seemed unlikely that both of us would get through.

So, you can see why it was not the sort of day that could be brightened by a ray of sunshine and a bit of blue sky. I was no longer living in Mr. Rogers's neighborhood, not since last week. I'd been moved onto Walter Kravitz's block.

At three o'clock sharp I strode into the seminar room, threw my briefcase on the table, and took out a yellow legal pad. Only then did I sit and take a look around the class.

It was a course on interest group politics, and all thirteen of my graduate students were present. They sat around the square table, and faced me at the head.

"Who's on for today?" I said, with no preamble.

It was nearing the end of the semester, and we were at the stage in the course where the students took turns making a class presentation. Their final papers would be a more complete analysis of their chosen topic, taking into account whatever criticisms or thoughts their oral presentations received. Thus far the students' offerings had been uninspiring and unoriginal. If that day's speaker repeated the pattern, I was in the mood to say as much.

A hand went up.

"I am."

It was Meredith Kospach who spoke, a third-year graduate student. She was short and round with bluntly cut brown hair. She wore big framed glasses that enlarged her dark eyes. Without a doubt she was the smartest student in the class, and, from the comments I'd heard from other colleagues, was one of the best in the entire graduate program. For a superstar student, however, she was unusually unassuming. Normally I liked her natural and easygoing manner, but that day I was determined not to be appeased by anyone, no matter how nice.

I flipped to a blank page on my pad. "Okay, Ms. Kospach," I said. "Shoot."

She took out a sheaf of notes and began. As she spoke, I gradually forgot about leaky boats, deathknell memos, and axe-wielding deans. Her topic was the use of media by environmental groups: how these organizations decided what particular causes to highlight in the national press, when they pooled their resources and when they did not, and the various ways the organizations managed to get free coverage. It was a good survey of the different strategies and calculations at work, and demonstrated how the environmentalists in these groups often managed to avoid dealing at cross purposes with one another. She concluded by giving her own assessment of the effectiveness of their strategies.

"These groups hire top-level professionals in public relations, and they do well in targeting issues that best lend themselves to high-profile exposure," she said. "Other interest groups could learn a lot from the environmentalists. As far as I can tell, they're the best at getting the publicity they want at minimal cost."

It was an accomplished presentation. When she was through she smiled and sat forward, hands folded, waiting for the critique. Her fellow students had first crack, and several brought up various points of argument. In most cases, they were more or less trying to show me they had paid thoughtful attention, but several remarks were downright testy. Graduate students were bottom feeders, after all, with no other prey than each other. Meredith came through the interrogation unfazed, demonstrating as much poise as intelligence.

I suggested a few more resources she could use, books I'd come across in my recent readings. Then it was time for the usual ten-minute break.

People sauntered out to get something from the soda machines or went downstairs and outside for a smoke. I stood up to stretch. Meredith was still in her seat, putting away her notes.

"You did a good job," I told her.

"Thanks, Professor Martin," she said. "I like working on this topic. In fact, I was wondering. . . . "

"Yes?"

She got up and came to the front of the room. "Do you have a second to talk?"

"Sure," I said.

"I've been thinking. For my doctoral dissertation I'd like to do a comparison of the environmental movements in the United States and Europe. By Europe I mean especially the Green parties in Germany and France. I was wondering if you'd agree to be my first reader."

"Really?" I said. I was flattered. Meredith was the sort of student who reminded me why I had chosen my profession in the first place. Part of what I was supposed to do at Patrick Henry was train future political scientists. And she was going to be a good one. After turning away Tony Donatello, I welcomed the chance to recoup some good feelings about myself. I wasn't such an ogre. I really was happy to help, when there was no risk.

"I'd love to direct your dissertation," I said. "But I must warn you—I come up for tenure next year and there's no guarantee that I'll get it. Are you sure you wouldn't rather ask someone with a more established reputation? When you go out on the job market, you know, there's a great advantage to saying you worked with a big name."

"I want to work with you," she said. "I thought *Bringing in the Green* was a great book. And I plan on being done with my dissertation a year from this May. I'm sure you will get tenure, but even if you don't, I'd be finished before you'd leave."

I nodded. "All right. Have you taken your comprehensive exams yet?"

"Yes. But I still have to take my oral exam. I'd like to get it done before the Christmas break, if at all possible."

"I'll see what I can do about scheduling one for you," I said. "Who do you want as your second reader?"

"What do you think of Professor Clark?" she asked.

Pam. I nodded. "I think she's an excellent choice. Professor Clark certainly knows Western European politics. But again, I caution you. She's even newer to the discipline than I am. She hasn't made her reputation yet either."

"I don't care," Meredith said. "In the end, it'll be the quality of the work that counts. Isn't that right?"

Not necessarily, I thought, but I didn't have the heart to say so aloud.

"Right," I said. "I'll look forward to working with you, Meredith."

"Thanks, Professor Martin. I really appreciate this."

"I'll talk to Professor Clark," I said. "I'm sure there'll be no problem."

The students began returning to the room; the break was over.

When all were seated I looked around with a smile and asked, "Who's next?"

Another hand went up.

That night in bed I closed yet one more political science journal and turned off the light. Still no idea for a new project had presented itself, at least nothing that merited a book.

What was wrong with me, I wondered. Had I become so bored with my own field?

I thought of Meredith Kospach. She was bursting with ideas. But how would she be in two years, after toiling all those long and lonely hours over her dissertation? Or, once she finished the degree, after five years of the assistant professor's life—five years of writing lectures, praying for publications, and then racing to meet the deadlines, and the incessant kissing up and playing down to all the whales—how would she be?

She'd be burned out.

Just like me.

The next morning, in my office, the phone rang.

"Hello?" I said.

"Hi, Lydia, it's Emily Willis. Look—" she went on quickly, "I'm sorry about what happened last Saturday night. I meant to call you Sunday but. . . . "

"That's okay," I said. "It wasn't any big deal, really."

"Well, I was wondering. Are you free for lunch?"

I paused. "You mean, today?"

"Yes. Everything here at the law school is just about shut down, with Thanksgiving tomorrow. We could have a nice long chat."

I wasn't so sure I wanted a nice long chat. It wasn't that I didn't like Emily. I did. But I was not about to confide anything to the wife of a colleague, no matter how well intentioned she might be. It would be like having a conversation with Karl, only indirectly and with lots of opportunity to let your guard down and screw up.

"I don't know," I said. "I have a class that goes until twelve."

"That's okay," she said. "We can meet at twelve-thirty. Or one, if you'd prefer."

"Okay. Let's say twelve-thirty. But I won't be able to take too much time," I said. "I'm handing back a quiz today and there'll inevitably be some students who'll want to complain about their grades this afternoon."

"They never do stop, do they," she said.

I smiled. "No. That's part of their charm."

"Okay. How do you feel about eating at the Fox Tail Inn?"

The Fox Tail Inn was a rambling prissy resort-type hotel with colonial trimmings, meant to evoke the days of Patrick Henry. It was a mile or so from the university, on the fringe of town. For a backdrop it offered views of the Blue Ridge mountains and the rolling foothills of the nearby countryside. It was a tourist industry dreamchild, where the rooms were booked for graduation by well-heeled parents three years in advance and where the university held its larger and more impressive conferences. It was not the sort of place that was conducive to an intimate *tête à tête*.

Which suited me just fine.

"Great," I said. "Twelve-thirty at the Inn, then."

"See you there," she said, and hung up.

When I arrived, Emily was already waiting at a table.

"Hi," I said, taking the seat opposite. "I hope you haven't been here long."

"No more than a minute or two," she said.

A waitress in a long yellow gingham dress with a white apron and bonnet arrived to hand us menus.

"Good afternoon, ladies," she said. "Our specials for today are baked Virginia ham with hot apple sauce, Chesapeake Bay crab cakes, and spinach and mushroom quiche. Would you like anything to drink? We serve Virginia wine by the glass from our own house selection."

"Just a Diet Coke for me," I said.

"Coffee, please," Emily said.

"I'll be right back with your drink orders," the woman said, and left.

I leaned over. "Do you think they serve Chincoteague pony steaks or Norfolk Bay jellyfish?"

Emily laughed. "This place is really sort of tacky, isn't it? I should have explained on the phone. My boss is thinking of having the Fox Tail cater a dinner for a conference next month and I wanted to check out the food. Do you mind?"

"No," I said. "It certainly is a change of pace from all those yuppie cafes sprouting up around the university these days. When

I first got here cappuccinos were still something of a novelty, and no one had ever heard of focaccia."

Emily set her menu down. Beneath the rippled red bangs, her blue eyes seemed unusually dark. I figured it was just a trick of the light.

"How long have you lived in Albemarle?" she asked.

"Oh, gosh—this will be my fifth year," I said. "It's funny, but I feel like I just got here."

"Really?" she said. "Do you think you'll ever feel at home?"

"Eventually, sure," I said. "Don't you think people always do?"

She sighed. "I don't know. I grew up in New England. My family lives outside of Boston."

"Where did you meet Karl?"

"At school. He was at Harvard and I was at Radcliffe. He stayed on for the Ph.D. while I went to work. And then we came here."

"Well, Albemarle is worlds away from Boston," I said. "Give yourself time. You've only been here, what? Just over a year?"

She nodded.

"Before you know it you'll be thinking you'll never want to leave," I said. "It happens to everybody. Albemarle has a way of growing on people."

"I hope so," she said. "Things are so different here. And it's not just the place. The work is different, too. I mean for Karl. I thought that once he started teaching we'd have more time to-gether, not less."

I shook my head. "It's a terrible business, academics, espe-cially in the larger research universities like Patrick Henry. There's lots of competition and pressure, and only your own self-discipline to make sure you do everything that needs to be done." I looked at her and smiled. "But, hey—hang in there. The first seven years are the absolute worst, before tenure. But the pressure will ease up significantly once Karl gets past that point."

She didn't smile back. "He's convinced he won't, you know," she said. "He's afraid he won't even get renewed next year, given what Shepherd said about having a partial manuscript in hand."

Uh oh, I thought. Forget worrying that Emily was going to pry into *my* affairs. Now I had the opposite problem. She was telling me things about Karl I was sure he wouldn't want me to know.

"He'll be fine," I said, and looked up to see our waitress heading our way. "Here comes Betsy Ross again. We'd better decide what we want."

We gave the menu a quick scan.

The bonneted woman set down our drinks and then flipped open her pad. "Are you ready to order?"

"Yes, I think so," I said. "I'll have the spinach salad."

"Your choice of dressing? The house specialty is mustard vinaigrette."

"That will be fine, but on the side, please," I said.

"The crab cakes for me, please," Emily said.

"Thank you," she said, and departed, her long skirts swinging.

I took a sip of my Diet Coke and then sat back. On the facing wall hung a huge portrait of Patrick Henry, his scarlet-lined cloak flung over his shoulder.

"My, my, my," I said. "Will you look at that."

"What?" Emily asked, and turned in her chair to follow my gaze. "Oh. Not *him* again."

"Yes, Mr. Give Me Liberty Or Give Me Death. I just don't understand this town's adulation of that man. I mean, okay—he was a great speaker and he had one good line. But otherwise! He was one of the area's largest slaveholders and didn't even release his slaves on his death. At least Thomas Jefferson let some of his go when he popped off. The two men hated each other, you know."

Emily looked back at me. "No. I didn't know."

"God, yes. James Madison hated Henry, too. In fact, he was afraid that Virginia would never ratify the Constitution because Henry was so adamantly opposed to it. Henry was a great supporter of states' rights, particularly when it came to regulating the possession of slaves. I read once that he walked out of a town hall meeting where people had gathered to debate the question of ratification. He turned at the door and actually yelled out, 'They'll take your niggers away from you, wait and see!'"

"You're kidding," she said.

"Doesn't exactly fit the glorious champion-of-the-republic image, does it?"

She grimaced. "I should say not."

"Oh, and there's more. His first wife went crazy and he kept her locked in the basement, with a slave to take care of her. She managed to die a year or two later. Then he married Dorthea Dandridge—she outlived him. In the end, between the two wives, he had something like seventeen kids. I think Dorthea bore eleven alone."

"Wow," she said.

"Yes. Can you imagine? And then the guy had the gall to try to prevent Dorthea from remarrying after his death," I told her. "He left a will saying she'd lose the inheritance if she took another husband, and all the property would go to Henry's executor, his cousin Edmund. Well, Dorthea was obviously no fool. She married Edmund, and, I assume, lived happily ever after."

"How do you know all this?" she asked.

I shrugged and sipped my drink. "It comes from living in Albemarle. Everyone picks up the local lore after a time. Plus, I love gossip, even when it's a couple of hundred years old."

"I've heard a lot of stories about Henry, but only the flattering ones."

"Yes, well, don't go repeating what I just told you to the university historian," I said. "He'd have a stroke. He's written the official Henry biography, and believe me, there's no mention in there about a crazy wife locked in the basement." I smiled. "You know the Sarah Shelton Henry Psychiatric Clinic at the hospital? It's named after her. I always thought that was a nice touch."

Emily laughed. "Honestly, Lydia. Sometimes I wonder how in the world you manage to keep your sense of humor."

"Sometimes I wonder myself," I said. "Now what about you? How's the law school?"

"It's okay, I guess," she said. "I like my job, but my boss is pretty demanding."

"Didn't you tell me you work for Collin McKenzie?"

She nodded. "Yes, *the* Collin McKenzie, the great expert on international law. He's always rushing off to The Hague to argue cases before the International Court of Justice. The man must have enough frequent flier points to circle the globe ten times over for free."

"And what exactly do you do for him?"

"I work for one of his research centers. Basically, I edit all his articles and books, including this casebook we just finished. It's not easy, believe me. The man may be a genius at arguing before the bench, but he can't write to save his life."

"Sounds like interesting work, though."

"Oh, it is," she said. "But he's away so much and he's stretched so thin that I end up frantically trying to meet a thousand deadlines at once. At least it seems that way sometimes. To top it all off, I don't think he even realizes how hard I work. He breezes in from these one- or two-week trips and just expects to find everything done, no matter how much he leaves behind. Then he's off again, leaving another avalanche of work."

"Does this guy ever teach?" I asked.

"Theoretically, yes, one or two courses every semester," she said. "Mostly he gets guest lecturers—government officials and other professors—to fill in. I've heard some people on the faculty complain because he's never around. But I don't think anyone would ever really protest. He's too big. There's even talk that he could be one of the next Supreme Court nominees."

"That *is* big," I conceded.

"I know," she said. "But can you imagine his family life? He's got a wife and two kids. They must never see him."

"Have you met his wife?"

"No," she said, "and he never talks about her." She paused. "You know, I look at him and I ask myself, Is this success? I mean, Karl keeps telling me that he'll have more time when he's tenured, but will he really? What if he turns out to be a success, too? He's applied for this grant to go to Strasbourg to study the European Economic Community. He wants to be there six months, maybe even a year. What am I supposed to do? Go with him? What about my job? What about my going to law school, or having a family? What about all those things?"

Her voice broke, and she abruptly stopped.

"Hey," I said, softly. I reached over and touched her arm.

She shook her head and put a hand up to cover her brimming eyes. She could do nothing, however, to hide the flush coloring her neck and cheeks.

"It's okay, Emily," I said. "It's okay."

Our waitress appeared, our plates in hand. We both sat back while she placed them before us.

"Here's your dressing," she said, "and some rolls. Enjoy your lunch." And she was gone.

Emily dabbed at her tears with a napkin. "I'm sorry, Lydia. I didn't mean to do that."

"I understand," I said. "Things can get pretty complicated. You should do what I do."

"What's that?"

I buttered a roll. "Live like a nun and don't own pets. In other words, depend on no one and let no one depend on you. It makes for a boring life, but it's as uncomplicated as you can get."

Emily gave me a trembling smile. "Is that really how you live?"

"Unfortunately, yes," I said, and took a bite.

She peered at me. "You don't have any boyfriends?"

"I used to, but not anymore. There was a guy I lived with when I was in graduate school—he's a political scientist, too. It ended up that he took a job at a school in Idaho, and I took one here. For the first year or so we tried commuting, but you can imagine how well that went. Now I only see him at conventions. I met his wife at the APSA in August. They got married last year."

"I'm sorry," she said.

I shrugged and poked a fork into my salad. "What was there to do? He didn't want to come live with me in Albemarle, and I sure as hell didn't want to move to Pocatello."

"And you've not met anyone here?" she asked.

"No. Oh, I've had a few dates, but nothing serious. Albemarle's not exactly teeming with interesting available men. It doesn't really matter now, anyway. I've got a lot of work to do in the next year, if I'm ever going to get tenure."

"You'll get it," she said. "I know you will."

"Well, I used to think that, but now we'll just have to see. Just between you and me, Julia Garshin wasn't too far from the truth Saturday night. Without another book, I could easily find myself in Walter's situation."

"Oh, forget Julia Garshin," Emily said, frowning as she cut her crab cake with force. "She's so full of bitterness, she thinks everyone else should be unhappy, too. She's my nightmare twin, you know."

I looked at her. "How's that?"

"You've seen how she and Victor are together, constantly picking at the old wounds from all the old wars. Julia can't forgive the years she worked to put Victor through graduate school, and then for being forced to raise the kids by herself, with no money, no time, no break. And Victor resents her just as much for reminding him of all her sacrifices and not appreciating his own. When I see Collin McKenzie I think of Karl, but when I look at Julia I wonder, will that be me in a few years?"

"Never," I said. "You could never be like Julia."

"I'm not so sure," Emily said. "We don't know what she was like way back when. Maybe she wasn't so different from me now."

I didn't have any response to that.

"Listen to me!" she said. "So gloomy! It must be the pressure from work that's done it. I can't tell you how much I'm looking forward to Thanksgiving. Four whole days out of the office! That's my definition of heaven. Are you doing anything special over the break?"

"No, I'll be around. In the library, if it's open."

"I wish we were staying home. Instead we have to head up to Philadelphia, to be with Karl's parents. It's their turn this year, and my parents get us for Christmas."

"Sounds equitable," I said.

She made a face. "I suppose. Someday I'd like to celebrate the holidays in my own home, you know? But until we have kids, our parents won't stand for any excuses. They'd be crushed, both sets."

"Yes, but then when you do have kids, they'll all want to come and spend the holidays with you."

"That's fine," Emily said. "Let *them* get stuck in standstill traffic on the beltway at eight o'clock at night. That's where we'll be, I assure you, in about seven hours."

"You're making the drive tonight?"

"Yes. We leave as soon as Karl gets home. He always says he'll come back early, but I can guarantee we won't be on the road until well past seven. And then he'll spend the whole trip yelling because the traffic's so bad. At least that's what happened last year."

"I'll bet the trip up to Boston for Christmas isn't any picnic, either."

"That's for sure. By the way, where are your folks?"

"Florida," I said. "They moved there a couple of years ago."

"Will you go down for Christmas?

"I'm not sure," I said. "Probably not. As I said, I have a lot to do between now and the end of next semester."

"I won't tell Karl you said that," she said, and reached for her coffee. "It makes him nervous to think of other people getting work done while he's on vacation."

"Let's just hope I actually *do* get some work done," I said. I took a last bite and then pushed the plate away. "That was good."

"The crab cakes weren't bad, either," she said.

"Does this mean the Fox Tail gets to cater your boss's conference?"

"I suppose so," she said. "I should try it one more time to be sure. This conference McKenzie's putting together is a really big deal. People will be flying in from all over the world."

"Maybe you should think about that new place, too—the one that just opened up downtown."

"The Cosmopolitan?"

"I hear that's where the local glitterati hang out—you know, all those famous writers and movie stars who've lately taken up residence in our fair countryside. The old Federalist estates are mixing a little Hollywood with their boxwood these days."

"I wonder if the food is as impressive as its clientele," she said.

"There's only one way to find out."

"Okay, I'll give it a shot," she replied. "But only if you come with me. I hate eating out all by myself."

"Sure, that would be great," I said, though I was a little surprised that the alternatives were me or no one. Didn't she have friends?

As if in answer, she said, "You know, I appreciate you letting me rattle on today. Both Karl and I are so busy, we haven't really gotten to know that many people. At least, I haven't. Karl has Danny and Felix and Victor, but I pretty much work alone. Sometimes I think I'm going to burst if I don't talk to *someone*. I didn't mean for it to be you—I mean, I didn't ask you to go out for lunch so that I could cry on your shoulder. But it looks like I did just that. I'm sorry."

"That's okay," I said. "It's good to let loose every once in a while."

"I guess," she said. "Anyway, thanks. Next time I promise, no violins."

"You've got nothing to apologize for." I looked at my watch. "I guess I should be getting back".

"Are you sure? I was thinking we could split a dessert."

"I'd better not. I've got students to see."

"Oh, that's right. The exam. No, no. Put your wallet away. This one's on the center. I've already cleared it with our accountant."

"Are you sure? Terrific," I said. "Thank you very much."

"Thank *you*. And don't bother waiting with me for the check. I can handle it from here."

I hesitated. "You don't mind?"

"Not at all," she said. "I'll call if I can swing another lunch at that new place. Otherwise, I may not see you until the department's Christmas cocktail party. You're going, aren't you?"

"Yes, of course."

"Great. Take care," she said. "Bye."

"Bye," I said, and left her at the table. I didn't really have to go—I could have stayed and shared a slice of pie. But that was what good friends did with each other, and Emily and I should not be good friends. She clearly did not know the boundaries, but I did, and I intended to respect them for both our sakes. As it was I'd already told her more than I should about myself, but it was hard to hold back in the midst of hearing another person's confidences. That was exactly the problem, you see. It's all too easy to get drawn in.

Now, of course, I had to accept the fact that all my minnow colleagues would know that I was living a life without sex. Emily would tell Karl—that was to be expected—and he would tell the others. That, too, was to be expected. It was the way of the world, especially the world of the sea.

I worked late in my office that night, writing letters of recommendation for various graduate students. If someone asked me to write a letter and I didn't think I could write a good one, I had my own way of telling them to forget it. I'd suggest they ask another professor who, I would say, knew them better and could thus give a more comprehensive assessment of their work. They always got the message.

But even for those I could gladly recommend, I hated writing letters. The problem was one of honesty. Not every student could be a brilliant thinker, or an extraordinarily gifted scholar, or a dazzling teacher. Yet anything short of such effusive praise opened a student to criticism and the ever-present and swiftly bestowed kiss of death. The whole system had come to suffer the equivalent of the spiralling grade inflation syndrome. Anything less than a B+ evaluation might as well be an F, and B+ wasn't so hot, either.

In going through the forms, I came across one from Tony Donatello. I stared at it for a moment and then put it aside. He had asked me to write him a letter a few weeks ago, but no doubt he'd rather I didn't now. I wondered which other professors he would ask. Certainly not Bill Tanner.

I remembered what Danny had told me last Saturday, that his advice to Tony had been to transfer to another school. It was an extreme suggestion. Starting over in another graduate program would set Tony back years. By the time he got his degree he'd be that much older than the other new Ph.D.s. It would be a mark against him. Departments like to hire young faculty; they like to think they're getting someone with the maximum number of productive years. Plus, people would look at Tony and wonder what took him so long. There was no getting around it. He'd be hurt.

I turned off my computer and put the remaining forms in a pile. I didn't like thinking about this business of age. My thirty-third birthday was coming up in the spring. If I failed to get tenure, I'd be in bigger trouble than Tony. With my years of experience a school would have to pay me more than an entry-level salary with a correspondingly higher proportion of benefits. And there were that many fewer years of teaching in me. So, to offer me a position, a department would either have to be extremely enthusiastic about me, or desperate because no one else would dream of teaching there.

I wanted to believe that my modest but growing reputation would see me through to another good institution, if need be. Over the years I'd heard stories of people who, after getting axed by Patrick Henry, ended up tenured at places like Harvard or Princeton or Berkeley. It happened. But could it happen to me?

I reached for my raincoat and purse. It was never a good idea to stay at my office too late, not when I had the long walk to my car.

As I made my way under the street lights to the parking lot, I silently cursed Walter Kravitz. If it hadn't been for him, the rest of us assistant professors would still be dreaming happy dreams about the future. But not now. Not since Walter went down. In a way, he was like Adam. His fall was going to make it a lot tougher on the rest of us.

I unlocked the car door, slipped in, and started the engine. It occurred to me then that I hadn't seen Walter since his tenure decision. Pam was right. Someone should call.

I headed for home.

6

The professional forecasters notwithstanding, the good weather held. Thanksgiving day dawned with clear skies and a soft southerly breeze. By mid-morning it was one of those glorious warm autumn days you often get in Virginia. I went for a short walk to the schoolyard at the end of the block just to be outside. There were lots of trees in my neighborhood. After the rain, they were almost all stripped to their bare boughs. Leaves, still too wet to rake, matted the grassy yards.

Back in my townhouse I curled up on the sofa near the window with my stacks of journals. I had once been a great fan of novels, but the days of pleasure reading had long since passed. Instead I paged through a lengthy article on the latest advances in windmill technology. Scientists had recently made enormous strides in mapping the wind, identifying areas of greater or lesser concentration. And windmills themselves were becoming more efficient, less noisy, and cheaper to build. Wind-power enthusiasts still had to address the problem, however, of matching production of energy to its consumption. There was no counting on the wind to blow faster or harder during a New York City heat wave when millions of people simultaneously cranked up the old air conditioner.

The article described a new group called Citizens For Elemental Energy (CFEE) that was leading the way in lobbying

Congress for additional subsidized research and development projects; specially targeted, of course, were the representatives of the windiest states, from Maine to Montana. The CFEE had become the latest addition to the interest-group melting pot, another bubble in the boiling brew.

In my mind I could hear a chorus of American Government 101 students asking, So? What difference does it make?

More than you might guess, I silently told them. You've heard of grass-roots politics. Here it is again, in a new context. Well, okay, so maybe CFEE members aren't exactly middle-America types. Your average voter doesn't know much about windmills, nor is he or she likely to write members of Congress to urge them to vote for more funding. But that doesn't matter anymore. The point is, these days everyone's an environmentalist. Everybody's in favor of cleaner air and water. All these Citizens For Elemental Energy have to do is hitch their wagon to that political star, and voila! Suddenly they represent the interests of millions—or at least that's what they'll tell the politicians in Congress. Of course, these Citizens have to somehow make themselves heard above the others claiming the exact same thing, like the lobbyists for solar, oil, gas, hydraulic, and nuclear power.

Still, I had a preference for windmills. There were some farms already operating in California. Scenes of them popped up occasionally in movies when a director wanted a particularly haunting effect, panning acres and acres of the sleek towers with whistling blades flashing in the sun. There was something about the sight of those giant steel pinwheels stretching in rows toward the horizon that evoked a sense of timelessness, of emptiness. . . .

The phone rang, breaking the trance. I leaned over and picked up the receiver.

"Hello?"

"Lydia, it's your mother. Happy Thanksgiving!"

"Happy Thanksgiving to you, too," I said. "I was going to call you later this morning. I thought you'd be busy in the kitchen just now."

"Oh, I've been ordered out by Maggie. She and Tom flew in yesterday with the kids."

Maggie was my sister. She and her husband had two children: three-year-old Suzie and Casey, age five.

"I'll bet they're enjoying all that Florida sunshine."

"Maggie says it's already nippy back in Minneapolis," she said. "It's so wonderful to see them. We just wish you were with us. Then the entire family would be together. We miss you terribly."

"Same here. But I really couldn't afford to take this whole week off."

"You work too hard," she said. "You need to have some time for yourself."

"Well, I was going to try and get maybe one day of skiing in, but I ended up having to scrap that plan, too. The department's just issued new requirements for getting tenure. Now it looks like I'm going to have to work flat out from here on in if I hope to have even a fighting chance."

"You're still planning on coming for Christmas, though, aren't you?"

I swallowed. "I don't think so, Mom."

"Oh, Lydia!"

"I know, I know," I said, closing my eyes and rubbing my forehead. I hated the disappointment I heard in her voice. "But you have to understand. It's my tenure year. If I don't do everything I can to finish another book, then *I'm* finished. I don't have any other choice."

"But you said the same thing *last* year when you didn't come. You said this year would be different."

"It would have been, except they went and raised the stakes again. Believe me, I want to come. You know how much I love being with everyone for the holidays. But I can't do it, not this year. If I get tenure, then I promise I'll never miss another Christmas again."

"Don't make promises you can't keep," she said. "What if you meet someone, get married?"

"Mom—"

"Unless you're going to tell me you have no plans for that, either." Her voice went to a higher tremulant pitch.

"Mom, come on. You're getting yourself upset."

"Why shouldn't I be upset? We never see you, Lydia. And it doesn't sound like you're getting out socially at all. You're such a beautiful intelligent girl. It isn't right. I worry about you."

"You shouldn't worry. I'm fine, really. I'm just at a stage in my career where I have to put some things first, and looking for a boyfriend isn't one of them."

"All right," she said. "But you have to give me your word, we'll see you sometime in the next year. You know, your father and I would be more than happy to drive up to see *you*, if you'd let us."

"I know that, and thank you," I said, my hold easing on the phone. The worst was over. "How's Maggie doing?"

"She's fine. She's standing right here next to your father, waiting to talk to you. You take care of yourself, dear."

"I will, Mom."

"Just remember, Lydia. Life is short, shorter than you think. Some things you put off, you may never get back to again. Now here's Maggie—"

Talking to my sister and father was a breeze compared to what I had gone through with my mother. Still, I could tell Maggie thought I should be there for Christmas even if it were for just a few days. After all, she and Tom both worked, and yet they were managing to schedule another trip. When it came time to talk to my father, I tried to explain how disruptive even a short visit would be for me.

"Okay, okay," he said. "But next year no excuses, young lady. Understood?"

I laughed. "Understood. Have a great Thanksgiving, Dad."

"You should smell the turkey we've got in the oven," he said. "My mouth is watering just standing here talking to you."

"When do you eat?"

"Noon," he said. "And afterwards Casey and I are going down to the pier for some fishing."

"Have fun."

"You, too, Lydia. Bye, dear."

"Bye, Dad. Love to everyone." And I hung up.

All at once I longed to smell turkey and pumpkin pie, and to hear the exclamations and clatter of plates when everyone sat down to eat. Casey and Suzie were getting old enough now to remember family gatherings, and my parents—they were also getting older.

Next year, I told myself.

The doorbell rang.

I frowned and got up to answer. Who on earth would call unannounced on Thanksgiving?

I had my answer when I peered through the peephole.

Frances.

Oh Christ, I thought. Now I'll have to explain why I'm not out, like I said I would be.

I put on a smile and opened the door.

"Frances, what a surprise," I said. "Happy Thanksgiving."

"Please forgive this intrusion," she said in a breathless voice, "but I'm afraid I must impose on you."

"Is something wrong?"

She had a two-handed grasp on her purse. "Would you mind terribly taking me to the emergency room?"

"Frances!" I said. "Are you sick?" Even as I asked I could see her face was pale and shiny with perspiration.

"I don't know," she said. "I don't feel that well. I have this terrible pain." She pressed a hand against her chest.

"Hang on—I'll be right with you," I said, and ran to grab my coat and purse. I closed the door to the townhouse. "You know my car. Here, I'll get your door."

She eased into my Honda Civic and reached back for the safety belt.

"You shouldn't leave your car unlocked," she said when I got behind the wheel. "Someone could steal it."

I started the engine and pulled away from the curb. "It's got 150,000 miles on it. I'm not worried."

Which was a lie, of course. I *was* worried—about her. She looked awful. There was a slight squeal of rubber as I sped out of the parking lot and into the street.

I glanced over to see Frances dab at her brow with a handkerchief.

"I'm taking you to Patrick Henry," I said. "It's closest."

"Thank you," she said, and leaned her head back against the seat and shut her eyes.

I ran two lights. Nobody else was out on the road, so it wasn't the daring move it might otherwise have been. In any case, I wasn't about to sit at some intersection with the motor idling while Frances had a heart attack in my passenger seat. When I finally swerved into the emergency room loop and stopped in front of its doors, several attendants rushed out to meet me.

"What's wrong?" one of them yelled at me.

"It's my neighbor. She has chest pains," I said.

Within moments they had Frances out of the car and into a wheelchair. One of them whisked her through the electric door while the other stayed behind with me.

"Are you okay?" he asked.

I blinked up at him. He was tall and lanky, with dark brown hair that fell below his collar. His eyes, however, struck me most. They were dark hazel, the color of moss.

I nodded and took a deep breath. "I think so."

"Then I'm going to have to ask you to move your car," he said.

"What?"

"Your car. You'll have to park it in the garage across the street. When you come back, you can fill out the forms."

"What forms?" I asked.

"I'll help you," he said. "If you don't see me, ask the nurse at the desk for Charlie. Got that?"

"Charlie," I said, climbing back into the Civic.

"See you in a few minutes," he said, and turned to go inside.

I numbly drove into the parking garage and found a space on the third tier. By the time I made my way back to the emergency room, Charlie was nowhere in sight.

The nurse at the front desk said he was helping a patient and would be out in a minute.

"Just have a seat," she said, and gestured toward the waiting room.

"The woman I brought in," I said. "Frances Taylor. Is she all right?"

"They're checking her now," she said. "We'll tell you as soon as we know."

There were only a handful of people seated in the waiting room area. Looking around I decided that most were like me— relatives or friends who were in no dire need themselves. One elderly gentleman in the row across from me caught my eye and smiled. The teeth were too perfect to be his own.

"Some way to spend Thanksgiving, huh?" he said.

I made what I hoped was a noncommittal noise.

"I'm waiting on my wife," he said. "She cut herself. I *told* her not to sharpen those knives, but she went ahead and did it. She said more accidents occur when knives are blunt, but I said no, that's not the way of it at all. Now we know who's right and who's wrong," he said, nodding. "Yes, sir."

Desperately I looked around for a magazine. They worked on airplanes. Did they work in waiting rooms?

"Yes, sir," he repeated. "All the way to the hospital I asked her, Who do you think is right now? She couldn't deny it. No, sir."

"Excuse me," I said, and got up. I walked to the drinking fountain. Where the hell was this Charlie?

"Still no word on Frances Taylor?" I asked the nurse.

"Still no word," she said.

All at once from outside came muted yelling that switched to loud the instant the electronic entrance doors swung open. A dozen college-age people burst in, carrying signs and shouting, "Humanity for animals! Humanity for animals!"

The nurse looked around. "Where the hell is Oscar?" she said, and then picked up her phone. "I need Security in the ER, stat!"

"Stop the murders! Stop the holocaust!"

The group spilled into the waiting room and stood over the startled people, shaking signs at them that read WANT TO KILL A RAT? DISSECT A VIVISECTIONIST and ANIMAL EXPERIMEN-TATION = BAD SCIENCE.

"Doctors of death work here!" one young woman yelled. She had spiky blond hair and full pouting lips. A coil of silver bracelets covered both forearms and gave a musical punctuation to every thrust she made of her poster. It was handwritten, and said DEAD MEAT STINKS on one side and VEGETARIANS FOR LIFE on the other. "Doctors of death! Right here in this hospital!"

The nurse stood up. "You better get out of here!" she said. "The police are on their way."

Another woman shouted to her companions, "Okay, every-body. Get ready for the cops." She looked older than the other protesters, in her late twenties. She had long brown hair that fell in one thick braid down below her waist.

She bent over the old man with the perfect teeth as he cowered in his seat. "Do you know what goes on here?" she cried into his face. "Do you? The torture of animals! The maiming of innocents!" She straightened. "All of you people, how can you be so blind? Don't you see the blood on their hands? These doctors are murderers, criminals. Don't you see it?"

From her pocket she pulled out a vial of red liquid and held it up high.

"The blood of innocents!" she cried, unstopping the bottle. With a great sweep she splattered those seated near her.

That got everyone up and moving.

"It's blood!" a fat woman cried. "She's throwing blood!"

The nurse was out from around her desk and ran toward the braided woman. "Stop it!" she cried.

"Humanity for animals!" someone yelled. "Free the prisoners caged in the labs!"

The woman with the braid saw the nurse coming and threw a splash of the liquid right at her. Red splotches and speckles made stark stains against her white uniform. The nurse looked down at her chest and held her hands away.

A bright light flicked on. Someone with a videocamera started taping the scene. The local TV station's logo was printed on the camera's side.

"Wake up, people!" the braided woman cried. Her eyes lit on me, and I could see her rearing back to give me a dose of whatever it was she was slinging.

"Hathor, stop it!" Charlie said as he stepped between us. "You're terrorizing these people!"

She kept a hold on her vial and leaned toward him. "So what? Their fear is nothing compared to what your lab animals feel."

A police siren sounded outside and then abruptly stopped. Several officers piled out of their cruisers and headed through the doors.

"You picked the wrong time and the wrong place," Charlie told her.

"Oh no, we didn't. Fairchild's on call. We know he's in there. This is all a diversion to give Amy a chance to find him. She has a little present for him."

"Nobody's going in there," he said, pointing to the corridor down which Frances had disappeared earlier. "I'm not going to let you scare sick people to death."

Just then a policewoman emerged from that very corridor marching the spiky blond in front of her. The young woman's wrists were bound with plastic ties, barely visible amid the maze of silver bracelets.

"Amy! Did you find him?" Hathor yelled at her.

Amy laughed and thrust her chin up and to the side in a Lookie There gesture.

Behind her strode a doctor, his lab coat and white shirt drenched in red. Even his white hair was speckled.

"Way to go, Amy!" Hathor cried.

"Keep moving," the policewoman said, and nudged Amy forward.

"Humanity for animals!" various protesters shouted into the TV camera as police wrestled to cuff them. An officer approached Hathor. She raised her vial.

"Want some of this?" she asked.

"Lady," he said, "you touch me with that stuff and I'll book you for assault."

Charlie plucked the bottle from her hand.

"Don't be stupid," he said.

"Fuck you, Charlie," she said, and the policeman grabbed her by the arm and hustled her away.

Charlie sniffed the liquid and then rubbed a drop between his fingers.

The doctor walked up, looking like the victim of a major gunshot wound to the chest. "What is it, Charlie?" he asked.

"My guess is red dye in water, Doctor Fairchild," he said.

Fairchild took a whiff, too. "Well, let's reassure these people, then," he said, and stepped forward. He raised his voice. "No need to panic, folks. It's just dyed water."

A security guard ran in.

"What happened?" he asked the nurse.

"Oscar, where were you?" she said. "We practically had a riot in here!"

"I just went out for a smoke," he said. "How the hell was I supposed to know?"

"What about Frances?" I asked Charlie. "Is she going to be all right?"

"She had an attack of angina, but she's fine now. Doctor Fairchild is going to schedule her for some follow-up next week. Turns out he's been treating her for a heart condition, and it seems she stopped taking her meds. He's sending her home to rest. You won't have much more of a wait. She'll be out in a minute."

All around us people were talking loudly as they gave statements to the police. In the corner I saw a pretty blonde with a lot of makeup and a microphone. She was interviewing the nurse. Charlie stared at her for a full minute and then looked away.

"Unbelievable," he muttered, and stuck his hands in the pockets of his white jacket.

"Wait a second," I said. "What about those forms?"

He looked back at me. "Ms. Taylor's given us all the information."

"Oh." It dawned on me that I wouldn't have minded filling in the blanks—not if Charlie were there to help. "Good," I said.

He started to walk away.

"Ah, excuse me," I said, stopping him. I noticed he kept glancing over at the TV woman. "What was this all about anyway? Who were these people?"

"Animal rights activists," he said.

"An animal rights group? Here in Albemarle?"

"That's right. They're called Humanity For Animals."

"Wow," I said, and paused to ponder the news. "No kidding."

"Look, I've got to go," he said. "Some of these people are pretty upset."

"Sure, sure," I said, and glanced at his ID. It had CHARLES WHITTIER, AUXILIARY in big black letters. "Thanks for taking care of Frances."

"Glad to help," he said, and waded into the crowd. The TV light switched off and I saw the reporter exchange a look with Charlie. She smiled and shrugged. He turned away without smiling back.

On the way home I could tell Frances was feeling better.

"What on earth was all that commotion?" she asked in a ringing voice.

"A demonstration of some sort," I said. "For animal rights."

"Animal rights?" Frances paused. "What was the purpose of demonstrating in the emergency room?"

"The hospital must have some labs or something," I said. "They had signs protesting animal experimentation. There was one doctor the activists were especially interested in—someone called Fairchild."

"Doctor Fairchild," Frances said. "He's my cardiologist."

I glanced over at her. "So you've had problems before?"

She nodded. "Yes, but it's been a while. I'm on medication—at least I should be. The last few months I've been feeling so well I thought I could do without the pills."

"But apparently you thought wrong."

"Apparently, yes." She sighed and settled back in the seat. "It's a tough business, growing old."

"You seem to be handling it well," I said. Up ahead was the turn into the townhouse drive.

"Thank you," she said. "My son thinks so, too. That's why he never comes to visit."

"I didn't know you had a son," I said.

"No, you wouldn't," she answered, and I didn't know if she were implying that such ignorance reflected poorly on myself or the son in question.

"Well, here we are," I said as I pulled into my numbered slot. I got out and went around the side to help her, but she was already up, slamming the door closed. I noticed she'd locked it.

"Thank you, Lydia," she said.

"What are neighbors for?" I said. "Why don't I come inside and make you a cup of tea or something?"

"No, no," she said waving me away as she started up the walk. "The doctor said to rest and that's exactly what I intend to do."

"Well, if you're sure . . . ," I said.

"I'm sure. I just hope I haven't spoilt your Thanksgiving Day plans. Your friends must be waiting for you." She fumbled in her purse for her house key and then fitted it in the lock.

"Uh, not exactly," I said. "It's a late supper."

"How fortunate," she said, and disappeared inside.

made a point of catching the local six o'clock news that night, a program I ordinarily never watched. The lead story was a house that had burned down somewhere out in the country. An unhappy couple told the interviewer—a moonlighting Patrick Henry student, I was sure, from the smirky look of him—that everything they owned had just gone up in flames.

"Along with your turkey dinner?" the young man asked.

The couple nodded. "That, too."

"I guess you must be thankful it wasn't worse." He turned to the camera. "Reporting live from Woodland Hills, this is Chris Mann for Channel Three ActionNews. Megan?"

"Thank you, Chris," lisped the anchorwoman as the scene switched back to the studio. She looked like a teenager who'd gotten into her mother's makeup and swiped some of her clothes.

Where do they *find* these people? I wondered.

She went on. "Earlier today a group calling itself Humanity For Animals staged a demonstration in the emergency room at Patrick Henry University Hospital, resulting in several arrests. Channel Three's Kathy Durban was on the scene and filed this report."

Tape of the demonstration ran while a woman's voice said, "Shortly after eleven o'clock this morning two dozen representatives from the animal rights group Humanity For Animals demon-

strated at Patrick Henry University Hospital. They were protesting the use of laboratory animals in experiments conducted in the
heavily guarded research wing of the hospital. The protesters specifically targeted cardiologist Doctor David Fairchild, well known
for his research on dogs." There was a shot of the red-dappled
doctor brushing away a woman's hand holding a microphone.
"Please, no questions—not now," he said, and hurried past. The
voice-over continued. "Several people present during the demonstration were frightened by the random throwing of what appeared
to be blood. Nurse Dorleen Wolanski had this comment."

It was the nurse at the reception desk. In the picture with
her was Kathy Durban, the pretty blonde. "It was frightening, it
really was," Dorleen said, the red stains vivid against the snowy
field of her uniform. "I think the whole thing proves we need better
security. Anybody can walk in here. Today we were lucky it was
just some nut throwing colored water. But next time it could be
some nut with a gun."

"Do you have any thoughts about the reason this group
staged their demonstration?" Kathy asked.

"What?" Dorleen blinked at her.

"Do you think they were justified in protesting the use of
dogs in experiments?" she said.

"Are you kidding? They're crazy," she said, and pointed to
her chest. "Just look at this!"

The picture cut to a live shot of Kathy outside the emergency room entrance.

"Megan, the police have arrested eight people in connection
with this incident."

"Kathy, was anyone hurt?" the anchorwoman asked.

"No, although several people were shaken up. When I asked
one of the Humanity For Animals members about these scare tac-
tics, she replied that such methods are necessary to bring attention
to their cause. I'd say they succeeded today, Megan."

"Thank you, Kathy," Megan said. "In other news. . . ."

I got up to make myself some pasta.

An animal rights group, I thought as I filled a pot with
water. Right here in Albemarle. What do you know.

That was precisely the question, of course. What *did* I know
about the animal rights movement? Not a whole hell of a lot. I'd

read about the boycott of fur coats in Aspen and I remembered hearing about illegal break-ins at various laboratories. But that was about it. I had no idea how well organized the movement was, or whether it had achieved any degree of political influence.

I set the pot on the stove and turned the burner to high. I did what you're not supposed to do—stare at it. But in this case it didn't matter. The water was at full boil before I even noticed.

The next morning I headed straight for the library. It was well past dark before I returned, weighted down with a new collection of books and journals. As I unlocked the front door, I heard Pam's voice in the middle of leaving a message on my answering machine.

"So if you get back in the next hour or so—" she said.

I dropped my satchel on the floor and ran to the phone.

"Hey!" I said, cutting her off. "Pam, it's me."

"Lydia," she said. "Did you just get home?"

"Just walked in the door this minute," I said. "How are you?"

"Fine," she said. "How are *you*? How was skiing?

"Oh, I didn't go," I said. "Too much work. Didn't I tell you?"

"No. I haven't seen you since. . . ." Her voice lowered. "Since Saturday night. I tried your office on Monday, but I must have missed you."

"Saturday night? You mean I haven't seen you since I got broadsided by Julia Garshin? Well, don't worry. The scars are healing nicely."

"You shouldn't joke about it, Lydia," she said. "It was awful, what she said. She had no right—"

"It's okay, Pam, really," I said. "To be honest, at the time it was pretty mortifying but now it's okay. I think I've come up with something."

"Really?"

"Yes. I think I've got a new idea." I threw down my purse, wormed out of my jacket, and carried the phone to the couch. "I'm talking about a *really* new idea."

"What is it?" she asked.

"Well, all this time I've been trying to come up with something, and nothing seemed to grab me, you know? But the problem was that I couldn't stop thinking along the same lines as *Bringing in the Green.* I've been attempting to recreate that first book, and it can't be done."

"Well, I can see why you'd try, though. It's a great study," Pam said.

"But it's over, written, and a sequel wouldn't have nearly the same impact," I said. "This environmentalist movement has come of age. Everybody's got an angle on it now. There's no new ground to break."

"I suppose you're right about that," she said.

"So, yesterday—Thanksgiving—I had to take my neighbor to the emergency room."

"The emergency room?" she interrupted. "What happened?"

"Nothing. She's fine. But I had to wait for her to get checked, so I'm standing there when all of a sudden the place is invaded by a bunch of animal rights activists from a local group called Humanity For Animals. Did you hear about it on the news?"

"No," she said. "I was up in Baltimore with my aunt and uncle. There's an animal rights group in Albemarle?"

"I was surprised, too," I said. "So there I am, in the middle of this wild demonstration, and I'm thinking, Hmmm, what *about* the animal rights movement? In the universe of interest groups, where does it stand?"

"On the outer limits, would be my guess," Pam said. "Right there with the quasars."

"That's what I thought," I said, kicking off my shoes and crossing my legs beneath me on the couch. "But the picture isn't that simple. So far I've only had a chance to browse through some books and a few articles, but I think I can see where this thing is heading. The movement's still pretty raw, as interest groups go. But it *is* slowly gaining some influence."

"If you ask me, that's not good news. An animal rights activist once stopped my grandmother on the street and screamed at her because she was wearing mink," she said.

"When was that?"

"About two years ago, in New York. My grandmother still can't talk about it without getting her blood pressure up."

"Well, from what I can see, the members of these groups fit right into the classic profile of extremists—and that's exactly who you'd expect to find in a movement during its first stages of getting organized. If I'm lucky, this local group could make for a good case study."

"A case study?" She paused. "Do you think you'd be able to finish something like that by summer?"

"Sure, if I work fast. First I've got to put out some feelers, find out if this Humanity For Animals is really a genuine organization. Nine times out of ten people show up for a demonstration and then scatter. Especially if they're students."

"I don't know, Lydia. Working up close with people like that would certainly not be my cup of tea. Nobody has the right to yell at old ladies, no matter how good their cause."

"The best part about it is there doesn't seem to be very much written about them, at least by academics. The animal rights movement is practically pristine territory. It's perfect!"

"Well, then—good," she said. "I guess I was sort of worried about you after Saturday. You have so many ideas and are so energetic, it never occurred to me that you might have problems putting together a new project. I always expect you to be on top of things, and look to you to give me encouragement when I need it. I never stopped to think you might need some support every once in a while yourself."

I winced. "That's okay, Pam, really. I'm fine. I just lost my momentum there for a while, but I'm back on track now, no problem. Oh, before I forget—I knew there was something I had to tell you."

"What's that?"

"Meredith Kospach. Has she spoken with you yet?"

"Meredith? No. Why?"

"I'm going to be directing her doctoral thesis, and she'd like you to be her second reader. She wants to compare the Greens in Europe with the environmentalists in the United States. Interested?"

"Yes, of course. That's a wonderful topic. I'd love to be her second reader."

"Great," I said. "I'll tell her we're all set then. See you Monday, probably."

"Okay. Maybe we can get together for lunch sometime this week?"

"Sure. Just come by. See you—"

I hung up and sat there for a moment, hugging my knees, and had a brief pang of doubt. What if this Humanity For Animals group didn't pan out? Then I'd be back at square one, scrounging for a hook—any hook—on which to hang an idea. I might even be driven to weep into the already tear-drenched shoulder of Pam Clark.

I stopped and shook my head.

No, I thought, clicking on the TV. I'd rather hang *myself* first.

T his is ridiculous, I told myself. There's no reason to be
nervous.

It was Monday afternoon and I was in my office. In a few
minutes Charlie Whittier was due to arrive.

I hadn't been nervous when I called him at home over the
weekend. When he'd answered, I'd explained in a matter-of-fact
way who I was and what I wanted to speak to him about. At first
he said he didn't have anything to tell me about Humanity For
Animals. He said he'd left the group over a month ago. That, of
course, only piqued my interest more. I requested a formal interview, and finally he consented.

At the time I'd been pleased. In writing *Bringing in the
Green* I'd relied on personal testimonies and accounts for most of
my research, and by the end had gotten quite good at making that
crucial initial contact over the phone. It was nice to know I hadn't
lost my touch.

As for conducting the interviews themselves, I'd discovered
I enjoyed listening to people talk. For me it was like the game in the
old coloring books called Connect The Dots. You'd draw a line from
dot to dot until you had a picture. A person's stories were like the
dots, and sometimes, when you connected them all together, you'd
see an image of people they themselves didn't even know existed.

That was the trick of it, you see. People usually like to talk about themselves—that's never the problem. But getting them relaxed, at ease, coaxing them to spill *all* their dots. . . . There lay the challenge.

I was eager to get back in the game. For me, that was normal.

What wasn't normal were my sweaty palms and accelerated pulse. It had been a long while since I'd spent any time with someone as good-looking as Charlie, and my libido was obviously delighted at the prospect of this new view from the convent walls.

Which is fine, I told myself. A totally harmless reaction, like sneezing from a whiff of pepper.

I looked around my desk for some easy distraction and finally lit on a rough draft of a seminar paper. I did my best to focus on the writing instead of the clock.

At five after three there was a rap on my door.

"Come in!" I called.

"Hi," Charlie said, stepping inside. He was carrying a bike helmet, worn very recently, from the look of his squashed hair.

I stood up and held out my hand. "Thank you for agreeing to talk with me," I said.

We shook hands and smiled. Up close, I got a good look at his eyes. They were the same lovely dark green I'd remembered.

"I don't know how much help I'll be," he said.

"You're giving me a start, and that's a lot of help in and of itself," I said. "I thought we'd walk over to the cafeteria for a cup of coffee and talk there. If we stay in the office, there'll be too many interruptions from students calling or stopping by."

"Sounds like you're a pretty popular teacher," he said. He had a lopsided smile that was absolutely charming.

"Ha," I said. "Come the end of the semester, everyone in possession of a grade sheet is popular with the students." I reached for my satchel. "Let me gather a few things and then we can be on our way."

His gaze wandered to my bookshelves.

"You've got quite a library here, Professor Martin." He reached over and pulled out a book. "This one has an interesting title."

I glanced at the white dustcover. "Yes. That was written by a colleague of mine here in the department."

He flipped open to the title page and read aloud, "To Lydia, and our mutual success—Walter." Charlie looked up at me. "Mutual success?"

"Um, yes. We both had our first books come out at about the same time. We exchanged copies."

He looked over the first page. "I'd like to read it. Would it be okay if I borrowed it?"

"Sure," I said.

He tucked it into his knapsack. "Thanks."

"I'm all set," I said, hoisting the satchel strap over my shoulder. "Shall we go?"

We headed for the food court in the student union building. It was a large eating area, and offered a step up from traditional cafeteria fare. The old assembly-line style of serving had been replaced with a mix of different fast food stands, dispensing everything from pizza to tacos to deli sandwiches. At that hour, the place was practically shut down. The Bakery Shop was still open, however. I ordered coffee and a blueberry muffin. Charlie just stuck to coffee.

"Are you sure you don't want something to eat?" I asked. "It's my treat."

"In that case . . . ," he said. He spoke to the large woman behind the counter. "Do you know if the glazed donuts were fried in vegetable shortening?"

She gave him a vacant look. "Sir?"

"I was wondering if the donuts were fried in one hundred percent vegetable oil, without any animal fat," he said.

"I have no idea," she said, wrinkling her broad nose.

"It's probably all right," he said, and took two.

My heart gave a little leap at this first sign of an activist spirit. I paid while Charlie carried the tray to a table. The woman handed me the change and stared after him.

"So!" I said, sitting down across from him and cracking open a creamer. "Are you ready to begin?"

"I guess."

I reached into my satchel and pulled out a miniature tape recorder.

"I'm supposed to talk into that thing?" he asked.

"You'll forget it's there once you get started," I said.

He took a bite of his donut.

"Ready?" I asked.

He nodded.

"Okay." I clicked the recorder on. "It's Monday, December first, at—" I glanced at my watch. "Three-twenty P.M. I'm speaking with Charlie Whittier. Charlie, what can you tell me about Humanity For Animals?"

He cleared his throat and sat forward. "It's an animal rights group. It's been around for about three or four years now."

"It's locally based?"

"No, it's a national organization. The Albemarle chapter was started by a woman named Hathor."

I wrote the name on a legal pad. "Hathor. Is that a first or last name?"

"Both. That's her name. Just Hathor."

"Oh." I looked up. "I remember now. She's the one who was throwing the blood in the emergency room, the woman with the long braid."

"Yes, that's right. Except it wasn't blood. Hathor wouldn't get near real blood."

"Why?"

"Because she doesn't believe in killing anything," he said, and took another bite of his donut.

"What about you?"

"What about me?"

"Do you share her views?"

"I . . . No, I guess I don't."

His hesitation interested me. I sipped my coffee and then set down the cup. "You said you were a member of Humanity For Animals. How long were you with the group?"

"Just for a year," he said. "I quit about a month ago."

"You work at the hospital?"

"I volunteer. I'm a medical student," he said. "I mean, I *was* a medical student. I dropped out after my first year, at the end of last May. Now I'm hoping to reenroll next semester."

"That's a quick turnabout. Why did you drop out?"

He took a deep breath and toyed with his remaining donut. "Well, actually I was kicked out."

"You were? What happened?"

His gaze met mine. "I said I didn't want to do any more dissections. I thought they'd let me substitute other kinds of lab work, but I was wrong. The dean expelled me."

"Wow," I said.

Charlie grimaced and looked back at the donut. "Yeah. Wow is right."

I paused for a moment, and decided to back up a bit. "Tell me, where are you from?"

He dipped the donut in his coffee. "Ohio."

"Really? I grew up in Illinois."

"No kidding. Where?"

"Chicago. I don't go back there very often, though. My folks moved to Florida a couple of years ago. Where in Ohio did you live?"

"Cleveland."

"And where did you go to college?"

"Antioch," he said, and sat back.

"That's a great school. May I ask how old you are?"

He grinned. "I guess I don't exactly look like a recent graduate. I'm thirty. How old are you?"

I was in the middle of taking a bite out of my muffin, which served as a small measure of cover against my surprise. "Umm," I said, dabbing at my mouth with a napkin. "I'm thirty-two."

His smile had worked its way up to his eyes. "Do you have tenure?"

"I come up next fall."

"Worried?"

I shrugged and reached for my coffee. The cup trembled as I lifted it, and immediately I went for a two-handed grip.

"I guess. Yes, sure. Everybody always is."

"I can imagine. I mean, your whole future rides on that one decision. Must be pretty stressful."

"As stressful as being expelled from medical school, I imagine," I countered. I didn't like the way our roles had somehow reversed. I was supposed to be *getting* dots, not doling them out.

The grin faded and he nodded. "Probably so."

"What did you do in those years after college?" I asked.

"I taught science in a private school outside of Cleveland. After a while I got bored and started taking pre-med courses at

Case Western. I did pretty well, so I decided to take a shot at medical school."

"That's when you came here?"

"Yup."

"Tell me about last year."

He shifted a little in his seat. "Well, at first it was great, you know? This place is really competitive and I was doing well in my classes. After a while my professors were telling me I could go into any specialty I wanted—neurology, or cardiology, or ophthalmology. I have a friend who says radiology is the best because you set your own hours and you never have to see patients."

"Sounds like you were a superstar."

"Right." Again the lopsided smile. "The only hitch was, I told everyone I wanted to be a family practitioner. That didn't sit too well, especially with my professors. People thought I was a low-class snob. You get the picture."

I nodded.

"So when I objected to the dissections nobody cared. I had to like it or lump it."

"None of the other students backed you up?"

"What, are you kidding? They were just waiting for something like this. The day after I refused to dissect a cat, my classmates got together and bought me a big box of Kitty Treats. Wrapped it with a bright red bow. I thought that was a nice touch."

"At that time you were a member of Humanity For Animals?"

"Yes."

"What led you to join?"

"I became a vegetarian about five years ago. When I moved here, a friend took me to one of the meetings and I liked it."

"You must have known medical school would pose this sort of problem."

He sat forward and rested his elbows on the table. He'd finished the donuts. "Not necessarily," he said. "Lots of schools have gone to videotapes or computer simulations of operations rather than supply each and every student with a fetal pig, for instance— not out of conscience but because it's cheaper. I knew there would probably be some stigma attached to going the alternate route, but I never expected to be expelled from the program."

"Have you thought about transferring to another school?"

"I've thought about it, but I can't afford to. I'm already neck-deep in loans."

"I see." I scribbled a note on my pad. "And those loans started coming due as soon as you quit school. Is that the reason you want to return, to get your degree and start earning a doctor's salary?"

He sat back, folded his arms, and looked at me. "What kind of question is that?"

I heard the anger in his voice and tried to keep mine as neutral as possible. "I'm wondering what led you to override your aversion to performing dissections and reenroll in medical school."

"Then why don't you ask me instead of putting words in my mouth?"

I set down my pen and leaned forward. "All right. What led you to override your aversion to performing dissections?"

He frowned. "I want to be a doctor. Is that so hard to understand?" He paused, as if expecting me to answer, and when I didn't he went on. "Look, if I tried to transfer, there was no guarantee another school would take me. Patrick Henry's already made it clear that if I'm willing to do the lab work, I can get back in the program. Once I have my degree, I'll be in a position to push for reform. Rather than being a voice outside the medical community, I can be one inside. It's a compromise, I know, but one I've decided is worth making. A lot of people don't agree, but that's okay. It's my life, not theirs."

Hey, I thought, no need to explain anything to me. I *wrote* the Roll Over Rule. You play along to get along until the day you're free.

"Is that why you left Humanity For Animals, because you decided to return to medical school?"

He looked past me across the room. A faint smile came and went. "No. I was kicked out of there, too. No vivisectionists allowed."

"I see." I picked up my pen and made another note.

"You keep saying that."

His gaze was fixed on me now.

I cleared my throat. "Do I?"

"Yes. What does it mean?"

"Um, I'm not sure I understand what you're asking."

"What does it mean, 'I see'? *What* do you see?"

"It means I understand the point you wish to make," I said.

"Really? Or are you forming your own judgments?"

"That too, I suppose."

He paused, then unfolded his arms. "What's this study of yours supposed to prove, anyway?"

"I'm not sure it's supposed to *prove* anything," I said, bristling slightly. "I'm interested in how a group like Humanity For Animals gets started and sustains itself."

"What about what it stands for? Does that matter?"

My brows arched. "For my research purposes? No."

He continued to study me.

"Look," I said. "I'm an academic. I don't evaluate causes, I analyze the people who are drawn to them. Members join groups for all sorts of reasons, and different groups will highlight different needs. Revealing those variances is interesting to me. Does that make sense?"

"So what has talking to me shown you? What have you learned from me?" he asked.

"I can't say yet," I said. "I haven't finished the interview."

He drained his coffee cup and sat up. "I'm afraid you have," he said. "I've got to go. I'm supposed to be at the hospital now."

"Oh," I said.

"So you can turn that thing off now." He nodded at the tape recorder.

I clicked it off. "I'd like to talk with you some more," I said. "Will that be possible?"

"Sure." He smiled. "But next time I'm bringing my lawyer."

"Oh, come on, was I that hard on you?" I said.

"Pretty hard. The way you asked me about those loans. . . ."

"I'm sorry. I shouldn't have assumed—"

"That's right," he said. "You shouldn't have." He held out his hand. "Well, thanks for the coffee, Professor Martin."

"Please, call me Lydia," I said. "All my victims do."

The smile broadened into a grin. "Okay, Lydia."

We shook hands, and he turned to go, his helmet tucked under his arm.

"Hey," he said, turning back. "How would you like to attend an HFA meeting? There's one in about two weeks."

"That would be terrific," I said.

"It's on December fifteenth," he said, "and this one will be at four-ten Rosehill Drive."

I wrote down the address. "What time?"

"Seven o'clock. Just don't tell them I sent you," he said. "Bye—"

"Bye!" I said.

When he was out the door I pushed the rewind button on my recorder and held on tight as I watched the tape spin. It was all there—the beginning of my new project.

I got up to order another cup of coffee.

It should have been champagne.

9

There was one last sprint in the academic calendar between Thanksgiving and the end of the fall semester, with only a week and a half of classes before the final exam period. It was a time of great stress for the students as they scrambled to complete papers, turn in projects, and bone up for an average of five three-hour-long written finals. In my few remaining undergraduate lectures, attendance was sporadic. For the last day of classes, however, the auditoriums filled to capacity. There were always some students who believed that, even though they had skipped every other lecture, if they made the last one they would surely pass the final exam.

I wrapped up my Intro to American Government course with a lecture on public policymaking in the current political climate, and gave an assessment of which trends I thought would become more or less dominant in the future. At the end there was the usual applause, a tradition at Patrick Henry after the last lecture. Then the students filed out into the halls. For them, the hard part was just beginning. They had a two-day reading period before the first round of exams began.

For me, with that last lecture I closed the book on my undergraduate classes. I'd already put together the final exams from questions my teaching assistants had drawn up. On the exam days themselves I'd be there to hand out the tests, but my T.A.s would be the ones to grade them. My only job was to record the grades by filling in the circles on the computer sheets, and then turn them in to the department secretary. Piece of cake.

My graduate seminar required more of me, but not much. Of the thirteen students in the course, only eight had finished their papers. The others had taken an incomplete. Some professors didn't allow incompletes, but I didn't mind. I told my students that if they wanted to take the extra time, fine. After all, they were minnows-in-training, and in the big blue sea no one stood over you to make sure you got your work done. There were some, of course, who ended up with more incompletes than grades, but I always thought this was as good an indication as any as to who was really fit to get a Ph.D., and who was not.

On the day before the exam period was to begin, I was closed in my office giving the seminar papers an initial read-through when there was a knock.

"Lydia? It's me, Pam."

I got up and opened the door.

"Hey, come on in," I invited, closing the door behind her. "How are you doing?"

"Okay," she replied, and sat down. She wore a dark blue suit with a gold-colored Christmas wreath pin in the lapel. "Well, actually, I'm exhausted. I was up until all hours last night. The students in my Western European politics seminar took me out for pizza and we got into this huge discussion that lasted until two in the morning. Don't students ever sleep?"

"Not during finals," I said.

She sighed. "I can't wait for Christmas vacation to begin. Are you going home?"

"No," I said. "I'm staying here. Too much work."

"How's the new project?"

"It's a little too early to tell," I said. "I've been reading everything about the movement that I can get my hands on. So far I've only done the one interview with the medical student, but I'm supposed to go to a meeting of the local Humanity For Animals chapter next Monday night. If I'm lucky I'll be able to line up some more interviews to do over the break."

"Sounds interesting," she said, yawning and shaking her head. "Excuse me. Gosh, I hope I can stay awake for the party tonight."

I looked at her. "Party?"

"Lydia, don't tell me you've forgotten? Tonight's the end of the year departmental cocktail party. How could you forget?"

"Is it really tonight?" I said.

"Yes! I can't believe you didn't remember. What if I hadn't come in here and reminded you?"

Now it was my turn to sigh. "I would have gone home, curled up with a glass of wine and a bowl of microwaved popcorn, and read about leg-hold traps, feed lots, and how steak gets made. Let me tell you, popcorn's about the only thing I can eat these days."

"Sounds grim."

"It is. But not as grim as chatting up Tom Shepherd over the punch bowl."

"Oh, come on, it's not so bad. It's only once a year."

"Twice," I corrected her. "There's the cocktail party every September to welcome the new faculty."

"Okay, okay. So twice a year you have to stand around and have a drink with your colleagues. Frankly, I think it's pretty pathetic that we get together so seldom. There are a couple of full professors I've never even *seen*."

"Well, they hide. This is only your first year, Pam. If you're lucky, you might spot them before you come up for tenure."

"I thought everyone was supposed to show up at these things," she said.

"They are," I said. "And those without tenure do. Those with tenure decide for themselves."

"I just don't understand it. You'd think you'd want to know the other people teaching in your own department."

I didn't respond. I'd decided long ago that, if and when I ascended into whalehood, I'd definitely take the absentee route for all optional departmental functions.

"I'm still working on getting people from other departments to give brown bag lectures to our faculty and graduate students. I think by next semester I'll have something lined up. It wouldn't be too elaborate, you know—just once a month get-togethers over the lunch hour to hear a talk. Do you think you could help me organize it?"

"Gosh, Pam, I don't know," I said. "I'm going to be pretty busy with this case study."

"Sure, of course," she said, and nodded.

I felt a stab of guilt, and gave it a firm push away. If Pam kept up these extra-research activities, she was going to overwhelm herself and go down on the tenure count. It was as simple as that. And my Red Cross training taught me never to grab hold of a drowning person—you're likely to drown, too. Better to swim alongside, leading the way out of the riptide, and hope the other person follows your example.

"Maybe you should let someone else get the thing off the ground," I said. "You're swamped as it is."

"I know," she said. "But no one else has managed to get anything going, *ever*. There's almost no interaction between departments at this university. It's really unbelievable."

Not so unbelievable, I thought. Most people knew better than to make that kind of effort.

There was another knock.

"Come in!" I called, and the door opened. "Hello, Meredith. Nice to see you."

"Hello, Professor Martin," Meredith Kospach said. Her big eyes behind the big glasses blinked and looked past me to Pam. "Oh, I'm sorry. I see you're busy."

"That's all right. We're just chatting."

"Hi, Meredith," Pam said. "How are you?"

"Fine, Professor Clark. And you?"

"Sleepy, but I'll live," Pam said, and gave her a warm smile. "Are you holding up under the end-of-the-semester crunch?"

"Yes, I think so," Meredith said. "Actually, I'm all done. My paper for Professor Martin's class was the last one I had to do."

"By the way, Meredith," I said, "Professor Clark has agreed to be your second reader."

"That's great," she said, turning to Pam. "Thank you."

"It's my pleasure," Pam replied. "You've chosen a fascinating topic. I'm looking forward to working with you on it."

"So, what's up?" I asked.

"I just stopped by to give you this." She handed me two typed pages. "It's my prospectus for the dissertation."

"Very good," I said, and glanced through the opening paragraph.

"There's a new book on the Green party in France I'd recommend you look at," Pam said. "Do you read French?"

"Yes. I audited a French class this semester to brush up for my language qualifying exam. I just passed it a few weeks ago."

"Good for you," she said. "The book's in my office. Stop by some time and you can pick it up."

"Thanks, Professor Clark."

"Which reminds me," I said. "You wanted to take your oral exam before the holiday break, right? Okay. I'll schedule something for next week, I promise. Call me Monday and I'll let you know what day."

She smiled. "Thanks. Bye."

"Bye, Meredith," Pam and I chimed together.

And she left.

"That's one bright young woman," Pam said.

"She should write a hell of a dissertation," I agreed. I looked at my calendar. "Maybe I'll try to schedule her exam next Wednesday morning. Say ten o'clock. Can you make that?"

"I think so."

"I'll have to check with Bill Tanner and maybe I'll ask Victor to come. Given her topic, it'd be good to have another comparative government person."

"You'll see them all tonight," she reminded.

I grimaced. "Right. What time do the festivities begin?"

"Five-thirty." Pam got up and stretched. "Don't be late, now."

"I'll have to stop off at home first and change. I also plan to grab a quick bite."

"Won't there be food there?"

"Sure. And if you can tell the difference between the egg rolls and the Swedish meatballs, you get a prize."

"Oh. That bad?"

"I've been through four of these already," I replied. "Trust me."

"Okay." She headed for the door. "See you tonight, then."

"See you tonight," I said, and settled back behind my desk to grade the next paper.

Our Christmas cocktail party was held every year in one of the older colonial pavilions that made up part of the original university design. We always had the use of the same large room, with French windows and a high, high ceiling. Spindle-legged chairs and brocaded loveseats were pushed up against the walls, and an enormous woven rug covered most of the parquet floor. The buffet table held chafing dishes with the interchangeable egg rolls and meatballs, and several vegetable dip platters. At the bar in the back of the room, your liquid version of holiday spirits was served up in a plastic cup.

Giving the scene a quick once-over when I walked in, I saw nothing had changed. As usual, the whale wives were out in force, this being one of the few occasions on which they made an appearance. They were older women who had raised their young and now pursued a variety of activities outside the university, which rendered them full of interesting conversation. Still, they made me nervous. They mixed more freely than their husbands, and you never knew when one would surface at your side.

As the chairman's wife and official hostess, Margaret Shepherd was circling near the door ready to greet all comers. She wore a blood-red dress of a conservative cut—no cocktail dresses at *this* cocktail party—and a salon-fresh hairdo. She gave me a standard smile and said, "Lydia, how nice to see you. There's a place to hang your coat in the back . . ."—as if the cloakroom had moved since the last party.

"Thanks, Margaret," I said, and walked down the hall to the rack of hangers. I took a moment to smooth my skirt and checked in the mirror to make sure no new banana stains had materialized. All was well. I hesitated and then buttoned up one more button on my blouse.

"That's a good idea," I heard a voice behind me say. I turned and saw Julia Garshin, her black hair falling over bare shoulders. She wore a strapless black dress with a side slit. "You show these old geezers some skin, they might keel over into the veggie dip. At least that's the effect I'm hoping for."

"Hello, Julia. Nice to see you."

"That's not true, but it's nice of you to say so," she said, and reached for a hanger.

Boy, she sure bolts out of the starting gate, I thought. I wanted nothing more than to get out of her way.

"Where's Victor?" I asked.

"He stopped on the way in to kiss some ass," she said, and turned. "Oh, here's my darling now. How was Margaret, Victor?"

"Fine," he said, not looking at her. He got out of his overcoat with a rough shrug. "Hello, Lydia. Good to see you."

"You, too," I said. "Well, I guess I'd better get out there and mingle."

"Yes, best to get it over with as quickly as possible," Julia replied. "Mercifully, anesthesia is provided. I intend to get myself a glassful right away. Unless of course *you'd* like to get one for me," she said to Victor.

"That's all right," he answered. "You've proven you're fully capable of helping yourself." And he walked out.

She smiled at me. "Gosh. It looks like I'm on my own."

"I'll see you out there, Julia," I said, and headed toward the main room.

I paused at the buffet table and pretended to look over the offerings while I got my bearings. It was a mistake.

"Hello, Lydia," came a deep voice at my side.

I turned. "Hello, Quincy. How are you?"

Quincy Burnbeck was an alpha whale. A towering slender man with a thick head of fading blonde hair, he had joined the department about fifteen years ago, having been bought away from Yale. At the time, people told me, he was considered quite a catch in the field of constitutional law, and as an inducement the university had offered him one of its most prestigious chairs. The only problem was that since he'd been hired he hadn't published anything. Nada.

"We haven't seen much of you lately," he said, and then looked past me. "Why, hello there, Hamilton. How are you?"

"Hello, Quincy, Lydia." Hamilton Farrell, one of two African-American professors in the department, was the senior person in congressional studies. Like Burnbeck, he, too, held a chair. But unlike Burnbeck, he published to beat the band. He tucked his hands in his pockets and rocked back on his heels to look up at Quincy. "Enjoying the party?"

"Always a nice little get-together," Quincy said. He turned to me. "Did you see the piece about Hamilton in the *University News*? He's been asked to testify before Congress."

"Really?" I turned to Hamilton. "On what?"

"Congressional/presidential relations," he said. "There's a subcommittee writing a report on how to improve communication between the two branches."

"How interesting," I said.

"Not as interesting as what Quincy here has been up to," Hamilton said. "I saw in the department newsletter that he's the featured speaker for the Learned Hand Award banquet this year." He smiled at Quincy. "Congratulations."

"Thank you," Quincy said.

It was then I realized I was caught in the middle of a classic whale jousting match. In this game, one person begins by flattering another, to which the other person responds with flattery of his own. In reality, however, each one is fishing for compliments as they vie in an ongoing contest for publicity. Whoever scores the most mentions wins, or, as in this case, whoever has the more prestigious mention. So far, Hamilton was ahead. The department newsletter was small beer compared to the more widely circulated *University News*.

"That's great, Quincy," I said.

He smiled and looked back at Hamilton. "So tell me what's new on the Hill these days," he said. "I'm taking my class to the Supreme Court on Friday."

"Can't say that I know," Hamilton said. "I haven't made it up there this semester—been too busy redrafting a manuscript on Congress and the Ford presidency. I had to make a few unexpected trips out to Michigan, to the Ford library. Last summer, during an interview, Gerry asked me to help reorganize the archives. Ever been?"

Quincy straightened his broad shoulders. Obviously neither one was about to give up the fight.

"Lydia! Lydia!"

It was Karl calling from across the buffet table. He beckoned with an urgent wave of his hand.

"Excuse me, please," I said, withdrawing from the field.

As I left I heard Quincy begin, "No, but I'd like to. In fact, Bill Rehnquist was telling me—"

Standing beside Karl was Emily. She wore a soft white sweater dress with a simple gold chain necklace. She looked pretty with her red curls and, for some reason, upset. Filling out the group were Felix, dapper per usual, and Gwen, whose ponytail had migrated up to a topknot.

"Have you heard the news?" Gwen gushed.

"No," I said. "What?"

All eyes turned to Karl.

"I got my Fulbright to Strasbourg," he said, beaming. "I just heard an hour ago."

"Karl, that's great. Congratulations!" I said. I glanced at Emily. She was trying hard to smile. "When will you go?"

"September," he said.

"Can you believe it?" Felix said. "What a lucky dog!"

"I'm so jealous," Gwen told Emily. "I suppose you'll put in for a leave of absence."

"I guess," Emily said. "I don't really know."

"But you *are* going, too, aren't you?" she asked.

"Well—"

"Emily, how can you even hesitate? Just think of the opportunities!" Gwen said.

"That's what I tell her," Karl said. "But she's worried she won't have anything to do."

"Good God, are you kidding?" Gwen said, rearing back slightly. "You could learn French, travel, take a cooking class!"

Emily frowned and twisted her necklace around a finger. "But I'm afraid I'll lose my job," she said.

"I thought you meant to quit it someday anyway," Felix said.

"Yes, but not next year."

"Felix is right. You should quit and just look for something else when you get back," Karl said.

"That's easier said than done," she replied.

"Well, you've got lots of time to think about it," I said. "It's a big decision to walk away from a paycheck."

"*I* think you're crazy," Gwen said, and turned to Felix. "Why don't you apply for one of these things?"

"I'll tell you where *I'd* like to go," Felix said. "Bellagio. You know, the Rockefeller villa on Lake Como, near the Italian Alps? It's the greatest academic boondoggle ever."

"Italy! Wouldn't that be fantastic?" Gwen said, clasping her hands together. "Say, maybe next year we could visit Karl and

Emily in France and then take a swing down to Venice. Would you mind visitors?"

"Not at all," Karl said. "The more the merrier."

Emily bit her lip and said nothing. Her freckles stood out against her pale cheeks.

To my left I caught sight of Victor and Danny.

"I'll be right back," I said. "I have to talk to Victor about an oral exam next week."

"When you're through, send them over," Felix said. "We can start planning our road trip to Strasbourg."

I crossed the room, edging my way past a pod of whales. They were gesturing to each other with meatballs speared on toothpicks. The clumps of meat were covered with a gooey red glaze.

"Hi, Danny, Victor," I said.

Victor turned at the sound of my voice and blinked hard at me. "Lydia," he said, and nodded.

"Hey, Lyd," Danny said. He was wearing a handpainted tie along with his ubiquitous gold earring. "Victor and I were just doing some sightseeing. Did you happen to notice who walked in a few minutes ago?"

"No," I said, glancing toward the door. "Who?"

"The new dean," Victor said. "He's over there, talking to Margaret Shepherd."

There was no difficulty locating Margaret. She was in earnest conversation with a balding plump middle-aged man of the nondescript variety.

"But that's Munsey," I said. "He's the assistant dean."

"Not any more, he isn't," Danny said. "Didn't you hear? He's been promoted. Word is the old dean pushed him through," Danny said. "And get this—he's been made a full professor as part of taking the position."

"A full. Just like that." I shook my head. "Wouldn't it be nice if it were so easy for the rest of us."

"I think he'll be fine," Victor put in, raising his chin. "I've always gotten along well with him."

"That's good," I said, taking a moment to register the implications of his statement. As dean, Munsey would have the final word on all tenure decisions, including Victor's and my own.

"Well," Danny said, "I guess it's nice to know that mediocrity has its rewards."

"Listen," I said. "I came to ask Victor something. I'm scheduling an oral exam for Meredith Kospach and I'd like you to be one of the examiners. Would Wednesday at ten be okay?"

"Sure. I can make it," Victor said.

"Great. I'll drop a note in your box to remind you, and include a copy of her prospectus. Thanks."

"Hey, what's with Karl?" Danny said. "He's whooping it up over there like he's actually having a good time."

"He's got some big news, but I'll let him tell you," I said. "Do you know if Bill Tanner's here? While I'm thinking of it, I want to ask him to come to this exam, too."

"I just saw him by the bar," Danny said. "Come on, Victor. Let's go check out Karl."

When I spotted Tanner he was talking to Emily, of all people. I figured she'd escaped Gwen and Felix by pleading a need for a drink and Bill had snagged her en route. He looked up as I approached, his light blue eyes making a quick skip from Emily to me.

"Hello, Lydia," he said in a pleasant voice. It had a depth of timbre that came across especially well on television. "Are you coming over to partake of the libations?"

"No, actually, I needed to ask you something," I said. "But I don't mean to interrupt your conversation."

"No, no," he said, turning back at Emily. "I was just telling Emily a few tales out of school about her boss."

"That's right," she said. If anything, her voice sounded more strained than ever. "Bill knows Professor McKenzie."

"Yes," he said to me. "Collin cuts quite a figure over at the law school. But I was telling her that in Washington, from what I hear from my friends in the administration, people look at him as being little more than a political groupie. He hangs around sniffing for crumbs, waiting for something to fall his way."

Emily frowned down at her plastic glass.

"I thought he had quite a good reputation," I said. "I've heard he's on the short list for Supreme Court nominees."

"Well . . . ," he drawled. "Don't believe everything people say. I understand lately he's been asking about openings for an ambassadorship or even a post to head up some delegation somewhere." He gave his boyish laugh. "My friends say they're considering him for an honorary position as White House pet. The President's parakeet died, you see, so the job is vacant."

I didn't laugh with him, seeing Emily's expression. She looked crushed.

"Say, Bill, before I forget, I've got a favor to ask you," I said, changing the subject.

"And what might that be?" he asked.

"One of my graduate students wants to take her American government qualifying exam before the break. Are you free next Wednesday at ten?"

"Let me see," he said, and pulled a small leatherbound agenda from his inner suitcoat pocket. He thumbed through it. "Ten on Wednesday. Yes, I can make it." With a quick movement he took out a pen and unscrewed the top. "These European pens are so clumsy," he said, though it looked, if anything, sleek and expensive. He closed up the book with a flourish and put away his pen. "Who's the student?"

"Meredith Kospach."

"Meredith Kospach?" He paused, smiling. "She's *your* graduate student?"

"Yes," I said. "She's asked me to be her first reader for her dissertation."

"She asked *you*?" There was still the easy smile, but I noticed the blue eyes had narrowed.

"Uh, yes. She was in my interest group seminar this semester. She's decided she wants to write about the international environmentalist movement."

"Sounds like a good topic," Emily said. "But she'd better make sure she can get something like that published when she's done."

But Bill did not seem to hear her. "So. I expect that means you'll want me to be her second reader."

"Well, actually, Bill. . . . " I was looking right into the blue daggers, now fully drawn. I went on in a rush. "She wanted me to ask Pam Clark. Pam knows quite a bit about the Green parties in France and Germany. I thought it was a good choice. Pam's already agreed to do it."

"Ah," he said. "Well. Yes, Professor Clark. I'm sure you made the right choice. It *is* just her first year with the department, isn't that right? I thought so. Hmmmm."

"I-I explained to Meredith the risk she was taking," I said. "I mean, after all, I don't have tenure either."

"Oh, you won't have any problem getting it," Emily said. "I'll bet anything you'll sail through. Don't you think so, Bill?"

A rush of blood flew to my cheeks. How could she ask such a thing in front of me? And of Tanner, of all people? An awkward pause followed.

"Certainly," Bill said.

The way he said it, though, I didn't think he sounded certain at all.

I took a deep breath. "Well, thanks for agreeing to sit in on the exam," I said, and stepped back. "You know, I think I will help myself to some of those libations after all. Excuse me—" And I headed for the bar.

I ordered a glass of white wine and took a couple of gulps before turning back around. When I did, Tanner was gone. Emily was still there, talking to one of the whale wives. I wanted to ask her if she'd noticed anything odd about Bill in that conversation, or if I were just imagining things. I decided it had to be the latter. Surely a guy like that would be only too happy to take a pass on yet another obligation, especially to a student.

In the near left corner I saw Tom Shepherd wrap up one conversation and look around. His eye lit on me, and he smiled.

Damn, I thought. Why me? I didn't want to hear more about his great expectations of me or my tenure file, not tonight.

I braced for what was coming—he'd taken a step or two in my direction—when suddenly he turned and hooked up with a couple of stray adjunct lecturers.

That's odd, I thought. Why *not* me? Then I looked to my right.

"We meet again," Julia said, and held out her glass to the bartender. "Could you fill that up, please?"

"Are you enjoying yourself?" I asked.

"You're kidding, aren't you?" she asked. "Thanks a lot," she said as she took her refill.

I decided I didn't feel like sparring. "All right. We'll skip that question. What are your plans for the holidays?"

She arched a brow. "Well, well, well," she said. "You can snap after all. And I thought everyone around here was always so excruciatingly polite."

I took another gulp of wine, furious with myself for allowing her to draw me out.

"Don't get me wrong," she said. "I find it refreshing." She paused, tilting her head. "Let's see. What are my plans for the holidays. . . . Well, we decided to skip Cancun, bag the Mediterranean cruise, and opt out of the Baja kayaking excursion. So I guess that means I'll be staying home with the kids and Victor. And you?"

"I'll be here."

"That's too bad. For you, I mean." She looked over and I followed her gaze to Victor. He was talking with Margaret and Tom Shepherd. "I don't imagine any of us will be going anywhere unless the assistant professor salaries get raised. I keep telling Victor it's not enough to suck up to people. He has to put himself out on the job market, get another offer, and make this place pay to keep him. But he won't—he's afraid the old boys will find out and think he's disloyal." She snorted. "He's such a fool."

"It's not so simple to get another job, you know," I said.

"He could at least try," she said. She shifted her glance and broke into a grin. "Hey! Look who just came in!"

I looked. Everyone did. There was a moment of absolute silence as Walter Kravitz walked into the room. Behind him was Pam.

Julia leaned over and said in a loud whisper, "I *told* you he had balls!"

He didn't even bother to take off his coat. He went to the buffet table, picked up a celery stick, and used it to scoop up a huge glob of dip.

Pam, with unerring radar, picked me out at once.

"Lydia!" she said.

It crossed my mind that I could get away with a cheerful Hi, Pam, and a wave, and just let her deal with Walter. It was obvious to everyone that she'd brought him, an act guaranteed to win her tar and feathers.

"Hi, Pam," I said, and was about to wave when, to my horror, I found my high-heeled feet making their way across the carpet. They took me right up to Walter.

"Hello, Walter. It's good to see you."

"Hello, Lydia," he said, wiping his fingers on a cocktail napkin. His dark hair looked in need of a trim and a comb.

"Hi, Lydia. Glad you made it," Pam said, slightly breathless. She turned to Walter. "Lydia almost forgot about the party. I had to remind her."

"Funny," he said to me. "I didn't forget. Wish I had."

"Oh, I wouldn't have let you!" Pam said, and gave a nervous laugh. People had stopped staring and were talking again, but in hushed tones. "I'm going to go hang up my coat. Do you want me to hang yours up, too?"

"No, that's okay," he said. "I don't plan to stay very long."

"Okay," she said, and scurried away.

He reached for a strip of green pepper and crunched into it. "So how's life been treating you lately, Lydia?"

"Okay," I said, and paused. "Listen, Walter, I didn't have a chance to tell you before. I'm sorry you were denied tenure. I was really surprised when I heard."

"Thanks," he said, and took another strip. "I was pretty surprised, too, let me tell you. I didn't think the bastards could get me."

I didn't want to respond to that, with all the whales so close by. "I read your book, you know. I thought it was great. Somebody else is reading it right now—I lent it out."

"That's all I've got, that book, to get me another job," he said.

"Have you started applying yet to other places?"

Technically, he still had his job at Patrick Henry for another year and a half.

"Sure, I've applied. So far I haven't made the short list anywhere. I can't even get hired for a non-tenure-track position, if you can believe that."

"Oh," I said. Where the hell was Pam? For that matter, where the hell were Karl, and Felix, and Victor, and Danny? I saw them huddled together in the corner, hands in their pockets, heads down.

"Shelly's not here?"

It was a stupid thing to ask, but I was desperate.

"No," Walter said, looking right at me. "She decided to skip this one."

"Here we go," Pam said, bobbing up at our side with drinks in hand. "I got you red wine," she told Walter. "But you can have the white if you want. I don't care."

"Well," I said, and made a show of looking at my watch. "I think I'll push off now. I'll see you guys around. And give my best to Shelly."

As I turned, Walter put a hand on my arm. "Take good care of yourself," he said. His eyes shone like black stones. "And watch your step. I wasn't smart enough to do that, but you are. Don't let them get you, too, Lydia. Don't give them any reason to care."

"Uh, okay. Thanks. Bye, now—" I said, and broke away. I headed straight for the cloakroom and grabbed my coat. I paused and glanced in the mirror, afraid of what I would see.

But it was only my face I saw there. My face.

Not Walter's.

A few minutes before seven on Monday evening I pulled up in front of 410 Rosehill Drive.

I cut the engine and sat as the cold seeped in. It had been a bad weekend. I'd slept fitfully, awakened by the worrying thoughts skimming through my mind. How in the world was I ever going to finish another book? If I could manage to complete a manuscript—a Herculean feat in itself—would that be enough?

I looked the house over. It was a small place made of brick, with a tiny yard. Someone, however, had managed to squeeze in a garden plot along the side. At the moment it was no more than a patch of dug-up earth.

This had better go well, I thought.

I reached for my purse and got out. On the porch were a couple of bikes and some empty flower pots. There was a sign on the door, handwritten. It said:

If you've come here to ask for money, we reserve the right to ask some from you—Humanity For Animals.

That ought to cut down on the door-to-door solicitors, I thought, and knocked.

A young woman in a rose-colored blouse and dark slacks opened the door. Her light hair was pulled back into a ponytail, her bangs stylishly feathered.

"Yes?" she said.

I paused.

"Kathy Durban?" I said.

"Yes?" she repeated.

For a moment I was flustered. What the hell was a television reporter doing here?

"Maybe I have the wrong address," I said. "I heard there was a Humanity For Animals meeting here tonight."

"Sure! Of course, come on in," she said. "Is this the first time you've attended a meeting?"

I entered and took off my coat. "You're a member?" I asked in reply.

"Card carrying," she said. "It's always a pleasure to welcome someone new."

"Thank you," I said, "but I really should explain why I've come. My name is Lydia Martin. I'm a professor at the university, and I'm working on a project involving animal rights groups. I'd like to sit in tonight as part of my research. Is that okay?"

She sighed and smiled while she hung up my coat. "I knew it was too good to be true. Attendance has really been dropping off lately, with the students getting ready to go home for the break. Look, have a seat and make yourself comfortable. Once the others get here we can decide if it's alright for you to observe a meeting. I'm going to make some tea."

"Thanks," I said.

When she was out of the room, I took a good look around. Against the side wall was a couch that looked as though it could use some reupholstering. Other furnishings included a couple of stuffed chairs and a ring-stained coffee table. Potted plants abounded; huge palm-leafed varieties sat in the corners and all sorts of ferns and ivy lined the mantelpiece and window sills. A fringed rug with bright South American accents lay in front of the fireplace. The fireplace itself was swept clean and looked unused.

Gazing at it I felt a shiver, and realized that I was cold. Didn't they have heat in the place? I peered at the thermostat. It was set for sixty degrees.

Spartan, I thought, and walked into the center of the room, rubbing my arms. Tacked to the wall over the sofa was a poster. It showed a picture of a live cat, its head in a vise with electrodes attached to its skull. A text was printed over the picture. It read:

> We have enslaved the rest of the animal creation, and have treated our distant cousins in fur and feathers so badly that beyond doubt, if they were able to formulate a religion, they would depict the Devil in human form.
>
> William Ralph Inge, "The Idea of Progress"

In the two weeks since I'd interviewed Charlie I had read a good bit of the animal rights literature, and had seen my fair share of poor creatures tied up, strapped down, and cut open. It was pretty horrific. I knew enough about media techniques, however, to be wary of such images and their calculated effect.

And speaking of the media, it interested me that Kathy Durban was an HFA member. When I thought back on her coverage of the hospital demonstration, one could say it had taken a certain slant, emphasizing the group's message over its behavior. Clearly, too, she'd exaggerated the number of protesters involved. At the time I'd put it down to error in the midst of confusion. Now I wasn't so sure.

The front door swung open and I heard a young woman's voice say, "Go on, get in there, George." An enormous gray cat dashed inside and across the room.

The spiky blonde with pouting lips followed.

"Oh, hi," she said. The plastic handcuffs were gone, but her armload of silver bracelets remained. They clinked as she threw off her coat and held out her hand. "I'm Amy. Who're you?"

"Lydia Martin," I said. "Nice to meet you."

"Some night, huh? It's freezing out there." She huddled in an oversized turtleneck sweater. "Hey, Kath."

"Hi, Amy." Kathy walked in carrying a tray with four steaming cups. "You met Lydia?"

"Yeah. A new person, right?"

"Lydia's a professor. She's doing a study of animal rights. She wants to know if it's okay to sit in on a meeting."

Amy shrugged and reached for a cup. "Okay by me. But Hathor may not like it."

"I know," Kathy said. "But I think we ought to talk her into it. It'll probably be just the three of us again tonight."

Amy bit a lip. I figured she was eighteen, if that. "In *that* case. . . . Lydia. That's your name, right? Mind if I make a little suggestion?"

"No, please, go ahead. What is it?" I said.

"Take off your shoes."

"Excuse me?"

"Oh, God, I didn't even notice," Kathy said. "You'd better give those to me—I'll put them in the bedroom. Hathor would have a fit if she saw them."

I was about to ask why and then instantly I knew. Of course. They were leather. I sat on the couch and quickly slipped them off.

"Here you go," I said, and handed them over. Kathy disappeared down the hall.

"Hathor can't bear the sight of animal corpses," Amy explained. "There'd be no way she'd stay in the same room with those shoes. If she knew they were stashed in the back. . . . "

"But you won't tell her, will you?"

"Nah." Amy put her cup down and sat on the floor on the other side of the coffee table. She hugged her knees, her bracelets glinting in the lamplight. "So you're a professor. What do you teach?"

"Political science," I said. "Are you a student at the university?"

"Yup," she said. "I haven't taken any poly sci courses, though. I'm a religion major. I graduate this May."

Kathy came back into the room. "All taken care of. There's nothing else, is there? Your purse?"

"Canvas," I said, lifting its strap. It was just by luck I'd chosen to bring it that night instead of the bulkier leather satchel.

"Good—"

Without warning the door opened again. In walked Hathor, wearing a faded denim jacket and torn jeans. Down her back fell the thick brown braid.

"Hi, everybody," she said, and started taking off her coat. She stopped when her dark eyes fastened on me. "Who are you?" she asked.

"I'm Lydia Martin," I said, and stood to hold out my hand. "Nice to meet you."

"I know you," she said, keeping her grip on the front of her jacket. "You were at the hospital."

Amy and Kathy looked at me.

"You were?" Amy asked.

"Yes," I said, lowering my hand. "I had to take my neighbor to the emergency room that day. That's how I learned of your group."

"Oh," Kathy said, and turned back to Hathor. "Lydia's a political scientist. She's studying the animal rights movement and she's asked for permission to sit in on the meeting tonight."

Hathor's eyes raked me from head to toe, and lingered on my stockinged feet. Then she turned her back and got out of her coat. She threw it on the chair next to Amy's.

"I think we ought to let her," Kathy went on. "We always talk about the importance of reaching out to as wide an audience as possible. Lydia's research could be another venue for us."

Hathor sat down in the chair farthest away from me and folded her arms against her chest. "What's your interest in Humanity For Animals?" she asked in a cold voice.

I sat up straight on the edge of the couch. "Well, as Kathy mentioned, I'm a political scientist at the university. My specialty is interest groups, particularly new ones. The animal rights movement appears to be in the early stages of getting off the ground, and I'm interested in how a group such as yours becomes established."

"Early stages," Hathor snorted to Amy and Kathy. "Shows you how much she knows." She turned back to me. "*You* may think the cause is brand-new, but some of us have been involved for a long time."

"I'm talking about the movement's political potency," I replied. "Surely you'd agree that the animal rights movement fails to enjoy widespread public support."

She didn't answer. She reached for a cup of tea instead.

"We're making some progress," Amy told me, resting her chin on her knees.

"That's right," Kathy said. "Here in Albemarle, for instance, it used to be that you could waltz into the animal shelter and take your pick of the strays for lab experiments. There's a city ordinance against that now. And the people sitting here in this room helped get it passed."

"I don't mean the movement is ineffective," I said. "But from my perspective you're still out on the fringes. You don't turn on the TV and hear folks arguing over vivisection, not like they do over global warming. Do you understand what I mean? You haven't penetrated the general consciousness yet. But saying that doesn't mean you never will."

"Do you support the movement?" Hathor asked.

"No," I said. "But I don't *not* support it, either. I want to understand its dynamics, get a fix on who's attracted to the cause and why. The most I can promise is a fair presentation of your purpose. That's all. You'll have to decide if that's enough."

For a moment there was silence.

"What do you think, Hathor?" Amy asked.

Hathor looked at her. "You and Kath want her to stay?"

"I think it's a good idea," Kathy said.

Amy nodded.

"Okay, then," Hathor said, and again her dark eyes rested on me. "You can stay."

I took a deep breath and reached into my purse. "Thank you," I said, and set my tape recorder on the table.

"You're going to tape us?" Amy asked, squirming slightly.

"Yes," I said. "But I won't use any names, not without your permission."

The three women exchanged looks. Then Kathy laughed.

"In for a penny, in for a pound," she said, and took a seat next to me on the couch.

"I'd also appreciate the opportunity to interview each of you individually," I said.

"Forget it," Hathor said. "We've got business to discuss."

"I meant later, at your convenience," I said, and glanced at Amy and Kathy. "It would help my work enormously."

"You can interview me," Kathy said, straightening. "I've got no problem with that. You can even do it after the meeting tonight if you want."

"That would be terrific," I said. "Thank you."

"Professional courtesy," she said. "I know how hard it can be to get people to talk to you."

"Are we going to start this meeting or not?" Hathor said.

I sat back and took out a small notepad and pen.

"Okay," Kathy said. "Let's begin. Amy, do you have those clippings from our Thanksgiving Feast?"

"Yeah," Amy said. She reached over to her coat and pulled some pieces of newspaper from its pocket. "Here. This one's from the *Albemarle Register*. It was pretty good. We actually made the front page of the second section."

She put the clipping on the coffee table. The headline read TURKEYS GOBBLE UP THE TRIMMINGS. Beneath that was a smaller headline: Thanksgiving Escapees.

"We saved a bunch of turkeys from a local farm," Amy explained to me, "and fed them a special dinner on Thanksgiving."

"Saved?" I asked.

"We bought them," Kathy said.

I was disappointed. An illegal raid would have been more interesting.

"I'd thought I'd talked the station into covering it," Kathy said. "Especially since I shot the video for them myself. It was supposed to run as a ten-second spot, but it got bumped by the emergency room raid."

"I tried to get the student papers interested, but they blew me off," Amy said. "I think it was because all the reporters were away for the break."

"Lazy bastards," Hathor said. "But I'll bet they wish they could have been at the hospital."

"I'm sure all the papers do," Kathy said. "It's too bad we weren't able to give people more notice."

"Look at this," Hathor said, pointing to another clipping. "The *City Weekly* covered the demonstration in their Who's News column, but they got our name wrong. Called us Humans For Animals. Typical."

"I don't mean to change the subject," Amy said, "but what about trying to get a speaker down from Washington? Has anybody been working on that?"

"I am," Hathor said. "HFA's national office promised us somebody, but not until late January, at the earliest."

"That's good," Kathy said. "Nothing's going on at the university that early in the semester. We should get a decent turnout, at least among the students. I'll make sure someone from the station covers it."

"Can you do that?" I asked.

"Not always," she said. "But something like this, where there's bound to be controversy. . . . Usually my boss goes for that kind of stuff."

"It would be especially controversial if you could arrange to hold it at the medical school," I said.

"I thought you were just supposed to listen and not say anything," Hathor said to me.

"Take it easy, Hathor," Kathy said. "She's allowed to make a suggestion." She thought for a moment. "You know, that's a great idea. Amy, can you check into reserving one of the auditoriums over there? Let's see how much resistance they give us."

"Okay," Amy said.

The cat jumped onto the couch, climbed up to the top of the cushions, and started kneading the fabric.

"If we handle the publicity right, we could get an enormous turnout," Kathy said.

"Especially if Hathor designs the flyers," Amy added. She looked at me. "You should see Hathor's calligraphy sometime. It's incredible."

"I'd love to," I said.

Hathor took another sip of her tea.

Then the meeting proceeded as the women went over future projects, which included recruiting more people to disrupt the hunting season and setting up booths at the next county fair to protest the annual rodeo. After another hour, they wrapped up.

They were only three people, but for my purposes a group was a group was a group. The tape in my recorder turned, capturing every word.

Humanity For Animals?

Secretly I had my own name for them: Tenure For Lydia.

"Nobody has to stay for this," Kathy said, tucking her legs beneath her. "I'll just be saying what you've both heard before."

I was busy putting in a new tape and making sure it was properly labeled.

"That's okay," Amy said. "I want to see what it's like to be interviewed. Don't you, Hathor?"

"I already know," she said. "It doesn't matter what you say, the interviewer always gets it wrong. People can't see past their own illusions."

I didn't exactly appreciate the remark, but I wasn't going to argue with her. I needed her cooperation as much as, if not more than, the others'.

"All right," I said, and switched on the recorder. "Ready when you are."

Kathy took a breath and closed her eyes, composing her expression. I figured it was a learned technique, something she did before the cameras were about to roll. Then she gave a great sigh and looked at me. "Okay."

"Why don't you start by telling me a little bit about your background, where you grew up and that sort of thing?"

She smiled. "Sure," she said, and began describing her family home in the Virginia countryside. Most people, when they give a spontaneous account of themselves, will move forward and then backtrack a little, saying, "Oh, I forgot to say this about then. . . ." But with Kathy, after the first few sentences it became clear she had spent the last hour preparing in her own mind exactly what she wished to say. There were no ellipses, no awkward transitions. She had a straight-line narrative, through her involvement with the environmentalist movement in high school, her conversion to vegetarianism in college, and her growing commitment to animal rights.

I was impressed, and disconcerted. She was too polished. She intended to show me only her very best dots.

"Then I finally came to the realization that our view of ourselves as a species is fundamental to all our problems," she said. "We think that as humans we're special, somehow set apart from and better than all the other living organisms in the world. But that perspective is simply another form of racism—let's call it speciesism. It's a blind prejudice, a false sense of superiority that has allowed us to trample on the rights of other animals and destroy the earth. But if we were to readjust our thinking, if we were to look upon ourselves as co-creatures, all with an equal right to a safe and healthy environment, then all the world's problems would disappear. There would be no pollution, no wars, no famine. And our enslavement of animals, their holocaust, would finally end."

"Wow," Amy said. "That's really beautiful."

Kathy blinked, her concentration broken. "Thanks," she said, and poured herself more tea. She glanced over at Hathor, who gave her a silent gaze in return.

"When did you become active in the movement?" I asked. "In college?"

"No, it wasn't until after I'd graduated. I'd moved to Ohio, looking for work," she said.

"Was there anything in particular that drew you to Humanity For Animals, such as a rally or lecture?"

"No. It was really because of my experience waiting tables in a fancy restaurant. I worked there to make some money until something opened up in one of the television stations. Being a vegetarian, I should have known there'd be problems. But the tips were extremely good, and I thought that so long as *I* stuck to my principles, that was all that really mattered." She peered into her cup and shook her head. "Well, I was wrong. The menu was grotesque—milk-fed veal, foie gras, steak tartare, calf's liver, the works. In the kitchen, the cooks pulled the legs off living crabs for fun and put live lobsters in the microwave to cook. I can still hear the sound of their claws slamming into the window. It was a nightmare."

"God," Amy said, and put her head in her hands.

Kathy looked up at me. "I worked there for a year, telling myself I needed the money too badly to quit. But then one day I snapped. Just like that. I was waiting on a couple of businessmen. One man ordered Hindquarter of Baby Lamb, Provençale. The other asked for Sweetbreads Supreme, and then said, 'Can you tell me how they're prepared?' and I said, 'Sure. What they do is, they take a calf—a baby cow—kill it and then rip out its thymus. That's the gland-like lymph tissue at the base of its neck that helps develop the immune system. Of course the calf doesn't need to worry anymore about its immune system. The animal is now dead, in order that you may enjoy this piece of tissue braised in a dry white wine sauce.' I turned to the other man. 'And would you like me to explain how your dish is prepared?' At that point, they yelled for the maitre d'."

Hathor grinned.

"I'll bet the restaurant didn't think it was so hot," I said.

"No," Kathy said. "Of course I was fired. The next week I went to work in a vegetarian restaurant, as I should have done in the first place. *That's* when I joined Humanity For Animals." She frowned. "It's funny, the sort of tricks we play on ourselves to try and justify behavior we know is wrong. I promised myself I'd never do that again, ever. I try to stay clear-sighted."

"And when did you finally break into television?" I asked.

"Just a few months later. But by then my focus had changed. It was becoming pretty clear to me that film is really the most powerful medium we have to communicate with one another, and I decided I wanted to be a shaper of the message, not just a receiver. In the year I've been with the station here, I've taken classes at the university in filmmaking. Eventually I want to make documentaries about animal rights. So that is the direction of my energy now." She paused. "With every passing day I gain more experience and knowledge. Someday I'll make a movie that will wake up the whole world. That is my dream."

She stopped. Her cheeks flushed a light pink.

I reached over and snapped the recorder off.

"God, Kathy," Amy said. "That was fantastic! And you'll do it, I know you will. You have the focus. God!"

Focus was right, I thought. She had the unmistakable intensity of a dedicated activist.

"Thank you," I said. "That was very interesting."

"Do you think you can use that?" she asked.

"Absolutely," I said, and started rewinding the tape.

"What happens next?" she asked. "Do I get to see what you write about me?"

"I'll let you look at the transcript of the tape, just to make sure everything's accurate," I said. "And I won't quote you without your permission. Sound fair?"

"Very fair," she said.

Amy gazed up at me. "When's my turn?"

"Whenever you like."

"Can we do it before I leave for Christmas vacation?"

"Sure," I said. "How about tomorrow?"

She shook her head. "I've got two exams tomorrow and another one on Wednesday. But I could do it Thursday. I leave Friday to go home."

"Okay. Just tell me what time and write down your address and phone number," I said, giving her my notepad.

"Why don't you come over for lunch?" Amy said.

"Sounds great." I took back the pad and squinted at it. "Where's Dogwood Lane?"

"It's off the highway going west, toward the Blue Ridge," she said. "Do you know Hunting Meadows Farm, where they hold the steeplechase races every year? Take that exit and go past Hunting Meadows. We're down the next road on the left."

"Wow. You're really out in the country," I said.

"Yeah," she said. "I love it."

Kathy stood up and stretched. "I hate to kick you out, but I've got to get up early tomorrow. The station is sending a crew over to Williamsburg. We're covering the governor's meeting with the state college presidents."

"Well, thanks for everything," I said, rising. I looked down at my feet. How was I going to leave without my shoes?

"Come on, Hathor, let me give you a ride home," Amy said, tossing over her denim jacket.

"If you'd stay just a moment, Lydia, there're some books I can lend you to read," Kathy said.

"That would be great," I said.

Hathor put on her jacket, watching me.

I swallowed. "It was nice to meet you, Hathor. Is there any chance I could interview you, too?"

She nodded. "Maybe."

"Great!" I knew my surprise sounded in my voice, but I couldn't help it. "Thank you."

She didn't break her stare. "You can get my number from Kathy . . . along with the rest of the things she intends to give you." Her gaze swept down and then, just as quickly, she turned. "Let's go, Amy. Mother's waiting."

"Bye!" Amy said, her bracelets jangling in salute. "See you Thursday."

Kathy closed the door behind them and leaned against it. "Whew. I was afraid you were going to have to leave barefoot. Thank goodness Hathor decided not to make an issue out of your shoes."

"You think she knew?"

Kathy gave me a look. "Of course. Hathor's no idiot."

"By the way, what does she do? Is she a student, too?"

"No."

"What is she, then?"

She smiled. "I think she should tell you, don't you?"

I said goodbye to Kathy and stepped out into the frigid night air. I was halfway down the walk when a dark figure turned off the street and headed right at me. I stopped, suddenly rigid.

The man approached.

"Hello, Lydia," he said.

"Charlie!" I cried, and let out a gasp of air. "What in the world are you doing here?"

"I was waiting for the meeting to break up," he said. "I thought everyone had left by now."

"They have. I stayed because Kathy had some books to lend me." I had a couple tucked under my arm. "Is she expecting you? She said something about turning in early."

"She'd better be expecting me." I could hear his smile. "I live here, too."

"Oh!" I said, and in a flash I saw the connection. Kathy had mentioned moving to Ohio after college, and that she'd only lived in Albemarle for a year. "You and she are together?"

"That's right," he said.

"Why didn't you say so?" I felt a burst of irritation and tried to cover it with a laugh. "I mean, you could have told me that the meeting was at *your* house."

"I guess." For a moment he said nothing. "What books did she give you? Here, let's move under the streetlight so we can see."

We walked toward the curb, our breath smoking around us.

"This is a good one," he said, tapping the spine. "You should read it first."

"I thought you were out of the animal rights movement," I said.

"I am," he replied, a slight edge in his tone. "But I can still recommend a book, can't I?"

I stood back, clutching the books to my chest. "Tell me, what does Kathy think about your decision to return to medical school?"

"She's not happy about it," he said. In the yellow light, his face looked eerie.

"I can imagine!"

He stiffened. "What do you mean?"

"I just interviewed her," I said. "She sounds pretty committed to the cause."

"So?"

I shrugged. "So, it would seem that living with a guy who's cutting up animals could be a problem."

He didn't say anything in response, but his breath came and went in great white puffs.

"Not that it's any of my business," I said, and smiled. "Well, I'd better be going. Bye, Charlie."

I walked to my car and got in. As I revved the engine, I caught his silhouette in the side mirror. He stood for a moment by the curb before heading back up the walk. To Kathy.

What I said was true, I thought. It really is none of my business. And I put my foot to the gas.

I leaned against the front edge of my desk and looked at my watch. It was almost a quarter past ten o'clock.

"Let's give him just a few more minutes," I said. "Then we'll begin."

The four of us were in my office—Victor, Pam, me, and Meredith Kospach. It was Wednesday, the day of Meredith's qualifying oral exam, and the questioners were all assembled except for Bill Tanner. He was late.

"Looks like you might have just the three of us to contend with," Victor told Meredith.

"Yes," I said, "but that also means we each get more time to ask questions."

"That's fine," Meredith said, and smiled.

"I'm sure you'll do very well," Pam said.

"Thanks, Professor Clark," she said.

She didn't look or sound nervous, which was good. I'd already advised her on what she should expect. Each university handled the oral exams differently, but at Patrick Henry the questions usually focused on the student's dissertation prospectus, given that one's general knowledge had already been tested in the written exams. I'd told Meredith to view her orals as an opportunity to discuss her research plans with more experienced scholars.

"Are you going home for the holidays?" Pam asked her.

"Yes," she said. "I leave tomorrow. I'm flying to Milwaukee."

"Milwaukee," Victor said. "I'll bet it's cold there."

"We've already had snow," Meredith said. "My parents called last weekend. There's over a foot on the ground."

Just then the door swung open and Bill Tanner walked in.

"Sorry I'm late," he said, setting his briefcase against the wall. "I had a call from one of the political correspondents at *Time* wanting to talk about the congressional campaigns. You know how it is."

Of course none of us did, but no one was going to say so.

"Good to see you, Bill," Victor said, blinking up at him.

Bill nodded back, taking a seat. With the flat of his palm, he smoothed his trousers and then crossed his legs.

I moved to sit behind my desk.

"Now that we're all here, we might as well begin," I said. "Meredith, if you'd please wait outside for just a moment...?"

"Of course," she said, and stepped out, closing the door behind her.

"Well," I said, "I don't think Meredith Kospach needs much of an introduction—I'm sure you're all familiar with her record. She's one of the department's outstanding students. Speaking from my own experience in the classroom with her, she's impressed me with her ability to absorb information and come to original conclusions."

Victor nodded. "What I've always liked is her written work," he said. "I had her in my international conflict management seminar. Her writing is as clear as a bell."

"I saw her give a presentation at the Student Forum Workshop a few weeks ago," Pam said. "She was great. She has a lot of poise for a graduate student. And she seems very committed to the profession."

"I believe that's true," I said. "She has the potential to be an extremely good political scientist. It wouldn't surprise me if she wound up as the department's number one candidate for the Patrick Henry University Fellowship next fall." It was the school's most prestigious award. "As for any weaknesses," I continued, "the only thing I could say is that I've noted a tendency to rush things a little bit, to fly headlong to her final point. She needs to linger a little more over the details so that her audience stays with her every step of the way."

I paused. I noticed that Pam and Victor were looking at me, but Bill's attention was fixed on something over my head.

"Is that an original Peter Max?" he asked, pointing.

I turned. He was looking at a poster tacked to the wall.

"Yes," I said. "Yes, it is."

He shook his head. "You should have it framed. Otherwise the edges will start to curl."

"Uh, okay. Thanks." I cleared my throat and glanced at Pam and Victor. Victor's face was totally blank. Pam's brows arched in a Don't ask me! expression. "Anyway," I said, "I assume you all have read Meredith's prospectus."

Pam and Victor had their copies sitting in their lap. Bill had nothing. He crossed his arms.

"You did get a copy, didn't you, Bill?" I asked.

"Oh, yes," he said, smiling, but made no move to produce it.

"All right," I said. "I guess we're ready to start. Victor, would you call Meredith back in?"

"Sure," he said, getting up and opening the door. "Meredith? You can come in now."

She entered and moved toward a chair in the corner of the room facing the rest of us. When she was seated she looked around with a small smile.

My plan was to begin by asking her to describe how she had first become interested in her dissertation topic. It was a way of putting her at ease, and of establishing an exchange without any pressure. I took a breath to speak.

Instead Bill Tanner said, "I suppose, as the senior faculty member here, I should get the ball rolling."

"Sure! By all means," I said, and sat back. It hadn't occurred to me that Bill would want to open the proceedings, but I had the feeling he thought it should have.

"Ms. Kospach," he said.

Meredith looked wide-eyed at him from behind her oversized glasses.

For a moment it appeared that was all he intended to say. He sat, his arms folded, mulling over Peter Max. Then he cocked his head to one side, dropped his glance to her, and smiled.

"I'm going to use the time allotted to me ask you a few questions about your understanding of the American political system. I want you to demonstrate the depth as well as the breadth of your knowledge, so don't hesitate to give lengthy answers. I expect them to be long. The subjects demand precise explanations."

Good God, I thought. What the hell is he doing? In principle, a professor was free to ask any question at the orals, on any subject related to the field. But it was an option that no one ever exercised. I had certainly not expected such questions, and I was sure Meredith had not either. I looked at her. She had one hand clasped in the other on her lap. Her knuckles were white.

"First, I'd like you to tell me what you think of the system of divided government," he said. "Does it work?"

She wet her lips. "Divided government," she said.

It was obvious she had repeated the words simply as a reflex and to give herself a moment to collect her thoughts, but Bill said, "Yes, divided government. You *do* know what I mean by that term, don't you?"

"Yes, yes, of course," she said, stammering slightly.

He's unnerving her, I thought, throwing her off stride before she's even begun.

"Then please answer the question." He paused ever so slightly. "Beginning with a definition if you would."

"Okay," she said, nodding. "Divided government is when the party that controls Congress is different from the party that holds the White House."

"Stop right there," Tanner said, holding up his hand. "'Is when'? Divided government 'is when'? That's the sort of locution I expect from a first-year student fresh out of high school. Divided government is a phenomenon, perhaps, or an arrangement of power, but not a 'when.' I asked you to be precise, Ms. Kospach. Now please continue. Does such an *arrangement* work?"

"It doesn't always work," she said in a quavering voice. "There have been periods in our nation's history of terrible legislative logjams. In fact—"

"So?" Tanner said. "Do you therefore prefer the British parliamentary system to the American separation-of-powers system?"

"No," she said. "No. The parliamentary system allows the majority view in the country to dominate without any kind of check. Laws get passed more easily and quickly, but they aren't always well balanced or—"

"Are you saying, then, that one is given to too much speed and the other too little? Is that your assessment?"

"Well, no, not exactly. There have been other times when the President and Congress have worked effectively together to pass lots of important laws even during periods of divided government. As an example—"

"I'm afraid you have me very confused, Ms. Kospach. What *is* your answer to my question?" He sat forward. "Let me repeat it, if that will help. Does divided government work?"

There was no mistaking the panic in Meredith's expression. "Sometimes it does. Sometimes it doesn't. . . . "

Her voice trailed off. For once Tanner didn't interrupt, but just let the sentence dangle.

"Sometimes it does, sometimes it doesn't," he repeated in a dry voice. "I'm afraid I don't find that response very illuminating, not without further clarification. I would like you to expound, including reference to the views of various experts on the subject, such as Mayhew, Jones, Fiorina, and Jacobson."

Meredith bit her lip. Her eyes were very wet.

After a long pause Tanner sat back. "Thank you, Ms. Kospach. I have no additional questions."

For a moment no one spoke. Victor pretended to look over the prospectus. Pam gazed at Meredith. I thought I saw the gleam of tears in her eyes as well.

Don't do anything, I silently warned Pam. Don't do anything, don't say anything.

Beware the whale.

"Well," I said, breaking the silence, "I guess I'll go next. Meredith, I was wondering if you'd tell us what led you to choose this topic for a dissertation."

She nodded but said nothing.

Okay, I thought. She can't talk yet, not without crying.

I made a show of paging through some notes. "I believe you've struck on quite an original idea. Why *did* the environmental movement result in the formation of a new political party in Europe but not in the United States? It's an excellent question that will no doubt shed some light on the fundamental differences between the American and European political cultures."

"Yes, it does," Meredith began, and swallowed hard. She kept her attention fixed on me and away from Tanner. "I guess I first got the idea a couple of years ago. . . . "

She went on to trace the origins of her project. But it was too late. The damage had already been done. Her confidence was utterly demolished. She stuck to short sentences and tentative explanations, not daring to show the slightest hint of panache. Pam and Victor threw her the softest of softball questions, but even then she pressed them to rephrase each one two or three times to make sure she understood exactly what they meant. All the while Tanner sat and watched and listened, and didn't say another word.

"Well, I guess that about does it," I said to Meredith. "Why don't you go out and stretch your legs for a few minutes? We'll call you when we've reached our decision."

She nodded and rose, not looking at anyone. Very softly she closed the door behind her.

For a moment the four of us sat there without saying a word. Then I picked up a pen and twirled it between my fingers.

"Bill?" I said. "Do you want to start?"

He pursed his lips and brushed an invisible speck of lint from his suitcoat sleeve. "Well, I don't see that there's really much to talk about," he said. "She obviously failed. She was unable to answer the simplest of questions."

"Only because you made her so nervous," Pam blurted out.

Tanner turned in his seat to face her. I saw his pale blue eyes take on a new focus. "I beg your pardon?"

"I think you made her too nervous," Pam said. "You kept interrupting her and never let her finish. Maybe you didn't realize it, but you were much too hard on her."

He stared at her. Then he said, "How many of these oral exams have you participated in, Professor Clark?"

She shifted in her seat. "This is my first one. Aside from my own."

He nodded. "I see. Do you know how many *I* have conducted? Scores. Keeping these facts in mind, do you still feel it is within your scope of competence to criticize me?"

"I just don't think she should fail, that's all," Pam said.

He smiled and looked back at Victor and me. "Well, I believe there's nothing further to discuss. Unless either of you would also care to differ with my evaluation."

Victor and I exchanged glances and said nothing.

"Fine," he said, and rose. "I'll leave it to you, Lydia, to give Ms. Kospach the regrettable news. I'm afraid such a task is one of those little unpleasant duties of being a dissertation advisor." He reached for his briefcase and straightened. "You know, you really ought to do something for poor Peter Max." And he went out the door, humming.

Victor stood up.

"What are you doing?" Pam asked.

"Leaving," he said. "The exam is over."

"Wait a second," she said. "You aren't going to let him get away with that, are you?" She looked at me. "Are you?"

"Pam, there's nothing we can do," I said. "He's the senior guy. If he says Meredith failed, she failed."

"But it's not fair!" she cried. "He browbeat her! She didn't have a chance!"

"Pam, it doesn't matter," Victor said. "It's over."

"No! It's not right! It's not fair! He kept tripping her up, picking her apart, asking her questions no one else ever has to answer."

"But which anyone should be able to answer," Victor said. "Meredith lost her cool and *allowed* herself to be tripped up. Tanner was hard on her, I'll grant you that, but part of being a professional is learning to handle yourself under fire."

Pam sat back, her mouth open. "So you two are just going to accept this? Are you, Lydia? What about all those things you said at the beginning, about how great Meredith is? You said she was the likely candidate for the Patrick Henry University Fellowship."

"Not anymore," Victor muttered.

"Look, Pam," I said. "I'll handle it, okay? She'll get another shot, and next time I'll make sure Tom Shepherd is here, too. With another senior person around, I don't think Tanner will pull the same stunt."

"Good idea," Victor said, and made for the door. "See you later." And he left.

Pam stood up. "I can't believe you're going to fail her," she said. "I can't believe you didn't say anything to Tanner in her defense."

"And what was I supposed to say?" I shot back. "He's entitled to ask her anything, you know that."

"But not in such a way that he intimidates her," she said. "As her first reader, you should have stepped in. You should have done more to protect her."

"And how was I to do that?" I asked, my voice rising. "Just how was I supposed to protect her? By telling Tanner to back off? What do you think would have happened then? Do you think he'd have said, 'Oh, excuse me—I'm sorry, I didn't mean to be so mean. . . .'? Is that what you think would have happened?" I threw my pen on the desk. "Grow up, Pam. This is the way the world works. You can't expect me to change it."

"I don't expect you to change the world," she said, grabbing her purse. "But I do expect you to act with decency. Letting Tanner fail Meredith on the basis of this exam is wrong. You know that."

"I told you, she'll have another shot. I'll make sure she gets through next time."

"Will you?" She looked at me. "And what if Shepherd decides to go along with Tanner, too? What then?"

"I'll handle it," I said. "It's not your problem, it's mine."

"No," she said. "It's not yours or mine. It's Meredith's. And I wish her a lot of luck."

She walked out, leaving the door open behind her.

Damn it! I thought.

For a moment I sat, head in my hands. Then I got up. It was time to talk to Meredith.

When I went out into the hallway, however, there was no one there. I looked up and down the corridor. Empty.

I reached for my purse and headed toward the Women's Room. When I swung open the door, I saw Meredith standing by the sinks, sobbing in Pam's arms. Pam didn't even look at me. She stroked Meredith's hair.

"It's all right," she said. "It's all right."

I turned around and made my way back to the office. There was a stinging in my eyes, but nothing worth noting. At my door stood a student.

"Uh, Professor Martin?" he said. "Do you have a minute? I'd like to talk to you about my grade on the final."

That's the thing about life in the ocean, you see. There's no treading water. You can sink or swim or do something called the Dead Man's Float. I decided Pam was working on that one.

"Sure. Come on in," I said, and paddled toward my desk.

L ate the next morning, I took the highway heading west toward
the Blue Ridge and watched as the smooth-shouldered mountains rose higher and higher the closer I came. They were in
their winter undress, patches of evergreen alternating with stretches
of dull brown. They didn't always look so drab. In the autumn,
hoards of tourists scurried down from Washington, D.C., to see the
changing leaves. This far south the colors were not as vibrant as
what you found in New England, for instance. Even so, the Blue
Ridge put on a pretty good show, and on peak weekends you could
count on heavy traffic along the mountain parkway.

There was no stampede that morning, however. When I
took the last exit before the road began its ascent, there were only
a few cars in sight. They whizzed by me as I slowed and made my
turn onto the ramp. The exit sign read Hunting Meadows.

Hunting Meadows was the site of a steeplechase racing
course. Twice a year—in the spring and fall—students and towns-
people gathered to watch horses jump rails and hedges, or miss
and tumble as the case may be. This time of year the place was
deserted, just empty green fields rimmed by dark wooden fences.
Looking at the scene, I thought, I should come out into the country
more often. It was nice to get away from town. Out here you could
forget the Meredith Kospachs and the Bill Tanners. Out here you
could find some peace of mind.

I glanced again at Amy's directions and looked for the next road on the left. It came up suddenly, around a bend. I swung into it, and immediately heard the rattle of stones and felt the car bounce in and out of a deep groove. Dogwood Lane, it turned out, was unpaved. At least I hoped it was Dogwood Lane. It was also unmarked.

The road wound uphill through a woods. The car swayed and shook as I gave it more and more gas just to keep it climbing. I didn't like the sound of my engine's strenuous efforts.

After a few more minutes, however, I started worrying less about the car and more about what I might find at the end of the road. What if this wasn't Dogwood Lane, but some private drive to some very private person's home? What if even now that very private person were loading up a shotgun at the sound of a trespassing Civic coming up the hill? I'd seen the movie *Deliverance.* I knew what could happen to city folk when they strayed too far afield.

The car jolted over a big rut and I braked to a stop at the edge of a grassy turnaround. There was no more road, no more woods. I was on a sloping meadow, and all alone as far as I could tell. I got out and called, "Amy?"

In answer I heard a huge deep bark. An enormous yellow dog burst through the tall grass and barrelled toward me. I managed to throw myself in the car and close the door before a smear of slobber covered my side window.

"Tyler! Tyler, wait!"

It was Amy's voice. I edged up from my crouch and peered out. There was Amy in hiking boots, jeans, and a ski jacket. She'd pulled the dog off my car and held it by its collar. When it saw me reappear in the window, it twisted against her grip and barked again.

I rolled my window down an inch.

"Who's that?" I asked. "Cerberus?"

Amy squinted and tilted her head to the side. "Who?"

"The three-headed dog who guards the gates to hell," I said. "You should know that. You're a religious studies major."

"I don't believe in hell or death," she said. "I study the Eastern religions. I believe in reincarnation."

Tyler tried to lunge again and gave another bark.

"I think he believes in death," I said. "The slow painful kind."

She laughed. "Who, Tyler? He's gentle as a lamb. I'm holding him so that he won't jump on you. All he wants to do is give you a kiss."

"A kiss," I said.

She nodded.

"You mean I can open this door and step outside and not be torn limb from limb?"

"I promise," she said.

"Okay. . . ." I opened the door and walked toward her. I held out my hand to Tyler. "Nice doggy, nice doggy—"

The next thing I knew, he leapt up, breaking Amy's hold. I glimpsed a gaping mouth rimmed with long white fangs and then, in the next instant, an enormous wet tongue. It swiped clear across my face. I fell back against my car, sputtering and blinded. With my coat sleeve, I wiped at my eyes.

Amy just about collapsed from laughing. "I told you all he wanted to do was give you a kiss."

I looked down at Tyler, who, mission accomplished, was now smiling up at me, wagging his tail. A long thread of drool hung from the side of his mouth.

"A kiss!" I said. "I feel like I've just come through a car wash! Even the inside of my ears are wet!"

"At least he's friendly," she said.

"Yes, well, next time remind me to bring a raincoat and umbrella."

"Let's get back to the house where you can wash up," Amy said.

I looked around. "There's a house here?"

"It's a cabin, really. It's just up this path at the top of the hill."

We started walking, with Tyler leading the way.

"I was afraid I had the wrong road," I said. "Especially when I got to the end and didn't see a car. I thought you had one."

"I do. My roommate borrowed it," she said. "Her last final is today."

"How did your finals go?"

"Okay, I hope. At least they're over with. I've just got one more semester to go, and then I'm out of here. I can hardly believe it."

We came to the end of the path. Ahead I could see a wooden shack sitting on the crest of the hill.

"Well?" she said, leading me the last few steps. "What do you think?"

I thought she was asking me about the cabin, until I looked west to the view on the other side. Looming up at smack-in-your-face range were the Blue Ridge mountains. They were huge and majestic, appearing far more rugged than their more muted long-distance profile. This close, you could see rocky outcrops and the crests of pine trees. I had to bend my head back to look all the way up.

"Wow," I said.

"The mountains aren't as near as they look," she said. "It's the air. This time of year it's so clear, it distorts distances."

"Look!" I said, shading my eyes as I pointed. "What are they, hawks?"

She laughed and shook her head. "No, 'fraid not. Those are turkey buzzards. They're the only ones that like to circle in groups like that. I'd get you my binoculars but I don't think you want to see them up close. They're *real* ugly."

"Oh," I said.

"But there are a lot of hawks around," she said. "We're on the migration route—the flyway. One spring a few years ago I even saw a golden eagle soar by. It was really something."

"I'll bet," I said. I looked over at the cabin and then back to the mountains. "God, talk about a view. How in the world did you find this place?"

"One of my old professors, Jeff, owns it," she said. "He used to live here until he had to leave the university. He teaches in Richmond now. He still comes up every now and again to meditate. That's part of the deal. He's into Tibetan Buddhism," Amy said. "He knows the Dalai Lama personally."

"He *had* to leave?" I asked.

"Yeah. He didn't get tenure," she said. "That was two years ago. He was really bummed out about it. He *still* is, in fact."

"I can imagine," I said. Another Humpty Dumpty who had a great fall, and not even the Dalai Lama could put him back together again. I felt a shiver run down my spine.

"Are you cold?" she asked. "Come on in and let me fix us some lunch. There's a fire going in the woodstove."

"Sounds great," I said.

Tyler bounded ahead of me through the door.

"It's a little cramped in here," she said, taking off her coat. I noticed she wasn't wearing her bracelets. Instead her fingers were covered with rings. "Jeff built this place himself, and I don't think he planned on having many visitors."

The cabin was indeed small. The main room served as kitchen, dining room, and bedroom, with a futon bed/couch in the corner. I took a deep breath. The place was filled with the smell of apples and cinnamon.

"It certainly is cozy," I said, and walked over to the futon. "Is this where you sleep?" I asked.

"No, that's Allie's bed—my roommate. Tyler and I use a small bedroom in the back."

At the sound of his name, Tyler wagged his tail.

"Is it okay if I wash up?" I asked.

"Sure," she said. "The bathroom's through there."

She gestured toward what looked like the door to a closet. I opened it. There was hardly enough room to step inside. Crammed in at an angle were a toilet, a very small sink, and a rack with clean towels. I washed my face and hands.

"Where's your shower?" I asked when I came back out.

"There is none," she said. She opened a tiny refrigerator and took out some covered bowls. "We shower at the gym at school. Why don't you have a seat at the table? This will only take me a minute to get ready."

I sat down, pulled out my tape recorder, and switched it on.

"I guess you have to use that thing, don't you," she said. "I can tell you right now I'm not like Kathy. I'm not very good at talking about myself."

"That's okay," I said. "I'm only interested in hearing how you became involved in Humanity For Animals—it doesn't matter how you tell me." I thought for a moment. "You know, there's something I've been wanting to ask you."

"Go ahead," she said.

"Why was it so important that you get that doctor during the protest—what's his name again?"

"You mean Fairchild?" Amy said. She cut thick slices from a loaf of dark bread. "He's one of the most notorious vivisectionists around. There's a dog lab at the hospital and he runs it. He uses the animals for heart experiments."

"But what did you hope to accomplish by throwing that stuff on him?"

She stopped slicing and looked at me. "It was symbolic— like marking him with sacrificial blood."

"Do you really think you can change someone's mind by doing something like that?"

"No." She placed the bread in a basket. "There's no point in trying to change *his* mind, but maybe we woke up somebody else that day. Most people don't know about the animal labs, and if they do, they haven't any idea what goes on in them. And that's exactly the way the vivisectionists want to keep it. The ambush on Fairchild got us attention. That's all I cared about."

"Did the police charge you with anything?"

"Sure," she said. "Trespassing, creating a disturbance, marching without a permit. The usual. They could have gotten me for assault, but Fairchild dropped the charges. I had to pay a fine and sign up for some community service, that's all."

"That was nice of him to drop the charges."

She shrugged and put some plates and silverware on the table, along with the basket of bread. "I don't know. He probably didn't want to bother. It would take up too much of his precious time."

I watched her for a moment. "I like your rings," I said.

She smiled and held out her hands. "Thanks. I only wear them when I think I need good karma. Like for this interview."

"You believe in that sort of thing? Good karma, bad karma?"

Amy laughed. "You make it sound so silly!"

"I didn't mean—"

"That's okay," she said. "I go through this all the time with my folks. But when you think about the concept, it's really no different from what they teach you in Physics 101. Actions beget reactions. Nothing happens in a vacuum. I believe we're all linked, everyone to one another. When we hurt others, we hurt ourselves, too."

"And the animals?"

"They're part of the same spiritual connection—all living things are. You know, in India there are people who sweep the ground before they take a step to avoid killing creatures underfoot. And they wear masks to keep from breathing in microbes."

"Sounds awfully confining," I said. "Is that a lifestyle you aspire to?"

"I guess so," she said. "What do you want to drink? We've got orange juice or mulled cider."

I glanced at the pot simmering on the stove. "Cider, definitely," I said.

"I guess that's one of the things I've had to come to terms with," she said. She poured a cup and then handed over a steaming mug. "I mean, that I'm not really there yet."

"There where?"

"Where those people in India are," she said. "Or Hathor. She really lives what she believes. No shortcuts."

I blew on my cider before taking a sip. Amy set the two bowls on the table, and then sat down. I peered into them.

"What's this?" I asked.

"Brown rice curry with vegetables," she said. "The other is a black-eyed pea salad. Help yourself."

"Vegetarian, I assume," I asked.

"Well, vegan, actually."

"Vegan. I've come across that word in my reading. It means—"

"It means I don't eat eggs or dairy products, either."

"And what's wrong with eggs and dairy products?" I asked.

"Have you ever read descriptions of how the chickens and cows that produce those things are treated?"

"Yes. Don't remind me," I said, and took a bite of the curry. "Mmmmm, that's delicious," I said. "I'd be a vegetarian, or vegan, or what have you, too, if I could whip up stuff like this to eat."

"Really? Then I could teach you how to make them. It's not so hard."

"I'm kidding," I said. "Which I suppose I shouldn't do. I've already had one interviewee accuse me of being overly detached from the causes I study."

"Who's that?" she asked. "Hathor?"

"No," I said. "Charlie Whittier."

She put down her fork and frowned at me. "You interviewed him? Why? He's not an HFA member anymore."

"No, but he was one," I said.

"I know, but. . . ."

"But what?"

She picked up her fork and poked at some rice. "He's turned against everything we stand for. You heard about his reenrolling in medical school?"

I nodded.

"It's awful. I don't see how Kathy can live with him. And I don't think she will much longer."

I swallowed a biteful of peas, and gave her a quick glance. "Really? Why do you say that?"

"Kathy told me. She says they fight all the time now. She said this has changed everything. It's really sad. I liked Charlie."

"And now?"

She paused, chewing, and then swallowed. "My teacher Jeff always tells me I shouldn't judge people," she said. "He says everyone is on a separate journey of spiritual evolution."

"I thought you just said we're all connected."

"We are," she said. "The universe has one ground of being, one source. But each life is its own unique manifestation, following its own destiny."

I wiped my mouth with a rough brown napkin and sat back. "You know, you haven't told me much about your background. What about your folks, for instance? What do they think about all this?"

She tsked, her full lips forming even more of a pout, if that were possible. "Oh, they don't understand me at all. But that's not so surprising. They're far far down on the evolutionary scale, spiritually speaking."

"Where do they live?"

"New York. Dad's a big shot Wall Street stockbroker and Mom's an even bigger shot lawyer. I remember when I came home my first year for Christmas break and they caught me meditating in my room. They completely freaked out—they threatened to pull me out of school. They said I was being brainwashed, which is a joke. I mean, who's got the more destructive lifestyle here? I'm not the one making money ripping people off, which is exactly what they do. And I don't eat up other creatures every day to get the energy to do it. That's what I told them."

Mom and Dad have obviously had a bit of a shock, I thought. "So you hadn't been involved with animal rights before you went to college?" I asked.

"No. It wasn't until I started studying Hinduism and Buddhism and Taoism—stuff like that—that I became aware. Jeff was a big influence on me. He taught me about how our souls could wind up anywhere in our next life—in a dog, a caterpillar, a mosquito. It really makes you pay a lot more attention to the living things around you."

"And when did you join Humanity For Animals?" I asked.

"My second semester," she said. "There was an announcement of a meeting in the student newspaper, so I went with my roommate."

"Did your roommate join?"

"Sort of," Amy said. "She goes every so often, like a lot of other people. It depends on what's going on—you know, whether there's a big march or demonstration."

"And what's Hathor's role in the group?" I asked.

"Oh, she's the one who started Humanity For Animals in Albemarle. Before her there wasn't any animal rights group around here, and for a while I think she was it—the only member. But she'll tell you all about that when you interview her. Has she said for sure yet whether she'll talk to you?"

"No," I said. "I have to call her."

Amy leaned forward. "Listen. If she agrees to see you, let her pick the day and time. And when you go to her place, bring a bag of barley and a bottle of wine. You got that?"

I blinked. "Barley?"

Amy nodded.

"Where in the world would I find barley?"

"The health food store up on Tenth Street carries it. It's in one of the bins—get the whole hulled kind. Don't ask me to explain, okay? Just do it."

"Okay," I said slowly.

"Trust me on this," she said, and grinned. She reached for the bowl of rice curry. "Do you want any more?"

"No, thanks," I said. "It was delicious, though." I picked up my mug and took another sip. "Just a few minutes ago when I asked you if you aspired to the same lifestyle as those Indians who sweep the ground, you said, 'I guess so.' Why so tentative?"

She sat forward and rested her head against one hand, gazing at me from a tilted angle. "I don't know. I'm still too self-conscious, you know?" she said. "Like, if I walked around with a surgical mask and broom, people would think I'm crazy. At the emergency room, when the police brought me out, everybody there looked at me like I had just crash-landed from Mars. That's hard. I figure it must mean I'm still caught in the wheel of life. Maybe in my next incarnation I'll be better. Don't get me wrong—I'm committed to animal rights, but I don't want to make the cause my whole life. After college, I plan to go out and get a job just like everyone else."

"What kind of job?"

"Well, I love baking, you know? Especially bread. So I was thinking—maybe I'll work for a bakery."

"Around here?"

"Not if I can help it." She sat up. "I've got this really great idea. A friend of mine makes desserts for a lot of the restaurants in town. He told me about this place in Italy, near Assisi, where you can study with monks. He said they have this whole philosophy about bread—how you release the essence of the grain when you mill it yourself, and how you can capture that energy by making bread out of it right away. Everything is done by hand."

"Sounds interesting," I said. "And expensive. How do you plan to get over there?"

"Well, I've already mentioned it to my folks. . . ."

Mom and Dad make their comeback! I thought.

". . . and they were pretty enthusiastic." She laughed. "I guess they were afraid I was going to run off to India or Tibet when I graduate, so Italy looks pretty good. They made me promise that if they paid for me to go that I'd learn Italian while I'm there. I figure I'll have to learn it anyway, to understand the monks."

I looked down at the dog sleeping by her feet. "What about Tyler?"

"I think my parents will take him," she said.

"Have they met him?"

"Not yet. I just got him from the pound at the beginning of the term. He's going home with me for the break, though."

"Good," I said, and reached down to stroke the silky coat. He opened his big brown eyes and thumped his tail against the floor. "I guess you're not so horrible after all, are you, boy. I'm sorry I called you Cerberus."

Just then the tape recorder clicked off.

"Is that it?" Amy said.

"Yes," I said. "Unless there's something more about yourself or Humanity For Animals you want to tell me."

"No," she said. "It's just that I don't feel like I've said very much that's important."

"Well, if you think of other things you want to add, we can always get together again."

"Okay," she said. "Anyway, I'll see you at the next meeting after the break?"

"You bet," I said, and got up. "Thanks. And thanks for the lunch, too. That was great."

"It was fun." She handed me my coat and picked up her own. "Tyler and I will walk you back to your car."

"Does Tyler insist on giving kisses goodbye?"

"No," she said. "That's just for saying hello."

"Okay," I said. "Then let's go."

That evening I played the tape one last time, comparing it to my transcription of the conversation. Hearing it again, I couldn't help but smile. The profile was classic—as typical as could be. In my interviews of environmentalists I had come across a multitude of young activists just like Amy. As the children of affluent parents, in railing against society's excesses they were just as often rebelling against their own upbringing as well. As they grew older, the shock value of their behavior inevitably dwindled, which created a corresponding drop in satisfaction levels. It's hard to feel superior about what you believe are personal sacrifices when no one's paying attention anymore. From what I knew of such upper-class radicals, in time most of them edged their way back into the fold.

It looked like Amy's parents were hoping to achieve this end by sending their daughter off to Italy to incubate. At the very worst, they'd hatch an Italian-speaking baker. But who knows? In a few years, they could also have an aspiring multinational executive on their hands, with dreams of launching an import gourmet food chain. Oh, there might still be talk of grains and essence and ground of being, but by then she'll have convinced herself that the only way she can make a real contribution is by getting into the capitalistic fray herself.

Maybe even as a lawyer. Or a stockbroker. Just like Mom and Dad.

When the tape ended I put away my notes, poured myself a glass of wine, and flopped down on the sofa. I groped for the remote control wand while I sipped my California red, and then turned on the TV. All of a sudden I heard a familiar voice, followed almost immediately by its familiar face.

It was Bill Tanner.

". . . truly a significant problem of our times," he said with a little nod for emphasis.

God, I thought, staring at him, my glass aloft. Every hair was in place without looking slicked or sprayed. How does he do that?

The camera pulled back to show his head framed in a screen. Ted Koppel gazed up at him from the *Nightline* anchor desk.

"So, Professor Tanner, I take it that you think there ought to be more regulation of special interest groups in Washington."

"Oh, absolutely," Tanner said, his baby blue peepers crinkling at the edges in a relaxed half-smile. No nervous blinking or bugged-out goggle eyes from this ace of the air waves. "The way things stand today, there's hardly anything separating Capitol Hill from the pressure groups. I've always said, A good lobbyist must know Congress, but now it's more in the biblical sense of the phrase, I'm afraid."

Ted chuckled. "Thank you very much, Professor." Tanner's image vanished from the screen, replaced by a shot of some other expert's head. "What do you think, Professor Greenwood?"

I didn't listen to Professor Greenwood's reply. I was still working over Tanner's words.

My words, actually.

Slowly I got up off the couch and reached for the university phonebook. I found Tony Donatello's number and dialed.

After a few rings a groggy voice answered, "Hello?"

"Sorry to wake you, Tony," I said. "I just wanted you to know, I'll be happy to direct your dissertation."

There was a pause. "Professor Martin?"

"Please stop by my office sometime tomorrow. That is, of course, assuming you still wish me to be your first reader."

"Yeah, sure, of course—but—"

"See you tomorrow, then," I said, and hung up.

You'll be sorry you did that, a voice inside me said.

I laid back down on the sofa and changed channels.

T he voice was right. The next morning I awoke on the couch, weak sunlight slanting through the windows. When I remembered the call to Tony, I sat up with a wince.

That had been stupid, I thought. Stupid, hasty, and reckless. Who cared if Tanner beat me out of a good line? It's not as if I'd ever have the chance to use it, at least not on *Nightline*. Of course, he did make me believe it *wasn't* a good line. Made it seem really bad, in fact.

The bastard.

Yes, but that bastard is too important to your future right now to get on his bad side, I warned myself. And I had a feeling that working with Tony Donatello would definitely do the trick.

After all, I'd already seen him grind up and spit out Meredith Kospach simply because she didn't choose him for her first reader. I could only imagine what he'd do to someone who accused him of plagiarism. Or to someone who helped that someone—like me.

There'd be nothing left to spit out.

I stretched my stiff back and debated hiding at home. I could call Tony and tell him I'd changed my mind. But I knew that was no good—I didn't have to be both despicable and cowardly. One was enough. Besides, I had only a few more seminar papers to grade, and they were at my office. Like it or not, I was going in.

I made my entrance into Russell around quarter to nine, which was late by minnow standards. There existed an unspoken rivalry among the assistant professors regarding daily arrival times. That particular semester Karl and Felix were competing for who could come in earliest, but I figured the only one they were impressing was the janitor. Shepherd never made it to the office before nine; the other whales moseyed in even later.

That morning I worked with my door open. Most of the students had left for Christmas vacation, so the halls were quiet. I sat at my desk, a seminar paper before me. As my eyes scanned the text, my mind was backstage, rehearsing.

I'm really sorry, Tony. I've reconsidered once again, and I've gone back to my original conclusion. I'm just not the right person to direct your thesis. Please try to understand. I'm *very* sorry. Have you tried talking to Professor Tanner and straightening things out?

That ought to do it.

So when I heard the sound of approaching footsteps, I set down the paper, folded my hands before me, and put on my most concerned expression.

If 'twere done, when 'twere done, well 'twere done quickly.

But it was not the soon-to-be-done Tony who appeared. It was Lady Macbeth herself.

"Hi," Julia Garshin said.

"Oh, hi," I said.

She crossed her arms and leaned against the door frame, her black curtain of hair swinging free. "Since when do you work with your door open? I thought all the professors around here liked to seal themselves in, like rats in their little holes."

"Some holes are nicer than others," I said. "This one doesn't have much of a view."

She stepped inside and looked out the window. The back of her coat bore the smudges of little hands. "The parking lot. Isn't that nice." She turned and gave my bookshelves the once-over. I assumed she was appraising my small but impressive personal library.

"Real wooden bookcases," she said, giving them a tap with a fingernail. "Victor's are metal—you know, the battleship gray kind. Did the department give you these?"

"No," I said. "I bought them."

"Figures," she said. "I didn't think they'd spring for anything so nice, at least not for a measly assistant professor."

"Hmmm," I said in my best noncommittal voice. I shuffled some papers and tried to look as though her being in my office was something less than completely irritating.

"So," I said. "What brings you to these parts?"

She cocked her head. "Is that a real Peter Max?"

"Yup."

"I'll bet that didn't come with the office, either."

"Nope."

"That's what you get when you don't have kids, I guess."

"A Peter Max poster?"

She actually smiled. "No. Money."

I shrugged. "I manage. Barely."

"Well, Victor and I don't. Thoroughly." She gave a different smile, a thinner one. "You want to know what I'm doing here? I just dropped off the little tykes. Victor's got them for the morning. He didn't know he was going to have them. He had no idea I had decided to get my hair cut. Poor man. He has to cope for two whole hours. He's awfully upset."

"Hmmm," I said.

"Yes. I'm just *too* cruel. Well, off I go. I mustn't be late." She stopped at the door. "You heard about Karl going to Strasbourg?"

"Of course," I said.

"Someone said Emily might not be going."

"She doesn't know what she's going to do," I said.

"Well, if I had to pick between France and this crummy backwater town *I* wouldn't have much of a problem making up my mind."

"Emily's worried about losing her job," I said, immediately rising to her defense. "And I don't blame her."

Julia arched her plucked thin brows. "Ah, well. To each her own." She thought for a moment and smiled to herself.

"Well, don't let me keep you," I said.

"Right," she said, and turned. "Bye, Lydia."

I watched my doorway and listened until her footsteps faded down the hall.

I finished the last of the papers, filled in the dots on the grade sheet, and then headed down to the department office to turn them in.

"Here," I said to Roberta. "All done."

She held the grade sheet at arm's length and gave it the once-over.

"Did you use a number two pencil, like you were supposed to?" she asked me.

"Yes," I said.

"Okay, Professor Martin," she said. "I'll get it to the dean's office this afternoon. I'm expecting a lot more to show up. Today's the last day, you know, for filing grades."

"I know," I said.

Just then the door opened and in walked Danny.

"Here you go, Roberta," he said, handing over two grade sheets.

"See?" Roberta said to me.

"Hey, what's going on in Victor's office?" Danny asked. "I walked by just now and I could swear I heard a baby crying."

"You did," I said. "Julia just swung through and dumped the kids with him."

"But we're supposed to play racquetball at lunchtime."

"Don't count on it," I said.

Two whales strolled in—Hamilton Farrell and Stanley Kitt, an expert in middle eastern politics. It was a rare sighting. Stanley only taught one course a year, and he absented himself from department meetings and from Russell Hall in general. Danny and I edged closer to the wall to let the two men pass. Hamilton shuffled through the mail in his slot among the cubby holes. Stanley leaned against the counter beside Roberta's desk. He had dark bushy eyebrows that looked like wooly caterpillars.

"Anything come in Fed Ex for me?"

"No, Professor Kitt," Roberta said. "Nothing so far."

"I'm expecting something rather urgent," he said. "It should be here by now."

"Well, no one's been by all morning," she said.

"I see." He paused. "Please let me know as soon as it comes in."

"Of course," Roberta said.

He turned to Hamilton. "Well? Are you ready to get some coffee?"

"Ready," Hamilton said.

They turned to leave and then had to rear back as the office door burst open with great violence. In came Victor. He had a toddler by the hand, and a wailing baby slung over his shoulder.

"Oh, sorry," he said to the whales. They looked at him unsmilingly.

"Hello, Victor," Stanley said.

He nodded, jerking his head. "Hello, Stanley. Hamilton. Uh, these are my kids."

"So I see," Hamilton said. He shifted his gaze to the toddler and fixed on the dark green spinachy stain covering the front of the child's overalls. "Boy or girl?"

"Uh, girl," Victor said. He hefted the baby. "This one's a boy."

As he jostled his son, a strong odor wafted from the diapers.

"Congratulations," Stanley said. "Now if you'll excuse us, we were just about to leave."

"Sure," Victor said. "Come on, honey," he said to his daughter. "Let the nice men get by. No, this way, honey. This way. That's right."

When they were gone, Victor let out a deep breath.

"Nice kids," Danny said.

"Oh, hey," Victor said. "About that game today. I don't think—"

"No problem," Danny said. "We'll try again later this week."

"Thanks," he said. The baby squirmed against him and continued his piercing cries.

"See you, guys," Danny said, and slipped out the door.

The little girl pulled away from Victor's hand. She looked up at me.

"Hi!" she said.

"Hi," I answered.

She ran to a pile of padded mailers stacked on the floor.

"No, no, sweetheart. Come over here." He turned to Roberta. "I've got to change Josh's diapers—"

"So I noticed," she said, and shot me a glance.

"And there's no place in the Men's Room to do it. Can I use this counter?"

"Absolutely not," Roberta said. "This is the reception area. You'll have to find someplace else. What's wrong with your desk?"

"It's covered with student papers, all arranged in a special order. I can't move anything." His eyes jumped about the office. "What about there?"

She looked behind her. "The Xerox machine? Are you crazy?"

"Come on, no one's using it. I'll put the cover down. Please?"

She shook her head. "What if Professor Shepherd comes in and sees you?"

"I'll watch for him," I said. "I'll go stand guard in the hall."

Victor looked back at Roberta. "Please?"

She shook her head again and sighed. "All right. But make it *real* quick. And be sure you take that dirty diaper out of here *pronto*."

"Thanks," he said, and then cried, "No, Caroline—put that down!"

I swooped the little girl up in my arms. "You'd better hurry," I said to him. "Caroline and I'll go stand watch."

"I appreciate this, Lydia. Really."

"Just hurry it up," I said, and went out the door.

A quick glance up and down the hallway showed the coast was clear. I looked back to see Caroline's big brown eyes staring right at me.

"Hi!" she said.

"We already did that, remember?" I said.

She stuck a hand in her mouth and with the other one started pulling on her hair. As best I could, I tried to hold her so that we had as little contact as possible. I didn't want any of that green stuff on me, whatever it was.

"You're a heavy little monster, aren't you? How about we try putting you down."

As soon as her feet touched the ground, she let out a howl. "Noooooo!"

"Okay, okay," I said, lifting her up again. "I get the message."

"Professor Martin?"

I turned to see Tony Donatello.

"Tony!"

"Hi. Who's this?"

"She belongs to Professor Garshin," I said. "I'm just minding her for a moment while he—takes care of some other business."

"Hi!" she said.

"Hi, yourself," he answered. "What's your name?"

"Caroline!"

"That's a great name," he said.

"Tony," I said, shifting Caroline in my arms. "I really need to talk to you."

"That's why I'm here. Hey, thanks a million for changing your mind about directing my dissertation," he said. "You've really saved my life."

"Uh, Tony, well—that's sort of what I wanted to talk to you about. You see, I've been giving this whole thing more thought and—"

He looked past me. "Hey, Professor Clark! It's great to see you!"

Pam came up and looked from Tony to me. "Hi," she said in a neutral tone. It was the first time she'd spoken to me in two days, since the oral exam. "What's going on?"

"Professor Martin changed her mind. She's agreed to be my first reader," Tony exclaimed.

Pam looked at me. "Really?"

"Well—I—"

Caroline jerked around to look at Pam. "Hi!" she said.

"Lydia, that's wonderful!" Her warm smile was back in place. "Oh, I *knew* you wouldn't let Tony down. I knew it."

"Hi!" Caroline said again.

"Hi there, Caroline Garshin," she said. "What are *you* doing here?"

"Tony," I said, "I really do need to talk to you—"

"Oh, Lydia, can I just borrow him for a little while first?" Pam asked. "I have some boxes of books out in my car, and I'm looking for someone to lend me a hand. A couple of them are just too heavy for me to carry all by myself. And I'm afraid I have to hurry. I'm in a No Parking zone."

"Sure, I'll help you," Tony said. "Is it okay if I come by this afternoon?" he asked me.

I sighed. "Sure. Of course. See you later."

"Bye, Lydia," Pam said, and gave my arm a little squeeze. "And *thanks*."

I watched the two of them head back down the hall.

"Yeah, right," I muttered. I looked back at Caroline. "It's all *your* fault," I said.

She giggled. Little bubbles formed at the edge of her mouth and trickled into a wet string.

"Okay, that's it," I said. "Down you go." And I started to ease her to the floor.

"Nooooo!" she cried again. She grabbed hold of my hair with both hands and kicked.

"Ow! Cut that out!" I cried, straightening, and tried to loosen her tight two-fisted grip.

"Lydia . . . ?"

None other than Tom Shepherd himself stood before me.

"Oh, hi, Tom," I said, trying to sound casual. I could barely see him for all the hair in my face. Caroline gave a hard yank. Smiling, I reached up and immobilized one of her fists.

"Is she yours?" he asked, squinting at me.

What did he think? I wondered. That somewhere along the way I'd gotten pregnant and given birth and he didn't know about it? I suppose such a thing *is* possible, I thought, in the sea.

"No," I said. "This is Caroline Garshin. Say hello, Caroline."

It worked. At once she let go of my hair and spun around to Tom.

"Hi!" she said.

Tom blinked. "Hi."

"Hi!" she said again.

This time he only nodded. He said to me, "I just need to get into the office."

"Oh, sure," I said, not moving. Victor had better hurry the hell up. "But I was just going to ask—" What? What? "—if you and Margaret were going to be around during the break."

He paused. "Yes, we'll be here. Why?"

"Um, just wondering. I thought maybe . . . maybe. . . . "

Caroline put her fist in her mouth again and spun back around to me. Her elbow caught me right in the chin.

He shifted his weight to the other leg. "Yes?"

"Maybe you two could come over some evening," I blurted out. "For dinner."

"I'm sure we'd love to," he said. "But you should call Margaret. She handles all our social engagements. Now, if you'll just excuse me—"

"Sure, *Tom*," I said as loudly as I dared. "See you later, then."

"Yes, well, I'm afraid I can't get by you. Would you mind . . . ?"

"Oh, of course." I gave up and stepped aside. "Sorry about that."

"That's fine—" he said, and put a hand to the doorknob. It flew away from him, opened from the other side.

"Oh, excuse me, Tom," Victor said. The freshly diapered Josh was slung back over his shoulder.

"That's quite all right," Tom said. "Please, you first."

"Thanks." Victor stepped out into the hallway.

"Have a good holiday, if I don't see you," Tom said to us, and then closed the office door behind him.

"Whew! That was close," Victor said. "How's Caroline been?"

"An angel," I said dryly. "Here you go."

"Daddy!" she cried, and opened her arms. Victor took her, balancing her on the other side from Josh. In one hand he grasped a brown paper sack.

"I've got to get rid of this," he said. As he spoke I saw Caroline wrap her fist about a lock of *his* hair. "And listen—thanks for helping me out."

"No problem," I said. "See you later."

He trotted off down the hall. I reached up and felt my hair. It was all sticky.

"Great," I muttered.

The office door opened once more. Roberta poked her head out and looked up and down the corridor.

"Any problems?" I asked.

"You mean with that baby? No. But have you seen Professor Willis?" she asked me.

"No. Why?"

"His wife Emily's on the phone. Could you talk to her? Sounds like something might be wrong."

"Sure." I followed her back into the office and picked up the receiver.

"Emily, this is Lydia. You're looking for Karl?"

"Yes." Her voice came across the line, breathless. "Have you seen him? I tried his office and he wasn't there."

"I haven't seen him this morning. He's probably working over at the library."

"No," she said. "The library's closed for the holidays. I already checked." She made a noise, like a sob.

"Is something wrong?"

"My car broke down—" Another sob. "And I'm in this gas station. I can't get back to work. I'm already l-late." This time she started really to cry. "Damn it!"

"Which gas station? The one over on Charles Street? Okay, hang on. I'll be right there." I hung up.

"She's got car trouble?" Roberta asked. "Poor thing."

"If anyone asks, just say I'll be back as soon as I can."

"Okay," she said. "But remember, I'm closing up the office early this afternoon—at two. And it won't be open all next week."

"Wow," I said. "Staff have all of Christmas week off this year?"

"No," she said. "Are you kidding? I'm adding some of my own vacation days."

"Well, I have to get going. See you later."

"Bye, Professor Martin," she said. "And have a good Christmas, if I don't see you."

"You, too," I said, and left.

When I pulled into the gas station, Emily was standing on the corner waiting for me.

"Thanks," she said, as she got in and slammed the door closed. She didn't look at me. She stared down at her hands instead. They were red with cold.

I noticed her eyes were pretty red, too.

"What happened to your car?" I said, turning back into the street.

"The timing belt broke," she said, biting off the words.

"That's not good."

"No. It's not. I was driving along and the car just stopped." She plucked a tissue out of her purse and rubbed her nose. "I was damned lucky I wasn't on the highway."

"Where were you?"

"On my way back from the Fox Tail Inn," she said, glaring at the road. "I went over for a meeting with their activities coordinator to get everything all set for that conference Professor McKenzie is holding next month."

"You were out by the Inn?"

She nodded. "And I had to get towed. All the way here. That was expensive."

"I'll bet," I said.

She turned in the seat to face me. "But it'll be nothing compared to what it's going to cost to get the car fixed. So you tell me. How can Karl expect us to get along for a whole year without two incomes? Things like this always come up."

I didn't know what to say to that, so I said nothing.

She crossed her arms and looked back at the road. "Karl says the Fulbright stipend will more than cover everything, especially when you figure in all the tax breaks. But that's assuming there'll be no surprises. And if there's one thing you can bet on in life, it's surprises. Believe me, I know."

I shot her a quick glance. She was twisting her wedding ring round and round her finger.

"It just isn't a good time to go away for a whole year," she continued, the edge in her voice softening. "Oh, I know everyone thinks I'm crazy, but sometimes you have to put practical considerations first. Do you know what I mean?"

"Sure," I said. "But what about Karl's book? He says a year in Strasbourg would help his research tremendously."

"I know that's what he says," she said. "But the truth is he'll just wind up being more distracted there than he is here. I can tell you this much—as it stands now, for all his late nights at the office he's got precious little on paper to show for it."

"Well, you've got to admit it's hard to write and teach at the same time," I said. "A year's break might be exactly what he needs."

She brushed back a curly lock of red hair. "Maybe. Maybe it's what he needs. But it's not what *we* need."

I made the turn up to the Law School. "Do you want me to drop you in front?" I said.

"That would be great." She took hold of her purse and waited for the car to stop before reaching for the door handle. "Thanks again, Lydia. I'm sorry you had to come get me."

"You won't have any problem getting home?"

"Someone here will drop me off, if I can't find Karl. Thanks—"

"Take care of yourself," I said as she got out of the car. "And have a good Christmas."

"You, too," she said, and closed the door. I watched her walk up to the main entrance, holding another tissue to her nose.

Something is wrong here, I thought. But I sure as hell was not going to be the one to say anything about it. I had enough problems of my own.

Like how to disengage myself from Tony Donatello and his cursed dissertation.

I have to get that matter taken care of *now*, I thought, and shifted the car into gear.

It was almost noon when I got back to Russell Hall. As I climbed to the third floor, I found myself thinking about Charlie. I could call. After all, we never did finish the interview. And in passing I could ask, How are things with Kathy these days?

A little obvious, don't you think? I asked myself.

So what? my libido shot back. You've already *been* pretty obvious. Charlie's not stupid. You just have to find out if he's also available.

I reached my office and was fishing for my keys when I saw a note stuck to the door. It read:

Professor Martin—Tony Donatello called to say that he won't be in to see you this afternoon. He caught a last-minute ride with someone to New York, and he had to leave right away. He said to tell you he'll be in touch after the break. He also put a copy of his prospectus in your box. Roberta

I tore it off, threw open my door, dropped my purse on the desk, and shot the crumpled note into the trash. So much for a nimble extraction from *that* little mess. If I let this matter drag on long enough, I'd be pulling myself out of a tar pit.

Not to mention that, in addition to everything else, I'd committed myself to having Tom and Margaret Shepherd over for dinner.

What else can I do, I wondered, to complicate my life?

Inspired, I sat down and reached for my phone book. I opened to the H's.

Just Hathor, Charlie had said.

Like she was Cher or Madonna or something.

I ran my finger down the column of names and came to a full stop. Sure enough, there it was. All by itself.

I dialled her number and waited. The phone rang three times before someone picked up.

"Who calls?" the voice on the other end said.

"Hathor? This is Professor Martin."

"Professor Martin," she said. "Do you have lots of animal corpses on today?"

"No," I said, eyeing my leather boots. I noticed the heels were getting awfully worn. "Look, am I catching you at a bad time?"

"A bad time? If it were a bad time, why would I answer? I'm not a slave to the ringing of a phone. Are you?"

"I don't think so," I said, which was another lie. I was always climbing out of showers or getting up from the dinner table to answer the phone.

"I suppose you're calling to ask for an interview," she said.

"Yes. Will you let me talk with you?"

There was silence.

"Hathor?"

"I'm thinking," she said.

"Listen, I know you don't like me—" I began.

"You mistake me, then," she said. "I neither like nor dislike you," she said. "But you're carnivorous, a habit which is repulsive to me. You smell of dead meat."

I frowned. "I do?"

"And you think you know everything already," she said. "I'm not sure I can help you."

"Your input will be of *tremendous* help, I assure you."

"That's not what I mean," she said.

This time I was silent. Of all the members of the group, she was the most important. Her dots were the ones I wanted above all. But how to get them?

"Then explain it to me," I said. "Please. I'll listen to anything you have to say."

Again she paused, and then I heard her exhale. "All right. But the meeting must be at the time and place of my choosing."

"Of course," I said, remembering Amy's advice. "Where and when are entirely up to you."

"Then come to my house at thirteen minutes before seven in the evening on Sunday. I live at 1003 Sycamore Street."

"This Sunday?"

"On that day and at that time, or not ever. Do you understand?"

"Yes, sure—thirteen minutes before seven at 1003 Sycamore."

"That's right. I'm through talking now," she said, and hung up.

I dropped the receiver and sat back.

"Yes!" I cried aloud, and tightened my hand into a fist. "Got you."

I decided to wrap up and head for home. After letting myself into the townhouse, I automatically glanced over at the phone. The message light blinked on the answering machine.

I hit the button and heard:

"Lydia? It's me, Pam. I'm just about to leave for San Diego and I wanted to call and say goodbye. I think it's really wonderful what you're doing for Tony. Did you know he was on the verge of quitting the program? Well, anyway, I just wanted to wish you a merry Christmas. I'll see you when I get back. Bye."

Great. That's just great, I thought as the tape clicked to a stop and rewound. Now, when Tony drops out, it'll be *my* fault.

I could feel the tar oozing between my toes.

No, I thought. I'm not going to get stuck. No way.

In a brief flash I remembered Pam's smile that morning when Tony proclaimed his good news. I sat down and rubbed hard at my temples. She'd never understand when I gave her the *real* news. But that was okay. She didn't have the right to expect so much of me.

We were all of us only minnows, after all.

14

scanned the row of bins. What the hell was all this stuff, anyway? A bunch of dried-up shriveled pebbly things, supposedly edible. I shook my head.

"Lydia?"

I started at the sound of my name and turned around.

"Kathy! My goodness," I said. "How are you?"

She smiled and pushed her loose blonde hair behind her ear. "I didn't mean to scare you," she said.

Beneath her coat she wore dress slacks and a silky blue blouse. There were also bold strokes of blush along her cheekbones, excessive for normal wear but probably exactly right for television.

"That's okay. I just didn't expect to run into anyone I know," I said.

"I shop here all the time," she said. "It's the best health food store in town. I don't think I've ever seen *you* here before, though."

"You haven't," I said. "This is my first visit." I looked back at the bins. "And probably my last. I don't know what half these things are, and the half I do recognize I'd never dream of putting in my mouth."

She laughed. "Is there something special you're looking for?" she asked.

"Yes," I said, and then hesitated. How weird was this going to sound? "Whole hulled barley. Ever hear of it?"

"Of course. It's right over there, in the last bin. What are you going to do, grow your own sprouts?"

"No," I said. I watched carefully for a reaction. "I'm supposed to see Hathor tomorrow night."

"Oh, well, in that case, you'll need a bigger bag than that." She took the small brown sack out of my hand and gave me a huge one. "When you fill it, make sure you leave some room to roll the top closed."

"I'm supposed to fill this thing?" I asked. It was as big as the grocery store variety.

"It doesn't really make sense to take just a little bit, does it?" she asked.

"No, no, of course not," I muttered. She seemed to think I was being rather dense. I moved to the bin and started shovelling scoopfuls of the hard brown grain into the bag.

Kathy opened another bin and filled a much smaller sack with some unidentifiable legume.

"How's your research going?" she asked.

"Fine," I said. "I have a copy of your interview, when you're ready to take a look at it."

"Great." She shook open another bag and scooped in some brown rice.

"Is Charlie here?" I asked as casually as I could.

"No," she said. The smile had vanished, replaced by an unreadable expression.

"He owes me the balance of an unfinished interview," I said. "Do you know if there's any chance I could reach him at home this afternoon?"

She closed the bags and placed them in her wire basket. "No. He won't be at the house. You could probably find him at the lab."

"The lab?" I set the sack of barley down and groped in my purse for my notepad.

"Fairchild's lab."

She practically spat out the words.

I had hold of my pad and uncapped a pen. "You wouldn't happen to know the number there, would you?"

She gave me a long look. "No," she said. "I wouldn't."

"Oh," I said, and paused. I capped the pen. "Okay."

"Look, I've got to go," she said. "You'll be at the next meeting?"

"You bet. When is it?"

"January twentieth, at Hathor's. You can bring me the interview then, if you like."

"Thanks," I said. "I'll see you on the twentieth."

"Great. Bye," she said, and headed for the checkout.

I looked down at my half-filled sack.

Here goes nothing, I thought, and went back to scooping.

The next night I bore the heavy bag of barley in my arms as I stepped out of the car. In my canvas purse I had stuck a bottle of wine, and as I walked it clunked against the casing of the tape recorder. I cast a glance up and down the street. It was an out-of-the-way neighborhood on the outskirts of town. Hathor's home was a modest single-story wooden frame, with old-fashioned gingerbread trim. It sat all alone on a huge lot.

I climbed the stoop and peered through the evening shadows at my watch. It was exactly thirteen minutes before seven. I raised my hand to knock.

The door opened before I touched it. From within I heard music—bells and a sort of hollow thumping. Hathor stepped out and raised her arms.

"Welcome, moon," she said.

I looked past her to the sky. There was a full moon on the rise, filling the horizon with a bright glow.

She lowered her arms, and held out her hands to me, the palms upturned.

"What gifts do you bring?" she asked, the words smoking on the air.

She was wrapped in something gauzy that fell in folds to the ground. Her hair, too, was wrapped in a turban that towered high above her head. Her arms, however, were bare. In the moonlight they gleamed white.

I stared at her.

"What gifts do you bring on this night of the change?" she said, her hands still outstretched.

I blinked. "I guess this," I said, and held out, with great effort, the bag of barley. "Oh, and this, too." I pointed my chin at the bottle of wine.

She reached into the sack, raised her hand, and let the grains fall from her fingers back into the bag. They made a rushing sound in the stillness.

I continued to hold the barley, trying to look as though I didn't feel like a complete fool.

She gazed at it and then me, her eyes shining.

"You have done well," she said. "I'm surprised. Now, follow me."

And I stepped into the house.

I stopped to take another bite of Karl's vichyssoise. It had the texture of not-yet-hardened concrete.

"And? And?" Emily said. "What happened next?"

"Give her a second," Karl said. "Can't you see she's trying to eat?"

I smiled and swallowed. Even Danny, usually so implacably unimpressible, perched at the edge of his seat.

"Come on. What happened when you went inside?" he asked.

"Well . . ." I sipped my wine and set the glass down. It was the evening after my interview with Hathor. Emily had organized a small last-minute dinner, with just the four of us: to make up for the last one, she had said.

"It was pretty eerie," I continued. "First thing I noticed was that all the electric lights were off. Instead she had about a hundred candles burning everywhere you looked. There was also a roaring fire in the fireplace, but that only warmed the front room. The rest of the house was freezing. And then there was this smell. . . . "

"Smell?" Emily wrinkled her nose. "Of what?"

"Spicy incense and something else, some other strong odor that I couldn't place. I started to get a little nervous—I'd never been inside such a spooky house. On the walls were long scrolls filled with hieroglyphs. I mean, she must have had fifty of these things with pictures of birds, snakes, pharaohs, you name it. It was amazing."

"Where did she get them?" Karl asked.

"She drew them herself," I said. "They were black ink draw-ings with simple, precise strokes. Anyway, she didn't let me look around too long. She told me to set the bag on this big table and motioned for me to put the wine down, too. Then she slid over this enormous wooden bowl and poured the barley inside it."

"Why?" Emily asked.

"Wait," Karl said. "Let her tell the story."

I sat back. "So, she hands me the bowl, and I almost drop it, it's so heavy, and she says, 'Let us now make our offering to Mother.'"

"Mother?" Karl asked.

"Mother," I said with a nod.

"Oh my God," Emily said. "She wanted you to feed that stuff to her mother? I would have bolted out of there right then."

"Actually, all I wanted to do at that point was switch on my tape recorder, but I couldn't, not while I had that gigantic bowl in my hands."

"So what happened next?" Danny asked.

"Hathor said, 'This way,' and I followed her down a long hallway. It was totally dark, except for a light way at the end of the passage."

"It's like that scene in *Psycho*," Danny burst in, "when she goes to find the crazy guy's mother. Remember? She creeps up to the chair and finally spins it around and Mother turns out to be a skeleton with hair."

"I have to admit I was beginning to be a little apprehen-sive," I said. "The smell was getting stronger and stronger—not the smell of incense, but the other one. It was almost acrid, really pungent. And the bells and the thumping drumbeat were coming from everywhere. She must have one hell of a stereo system. So we go through this hall, and Hathor slows up and has us move just one step at a time, like we're bridesmaids pacing ourselves down the aisle, and I'm praying I won't trip and spill the ten pounds of barley. I'll tell you, my arms were getting pretty tired at this point, too. I wasn't sure I could hold that bowl up much longer." I paused and smoothed my napkin on my lap. "Then, at last, we reached the end and there she was." I opened my hands, palm up. "Mother."

"Was she a rotting skeleton in a chair?" Danny asked.

I smiled. "No. She was very much alive. She was actually quite beautiful, with huge brown eyes, silky skin, and lovely long floppy ears."

"Long floppy ears?" Emily said.

"Yes," I said. "Mother, you see, is a cow."

"A cow!" Karl said. "She had a cow in her house?"

"Yup. A bona fide bovine."

"What did you do?" Danny said.

"I placed the bowl in front of her and watched her eat. Hathor even let me pat her."

"What the hell is she doing with a cow in her house?" Karl asked.

"Hathor explained that she herself is an avatar of the Egyptian goddess by the same name."

"And what in the world is an avatar?" Emily asked.

"A human incarnation. Hathor thinks she's the goddess come back in human form. The cow is her symbol. According to the religious beliefs of ancient Egypt, Hathor's first manifestation was as a divine cow who inhabited the heavens, and it was she who gave birth to the universe. With her milk she nourished all living creatures."

"Weren't you afraid?" Emily asked.

"No," I said. "Not at all. Mother was quite gentle, albeit a little mangy."

"I wasn't talking about the cow," she said. "I meant, weren't you afraid to be all alone with that woman?"

"Hathor?" I paused. "No, not really. She gave me a cup of Mother's milk. It tasted rather sweet."

"Yeah, but where did she *get* the cow?" Danny asked.

"From some farmer in the area whose dairy went under," I said. "He put the cows up for sale. Apparently Hathor scraped together the necessary funds and bought Mother. The other cows ended up in the slaughterhouse."

"Sounds like Mother got damned lucky," Karl said.

"So then what did you do?" Danny asked. "Did you ever manage to get your tape recorder on?"

"Yes," I said. "Once Mother finished eating, we went back to the main room and I got it going."

"Hathor didn't mind?" he asked.

"From what I could tell she paid absolutely no attention to it. She sat on the floor in front of the fire, poured us both some wine, and then just started talking without any reluctance whatsoever. She was in a festive mood. Turns out, yesterday was the winter solstice—that's what she meant at the very beginning when she called it 'the night of change.'"

"What did she tell you?" Emily said.

"I asked her about the music," I said. "They were tapes she'd recorded of herself playing the sistrum and flat drum. The two together were quite nice, once I got used to the staggered rhythms."

"I never heard of a sistrum," she said.

"Or a flat drum," Danny said.

"Well, I hadn't either, but that was no problem. Hathor got up and produced the genuine articles. A sistrum is like a small tambourine on a stick that you shake, only the bells are strung through the inside of the frame. And a flat drum is just a big flat drum. You tap it with the tips of your fingers and it makes this hollow thumping kind of sound."

"Why those two instruments?" Karl said. "When she was a little girl, her parents insisted on sistrum lessons?"

I laughed. "Oh no. Surely you should be able to guess why. The sistrum is a fetish of this particular divinity. Hathor told me that sometimes the goddess actually takes the shape of the sistrum. She literally embodies it."

Karl raised a brow. "Was Hathor talking about herself at this point, or of the ancient Egyptian version?"

"I don't know," I said. "It was hard to tell. I don't think she makes that distinction. As for the flat drum, that's another favorite instrument of the goddess. In Egypt there are lots of hieroglyphs on various temples depicting Hathor playing one. She pointed out some copies she'd drawn among the scrolls on the walls."

Karl sat back and looked at me. "I'm telling you, Lydia, she sounds absolutely mad."

"Maybe. At least she was helpful, which was a surprise. Remember, this is the woman who said I smelled of dead flesh. Just to be on the safe side, I didn't eat any meat that day, in case she really *could* smell it on me. I wasn't about to take any chances, not with someone whose cooperation was going to be so critical to my research."

"So what did she tell you?" Danny said.

"She talked a lot about the other members of the group and the differences among them," I said. "She was very critical of Charlie, Kathy, and Amy for having pets. She doesn't believe in keeping 'companion animals,' even if you get them from the animal shelter. She thinks it perpetuates a master/slave dynamic and is no different from other forms of exploitation of animals by humans. Animals should be free, period."

"And how does she justify owning her own cow?" Karl asked.

"She doesn't own the cow," I said. "The cow is Hathor's familiar, sent by the gods to mark her divine origins. Mother is a sign, I guess you'd say. A gift from the source."

"I don't know," Emily said, frowning. "She sounds like she's *way* out there."

"As a research subject, she's absolutely fascinating—the most extreme adherent to an ideology I've ever met," I said. "She's uncompromising when it comes to animal rights. To give you an example, she's read up on all sorts of drugs, and will take no medicine that was developed through animal experimentation. That knocks out almost everything."

"What about her background?" Karl asked. "Did you get any information about her parents or where she grew up?"

"Some," I said. "Her parents live in Chicago Heights. Her father is a professor at the University of Chicago. Her mother is an artist."

"What does her father teach?" Karl asked.

"Psychology," I said.

"Add them up and what do you get?" Danny said. "A calligrapher who thinks she's a cow goddess. They must be *real* happy."

"Does she see much of her folks?" Emily asked.

"No," I said. "They disowned her a few years back when she started tracing her family tree through Ra and Isis rather than through Mom and Dad."

"How does she support herself?" Karl asked. "Does she have a job? How does she live?"

"Well, she works a lot for the Shelter For Battered Women. You see, the Egyptian goddess is supposed to be a great protectress of women. She's also very active in helping the newly dead adjust to the afterlife, being the first to welcome them to the other world. So, this Hathor volunteers at the local hospice, caring for the terminally ill."

"That's pretty noble," Emily said.

"I'll bet the hospice administrators don't know much about her or she wouldn't be there," Danny said. "I mean, would you want someone like her hanging around your deathbed? I'd be afraid I'd wind up wrapped in a sheet with all my vital organs sealed in jars."

Emily shrugged. "I still think she deserves some credit for that sort of thing. *I* certainly couldn't do it."

"You're Collin McKenzie's administrative assistant," Karl said. "To hear Bill Tanner tell it, you already work with the living dead."

"Very funny," she said, flushing.

Danny twirled a spoon between his fingers and gave me an appraising look. "You know, Lydia, you could have stumbled onto something very big here."

I half-smiled. "Really? What do you mean?"

"I mean, people are fascinated by weirdos. Normal folks like being reminded of just how normal they are. And what the general public likes, editors and publishers are sure to love."

"So, what are you suggesting?" I said. "That I make Hathor the centerpiece of my study?"

"Yes," he said. "And that you might consider trying the commercial presses first."

Emily turned to me. "Lydia! Maybe this could be a bestseller! You'd be rich!"

Karl shook his head. "I think you should stick with an academic publisher, no matter what," he said. "No one's going to take the scholarship seriously if you go with a popular press."

"Oh, come off it! That's not true," Danny said.

"It *is* true!" Karl shot back.

I rested my chin in my hand as they fought over my future. Should I or should I not appear on *Oprah*—that was the question. All music to my minnow ears.

That night I lay in bed and looked out the window. The moon was high in the night sky, one edge slightly clipped from full.

What if Hathor was right? I wondered. What if we're all recreations of some previous being, extensions of someone else's past?

I hadn't mentioned to Emily, Karl, and Danny my parting with Hathor that night. She had walked out with me into the front yard to say goodbye and turned to stand against the moon. With her high turban, she looked like a hieroglyph in silhouette. I was surprised when she held out a closed fist and reached with her other hand to pull forward my own.

"A gift from Mother." She put something in my palm and closed my hand tight around it. "Serve us well," she said, and then went back inside.

It had looked the same in the moonlight then as it did now, hanging from my bedpost. The dark burnished beads glowed, instantly recognizable. Hathor had given me a necklace of strung barley.

I reached out and fingered the kernels. Maybe she's right, I thought. Maybe the past does determine the future.

Whatever, I thought. My eyes started to close.

Just please don't let me find out I'm really a cow.

I thought of Mother. At least she wasn't alone.

C hristmas Eve day I drove up to school. I had managed to finish a preliminary outline of my new project and wanted to run it off on the department's laser jet printer. Its fancy fonts and clean finish made even the roughest drafts look good.

I drove past the stadium parking lot and headed closer in. Since the university was officially shut down for the holiday week, I could park in the whale lot behind Russell with impunity. A few other cars were already there—I spotted Felix's Subaru next to Karl's rusting and dented Rabbit. I veered away and pulled into a slot on the other end beside a late-model Volvo. On its backside was a white oval sticker marked with a black S: international code for I BOUGHT MY VOLVO IN SWEDEN. WHERE DID YOU BUY YOURS?

What a happy life it could be in the deep deep sea!

Inside Russell the halls were quiet. I walked toward the main office, the sound of my footsteps ricocheting down the corridor. A door up ahead opened.

"Oh, it's you," Felix said.

"Hello to you, too," I said. "Who were you expecting?"

"Roberta." He ran a hand through his hair, which looked, for once, as if it hadn't been combed. His clothes were also uncharacteristically rumpled. He wasn't even wearing a tie. "Where the hell is she?"

"Home," I said. "She's got this week off. It's Christmas, remember?"

"Christmas isn't until tomorrow, goddamn it! Some of us have work to do."

I gave him my most quizzical look. Not only had I never seen him look so ungroomed, I'd also never heard him swear. "Having problems?"

"Problems! Problems!" He threw up his hands. "I've got nothing *but* problems, if you want to know the truth. I have a paper that was due last month—it's for this big conference coming up in February. I'm supposed to send my final version *today without fail* to the panel chairman on a computer disk with all the commands stripped from it. I have absolutely no idea how to do that. I expected there'd be someone in the office to help me!"

He was practically shouting.

"Take it easy," I said. "So you send it the day *after* Christmas. What's the big deal?"

"You don't understand," he said. "I've already—" He paused, and went on in a low voice, "I've already put this publication on my vita and if I fail to make the deadline, I'm screwed."

"You mean, you listed it as a forthcoming conference paper?"

"No, as a chapter in a book."

I stared at him. "You what?"

"Well, that's what it's going to be, eventually," he bristled. "The guy who's running the conference is sure he'll find a publisher any day now, no problem. It's not like I'm lying or anything. I'm just pushing things up a bit, that's all."

I glanced around to make sure the halls were as deserted as their silence implied.

"Why don't you wait until the book is actually out, then?" I asked, whispering. "Especially if you're so sure."

"Because Shepherd just asked me for an updated vita and I had to show something new I've accomplished," he whispered back.

I shook my head. "You shouldn't have done that," I said.

"Jesus Christ, Lydia," he said in something much louder than a whisper. "Don't you see? I *had* to. You got your doctoral dissertation published. That was nice. Makes things a lot easier for you. Some of us aren't that lucky."

"Well, what about trying to get *your* dissertation published?"

"It's too late. My book has already been published."

"You mean someone else wrote on the same thing?"

He nodded, staring down at the floor. "Yes. William Chase Lake, the number one constitutional law scholar in the country, wrote an article for the *Harvard Law Review* using my exact same argument and citing all my sources. If I sent my manuscript out, it would look like I ripped off his ideas."

"That's terrible," I said. "What awful luck!"

"I'm not so sure luck had anything to do with it," he said, lifting his eyes to mine.

I blinked. "Are you suggesting—"

He cut me off. "I sent my dissertation to a publisher last year. It didn't get accepted, but I'll bet anything Lake was one of the reviewers." He paused. "He carved out its core and published it himself as an article, taking all the credit."

"But you don't *know* that," I said. "It could be that you and he just happened to hit on the same idea."

He folded his arms. "The *exact* same idea? I don't believe in those kinds of coincidences. Not in this business. Anyway, it doesn't matter. The point is, my dissertation is dead on arrival. I'll have to use my leave next semester to write a different book. If I manage to get it published, and if I have the odd conference paper and some chapters in other books as well, then maybe I'll stand a chance of getting tenure. Maybe."

"At least you have some time," I said.

"I used to think I did, until the department raised the publishing standard," he said. "Two years seems awfully short now."

I tapped the computer disk in his hand. "Well, the good news is I can help you with that."

"You can?" Eagerness replaced the look of doom in his eyes.

"Yes," I said. "Stripping codes is easy. Let's go into the department office and use Roberta's computer."

"Terrific!" he said. We headed down the hall. "If I'm able to Fed Ex this thing before the end of the day, then maybe my vita will be something less than a totally fraudulent document."

Again I glanced at the closed office doors lining the corridor. "Aren't you afraid someone might hear you?"

He laughed. "You don't honestly think any of our more exalted colleagues are around, do you? On Christmas Eve? Hah!

That's a good one. Speaking of which, guess where Stanley Kitt's hanging his stocking. In Aruba. I was there in the office when he left his hotel number with Roberta." He dropped his voice to a deep bass. "In case I get any important messages." The pompous tones were vintage Kitt. I laughed while Felix rolled his eyes. "He's probably savoring a salty Margarita even as we speak. The only tan I'll get this year is what I pick up from the radiation leaking out of my microwave oven."

"I thought someone told me you and Gwen were going to Key West for the break."

"We were. But after what happened to Walter, I decided I'd stick around and work."

"Does Gwen mind?"

"Of course, but what am I going to do? I had to finish this paper, and I've got to get started on a book. I told her, for the foreseeable future I won't have time for that 'togetherness' she talks about so much. At the moment she's threatening to go to Florida without me."

"Do you think she'll really do that?"

He shrugged as he unlocked the department office door. "I don't know. I would if I were her, just to get away from me. The way I've been acting lately, I wish I could get away from me, too."

We went inside.

"Well, well, well," Felix said as we entered. "Look who's here."

Karl sat at Roberta's desk, going through a stack of papers.

"Hi," he said, barely glancing up at us. A deep crease cut across his brow.

Felix perched on the desk corner. "What's up?"

"Hey, careful," Karl said, and pulled the corner of a page out from underneath Felix's leg. "I want to keep all this stuff organized."

Felix cocked his head, trying to read upside down. "What stuff?"

"Forms for my Fulbright, all right?"

"Jeez!" Felix said, getting up. "Did we forget to take our Prozac this morning?"

"Give me a break, will you?" Karl said, and went back to his papers. "I've got to finish this before we drive up to Boston. We should have left hours ago."

"There's just one small problem," I said.

His bloodshot eyes turned warily to me. "What's that?"

"You have to change desks. We need to use Roberta's computer."

His lips formed a thin line. "Right this very second?"

"Hey, you're not the only one pressed for time, you know," Felix said. "I'm under a deadline I absolutely can't miss."

Karl's frown tightened, along with every visible muscle in his face and neck. He pushed back Roberta's chair and stood up. "Fuck your deadline!" he said, grabbing at the sheets he'd laid out on the desktop. He flushed a dark red. "And fuck you! Both of you! I'll never get out of here. Never!"

He strode to the door and slammed it behind him.

Felix and I looked at each other.

"Seems like our friend is under a bit of a strain," I said.

"No more than the rest of us," Felix said, moving to take the seat Karl had just vacated. "And pretty soon he won't *have* any friends if he acts like that."

"I don't envy Emily's drive with him today," I said.

"I don't envy her, period," he said. He booted up the computer and slipped in his disk.

"Think one of us should go talk to him?"

"Later," he said. His fingers hovered over the keyboard. "First you've got to help me."

"Okay," I said.

At least Felix had a problem that could be solved. I pulled up a chair to sit beside him and started giving instructions.

I didn't think of Karl again until much later, when I left Russell and made my way to my car. The beat-up Rabbit was gone, and I hoped it was well on its puttering way to Boston. The weather didn't appear to favor anyone's holiday travel plans. Low gray clouds blanketed the sky, plunging the day into an early dusk. With them had come a stiff wind. I leaned into it and felt the sting of tiny needles against my face.

Snow.

I managed to get home before the traffic snarled. People in Albemarle weren't accustomed to driving in snow, and, coupled with the fact that no one bothered with snow tires, conditions out on the road could often turn downright hazardous.

At six o'clock I switched on the local news. Already there were reports of fender benders on the side streets. The station even had a crew shooting live tape of cars fishtailing on the main thoroughfare. Kathy appeared on the screen, all bundled up in a ski parka and scarf.

"The police are advising motorists to stay off the road tonight," she said. "Those who must travel should make sure their cars are equipped with chains."

The screen cut back to the gamine anchorwoman. "And those of you who are driving to work tomorrow morning should give yourselves lots of time—"

I flicked the TV off. Maybe it was just my imagination, but Kathy's eyes had looked awfully watery.

Probably from the cold, I thought.

I settled back into an armchair to read for an hour or so before making dinner. Outside, big flakes flew by the windows. A pane rattled. Without realizing it, I forgot all about the opened journal in my lap. I stared after the bits of white streaming down, falling without end.

I was revising my regrets of just a few nights ago, when I'd envied even the companionship of a cow. Instead I contemplated the plight of married assistant professors. There was Felix, packing off his wife for a long lonely vacation, metaphorical and otherwise, while he stayed home and padded his vita. There was Karl, who was just as happy to go away himself, whether Emily wished to or not. And then there was the department's trophy couple, Victor and Julia. One could not fail to include them in the list.

Fools.

They should have waited, all of them. They should never have fallen in love, not before they'd survived the sea. It was their big mistake. All they had to do was wait. Was that so very difficult?

Just then there came a knock. I sat up.

"Lydia?"

It was Charlie's voice.

When I opened the door Charlie was stamping the snow off his feet. Behind him the flakes fell in a hissing shower. Already the walkway was lost beneath a white pillowing softness.

"Hi," he said.

My expression must have registered complete shock, because he added quickly, "I should have called first. I'm sorry."

"No, that's okay," I said. "I wasn't expecting anyone, that's all." Least of all you, I thought.

"I just came by to return this," he said, and held out the white dust-jacketed book.

"Thanks." I reached out, and Walter's book dropped between us. In the next instant we were both crouched down on the doorstep, holding the book together. We were so close, I could feel the cold radiating from him.

"Sorry," he said softly, and let go.

We straightened. I took the book and pressed it against my chest.

"Can you come in for a minute?" I asked, hardly daring to look at him.

"Sure."

I held the door wide and then closed it behind him.

"Let me take your coat," I said.

"Thanks," he said. He rubbed his hands together hard.

"Don't tell me you rode your bike in this weather," I said.

He shook his head. Drops of melted snow gleamed against his dark hair. "No. I walked."

"You must be freezing! Would you like something to drink? I can make tea, or hot chocolate, or coffee."

"Coffee'd be great," he said, and stepped into the living room. "Does your fireplace work?"

"I don't know," I said. "I've been meaning to try it. There's some wood stacked in that far corner. Are you good at building fires?"

"I was a boy scout once, if that's any recommendation."

"Well, you're welcome to give it a shot," I said, and went into the kitchen.

Once there, I prepped the coffee machine and waited for it to work its usual magic. Over the sink was a window. I leaned toward it to catch my reflection in its dark pane.

Good God, I thought, and tried to comb my hair with my fingers. Useless. Then I glanced down at my clothes. I was wearing sweatpants and an over-sized fleece top—very comfortable and about as unsexy as you could possibly get.

When the coffee was ready, I put everything on a tray and carried it out into the living room. Charlie knelt by the hearth, poking a stick into the heart of a few tentative flames.

"Congratulations," I said. "I think you qualify for a badge."

He got up and dusted off his jeans. "Let's wait and see if it takes hold. Right now I'd say it's off to a mighty feeble start."

"Here you are," I said, and handed him a cup. I sat down on the couch and he took a seat beside me.

I raised my mug. "Merry Christmas," I said.

He saluted me back. "Merry Christmas."

There was a moment of silence while we sipped. Then Charlie sighed and settled back, gazing at the fire.

"So tell me," I said. "How's work?"

"Good," he said. "I spent most of the day in the ER, which means with any luck I won't have to show up tomorrow."

"Is Christmas busy there?"

"It can be," he said. "You saw what it was like on Thanksgiving. There's always trouble when people get together and drink too much, especially if they're related to each other."

I laughed. "That doesn't say much for family reunions."

"What about you? Are you planning to fly home to Florida in time for Christmas dinner?"

"No, I can't this year," I said, pleased that he remembered that small fact about me. "Too much work."

"How's the research going?"

"Terrific," I said. "People have been incredibly helpful, especially Humanity For Animal members." I looked at him over the rim of my cup. "You know, you might have mentioned Mother."

He laughed. "I thought it would be more fun for you to discover her yourself. And anyway I wasn't sure Hathor would want you to know. You must have gained her trust."

"I think so," I said. "She certainly told me a lot about herself. It's not often I hear several life stories at once. From the same person, I mean."

"Hathor's a trip, that's for sure," he said.

"Yes. I plan to give her a lot of play in my book."

Charlie lowered his coffee. "You aren't going to talk about Mother, though, are you?"

I reared back slightly and frowned. "Of course. Are you kidding? Without Mother, Hathor's just your run-of-the-mill Egyptian avatar. I *have* to talk about Mother."

He didn't seem to get the joke. "But if you do that, Hathor will lose her for sure. She's not exactly in line with city zoning restrictions, you know."

I shrugged. "Then I'll give Hathor another name. What do you think of Isis?"

"No matter *what* you call her, anyone who cares to look into the local HFA membership will figure out who she is pretty fast," he said.

"Look," I said. "I'm a researcher. I study interest groups. They don't come in globs—they're made up of individuals. In order for me to present an analysis of a cause, I have to also present the people who promote it. Besides, if worse came to worse Mother just would have to relocate to some barn out in the county, that's all," I said. "It wouldn't be the end of the world. But consider *my* position. My career is on the line with this book. If I don't get it published, I'm finished at Patrick Henry. Once I get tenure, *then* I can afford to be generous to others, cows included." I paused. "You understand, don't you? Anyway, you should. You're in the same bind as me, having to bite the bullet and do the dissections."

He took a deep breath and then released it. "I guess you're right. They're both terrible means to a supposedly good end."

I didn't think I was being so terrible, but I didn't disagree. I still remembered Hathor's last words.

Serve us well.

And she didn't mean as opposed to rare, either.

I went on. "Anyway, I'm making lots of progress. Recently I decided to broaden the scope of my interviews to include other local activists—feminists, gay rights advocates, and environmentalists—to find out if they identify with or feel any connection to the animal rights cause."

"Who've you talked to?"

"Well, no one except HFA members so far," I said. "I've just been setting up appointments. Everyone wanted to wait until after Christmas to meet. Most folks do try and make it home to their families for the holidays, no matter how hazardous it may be to their health." I paused. "Are you looking forward to starting back up in medical school next month?"

"Sure. I guess so." He got up and placed a small log cross-wise upon the struggling fire. With a turn of his head I saw his gorgeous green eyes rest on me. "What I mean is, I'll be glad when I'm through."

"You've got two more years," I said.

"Yes."

"I'm sure it'll go by fast," I said.

"By then you'll have tenure."

"Let's hope," I said, and smiled. "Doctor, lawyer, Indian chief. And professor."

He didn't return to the couch, but instead stretched his legs out on the carpet, propped his back against the sofa, and shifted his weight to half-turn in my direction.

"Aren't you going to ask me about Kathy?" he said.

I was just putting my cup on the table, and for a second it remained poised in mid-air. Then I completed the motion and sat back, tucking my legs beneath me.

"I didn't think I should," I replied.

"We've split," he said. "I moved out a couple of weeks ago, almost right after I last saw you."

"Oh," I said, and squirmed slightly. I was keenly aware that he was watching my reaction. "I'm sorry to hear that."

"But not surprised, I bet," he said. The firelight lit up the near side of his face and cast the other half in shadow, making it difficult for me to read his expression. "You were right, after all. There really was no room for compromise. I remember how angry I was with you that night for pointing it out."

"I'm sorry. It wasn't my place to say anything. I-I don't know why I did."

"You don't?"

My lips felt dry. I was suddenly aware that my chest was visibly rising and falling from too shallow breathing. I reached for my coffee. As I grasped the ceramic handle, Charlie's hand was there, too, covering my own.

I didn't move. His fingers crept around mine, easing them from the cup. I watched as our fingers intertwined, separated, and intertwined once more.

I kept my eyes on our hands, unable to decide what to do or say. Such things shouldn't happen so quickly, I knew. But then again, there was nothing quick about it. I'd already waited years.

His grasp tightened.

This is a mistake, I thought.

Then I slipped down from the cushions to kiss him.

Later, in the bedroom, I woke to a wash of light. Sometime in the night the moon had broken through the snowclouds. Now it hung outside my window, riding low in the sky.

Beside me Charlie stirred. I reached over and tugged the blanket back up around him, and then wormed under the covers myself.

I've got him, I thought. Even if only for one night.

And at that moment I would have sworn, one night was truly enough.

"Lydia? Lydia? Wake up," Charlie said.

Before falling back to sleep that night I had tried to prepare for any number of morning scenarios. But I never quite imagined what *really* awaited me: the sight of Charlie wrapped in a blanket, squatting by the window.

"Look!" he said.

I sat up, holding the sheet against my bare chest.

"What?" I said, squinting.

"Can you believe it?" he asked.

Outside, deep drifts of snow gleamed with blinding whiteness.

I leaned forward and stared. "My God, how many feet did we get?" I said.

"Three, easy." He jumped back into bed, threw the blanket over both of us, and wrapped his arms around me. "Merry Christmas," he said, smiling.

I smiled back and ran my fingertips over the dark stubbles bristling along his cheek. How long had it been since I'd felt a man's morning shadow?

"Hey, are you okay?" he said. "All of a sudden you're trembling."

"I'm just a little cold," I lied. "It's all right."

"Here," he said, holding me closer. "How's this?"

"Wonderful," I said, kissing him. "Absolutely wonderful."

We ate a breakfast of toast and coffee in front of another fire.

"You're improving," I said. "It didn't take the whole Sunday edition of the *Albemarle Register* to get this one going."

"Are you criticizing my technique?"

I rubbed my foot against his leg. "Never. Your technique is perfect."

It was the typical silly thing that lovers say, and I was delighted once again to have the privilege.

"Do you mind if I make more toast?" he said, leaning toward me.

I laughed. "More? Do you always eat this much for breakfast?"

"No," he said, starting to kiss me. "Something must have happened to my appetite."

The phone rang. We drew back and looked at each other.

"Your boyfriend?" he said.

I gave him a shove and stood up. "No. Probably Mom and Dad." I was wearing my bathrobe, and I tightened its sash as I crossed the room toward the phone.

"Hello?"

"Merry Christmas, dear," came my parents' voices simultaneously over the line.

"Merry Christmas to you, too," I laughed.

Charlie, wearing nothing but boxer shorts, padded into the kitchen.

"We heard on the news that Virginia got socked with a big snow storm last night," my father said.

"You heard right." I glanced out the windows. "Three feet already and it's still flurrying."

"You aren't going out today, are you?" my mother asked. "The roads will be awful."

"Don't worry, Mom," I said. "I'm not going anywhere today."

"We do wish you were here. Your father and I were just thinking—"

A loud clatter of pans cut her off.

"Are you cooking?" she asked.

"No, I—"

Charlie's head poked around the doorway. "Sorry!" he whispered. "I'm looking for some maple syrup."

I put a hand over the phone's mouthpiece. "It's in the refrigerator. Now shhhh!"

"Lydia?" my father said. "Who are you talking to? Is somebody there?"

"Um, yes. Sorry. Go on. You were saying?"

There was a pause. I could sense their confusion.

"We're so glad you're not spending the holiday all alone," my mother said, casting out the first feeler. "Is it your friend Pam?"

"No, no. No one you know."

But she was not to be deterred. Cutting right to the chase, she asked, "Is it a man?"

I rolled my eyes and turned toward the wall, hoping my voice wouldn't carry. "Yes, Mom. It's a man."

From the kitchen came more clangs. What in the world was Charlie doing?

"Well!" my father said, his voice beaming. "We won't keep you."

"Yes, dear," my mother said. "We can talk later. Have fun!"

"And give our best to your young man," my father added.

"Okay. Thanks for calling. Love you—bye."

I hung up. Once, having a male in the house would have grounded me for weeks. Now they were probably dancing a jig. Time is a revelation, I thought.

There was another big clatter.

"What's going on in there?" I asked, crossing to peer into the kitchen. Charlie crouched before one of the lower cabinets, knee-deep in saucepans.

"I'm looking for a skillet," he said. "For pancakes."

"You want to make pancakes?"

"Yes, to impress you. They're my specialty."

"Well, then, here you are," I said, sliding open the drawer below the oven. "There. My best frying pan."

He pulled it out. "Lydia, the price sticker is still on this thing. It's brand new."

"Not exactly. I've had it a few years."

"A great big skillet like this, sitting around gathering dust." He shook his head. "Good thing I came along. Now you just take a seat and watch the master at work." He started rummaging through more cabinets. "Where do you keep your flour? Ah, there it is."

I smiled, poured myself a cup of coffee, and sat down at the table to watch.

"Voila!"

"Good Lord, Charlie," I said. "You call this a pancake? It's gargantuan! It's even too big for the plate—look how it overlaps the edges."

He pulled up a chair close to mine and handed me a fork.

"That's right. A mutant flapjack. The Godzilla of all pancakes. My specialty."

I laughed. "I can't eat this thing."

"Not all by yourself, anyway." He held up his fork. "At your assistance. *You* can pour the maple syrup."

"Thanks," I said, squeezing out a small lake of the stuff. "That enough?"

"Perfect!" he said, and tore right into the pancake's very heart. "Come on. Dig in! You'll need the energy."

"Oh?" I gave him a coy look.

"You bet. We've got to get out there and get busy."

"Out there where?" I said, blinking.

"Out there!" He motioned with his fork toward the window. "Outside. You don't want the neighborhood kids to have all the fun, do you?"

"You mean . . . ?"

"Snowmen," he said through another big bite. "We're going to build the best on the block."

It was dusk before we made it back. We had meant to call it quits much earlier, after the third snowman, when we followed riotous shouts and squeals to the next street over. Milford Avenue was on a steep slope and overnight had been transformed into the hot spot in the neighborhood for sledding. Charlie talked a couple of the kids into giving us some turns, which worked out well until we rammed into a telephone pole. The sled was unhurt and so were we, but after that no one was willing to let us have another shot.

"Wait a second," I said as we slogged up the walkway to the townhouse. "Just one more."

I flopped on my back onto a plane of smooth snow and waved my arms up and down.

"That's real nice," Charlie said. "That's the best angel yet."

Just then an outside light flicked to life and a door opened. Frances appeared, craning her head.

"Oh, it's you, Lydia!" she said. "I didn't recognize your voice. Merry Christmas."

I got up and brushed myself off. "Merry Christmas to you, too, Frances," I said. I hoped a simple exchange of holiday greetings would suffice for the situation, but I was wrong. She remained on her doorstep and looked at Charlie.

He removed a mitten and held out his hand. "Hello, Mrs. Taylor. You probably don't remember me."

She squinted at him, and then her wizened Christopher Robin face broke into a smile. "Yes, of course I do. From the hospital." She took his hand.

"Charlie Whittier," he said as they shook. "Merry Christmas. I hope you're feeling better these days."

"Oh, much, thank you," she said, and smiled from him to me. "What a nice surprise. Have you been out admiring the snow?"

"More than that," Charlie said, and gestured toward my front yard. "We've been adding to the snowman population."

"My, that's quite a large one," she said. She looked back at me. "I didn't know you had such talents."

"Me either," I said, and straightened. "Well! We mustn't let you stand there with your door open. It was nice to see you."

Instead of moving back, however, she took another step out.

"Would you like to come in?" she asked. "I've made some hot chocolate." She gave a rueful look at Charlie. "Eggnog's off limits, unfortunately. All that cream."

"That's awfully sweet of you," I said quickly before Charlie could answer, "but I'm afraid we can't. Thank you, though, very much."

"Yes, thank you," Charlie said, and took her hand again.

"Some other time, then," she said. "How wonderful to see you again, Charlie. I do hope I'll have another chance soon."

We exchanged a wave before I moved to unlock my door and she disappeared behind her own.

"Whew!" I said once we were safely inside. I started peeling off my sodden mittens. "For a moment there, I was afraid we were going to be stuck."

Charlie shrugged out of his coat, sat on a chair, and used both hands to pull off his boots. "I don't know. Maybe we should have accepted. She seemed sort of lonely."

"Oh, she's always that way," I said, and hung my coat beside Charlie's. I rubbed my hands. "Let's see if banking those coals worked."

"How's her heart these days?"

"Fine, I guess." I reached for the poker and gave the ashes a stab. "Hey, look! We're still in business."

He walked over in his stockinged feet, crouched beside me, and helped feed kindling to the embers.

"Haven't you asked?" he said.

"What? You mean about her health? No, and I don't intend to," I said. "I don't want to know."

"Aren't you being a little. . . . " He searched for the word. "Cold? She *is* your neighbor, after all," he said.

I shook my head. "No. Look, it's like I was telling you last night when we talked about Mother. I've got too many problems of my own to concern myself with anyone else's. It just leads to *more* problems. Believe me, I know."

I thought of Tony Donatello.

When Charlie didn't respond I glanced at him. He was back on his heels and appeared to be studying the sticks in his hands. There were two lines between his brows I hadn't noticed before.

"Might as well throw those in, too," I said.

He roused. "Sure." And he tossed them on the fire.

"Well," I said, getting to my feet, "why don't you take over here while I make us some dinner. Pasta sound good?"

"Great," he said.

I paused. Something was . . . different. "Are you okay?" I asked.

He gave me a quick smile. "Of course. Do you want a hand in there?"

"No, you've already demonstrated your culinary skills," I said. "Us amateurs deserve a crack."

A half hour later I reemerged, bearing a large ceramic bowl filled with steaming pasta. Charlie was on the couch writing in a spiral notebook. When he saw me, he shut it and made room on the coffee table for the bowl.

"Working?" I asked. "On Christmas? And I thought *I* was bad."

"Nah, just scribbling," he said. "Ummm, this looks terrific. What do you have in there, garlic?"

"And olive oil and flaked red peppers. Strictly vegetarian." I went back for a couple of smaller bowls and silverware.

"So what were you scribbling?" I asked. I handed him a napkin and sat down so we were both facing the fire. "Taking notes?"

He chuckled. "No. Not exactly." I lifted a serving of spaghetti between two large spoons and he quickly held out a bowl to catch it. "It's my journal."

"You mean, like a diary?"

"Please," he said, wincing. "I prefer 'journal.' It makes me sound more like Henry David Thoreau and less like a moony teenager."

"Huh," I said, filling the other bowl. "I didn't know people still did that sort of thing."

"You mean people other than moony teenagers." He took a bite. "This is good. Hats off."

"Thanks." I twirled some strands around my fork. "So tell me more about this journal of yours. You write in it every day?"

He nodded, chewing, and then swallowed. "Just about. It's a habit now, I guess. Putting things down on paper helps me focus my thoughts—I try to sort through what's important to me and what's not."

"Interesting," I said, and took a bite. For a moment neither of us spoke. "So how long have you been writing in your journal?"

"Years," he said. "Since college."

"No kidding," I answered. I picked up the spoons. "More?"

"Absolutely," he said, again raising his bowl.

I dropped in another serving and we went back to eating. "Listen," I said. "Would you let me look at it sometime?"

That stopped him. He put down his bowl and turned to me.

"You want to read my journal?" He smiled. "You don't really think I'm taking notes, do you?"

"No, no, of course not," I said. I cocked my head and watched my fork turn around another mouthful of spaghetti. "I just thought it could be useful. You know. For tracking what led you to the animal rights movement, your decision to go to medical school, and then all that's happened in this last year."

He stared at me.

"I don't mean you'd give me the whole thing," I assured him. "Just whatever parts you think might be helpful. It would be a way of finishing off your interview."

"You want to read my journal as part of your research?" His voice sounded strained.

I frowned. "You're looking at me like I've just asked you to commit a major felony or something. It's no big deal."

"Lydia, I thought that what was happening between us was private. I didn't realize *you* were still taking notes."

"I'm not! Look, just forget I ever asked, okay? Really. Let's just forget it."

He let his gaze drop to his bowl. "Okay," he said, and picked up his fork. He moved it back and forth among the strands.

I watched him for a moment, and then gave my own pasta an enthusiastic twirl. "You aren't going to believe this. I looked in the paper and guess what's on TV tonight?" I said. I didn't wait for an answer. "*Holiday Inn.* Don't you love that movie?"

He didn't say anything.

"You know which one I mean. Bing Crosby and Fred Astaire fight for the same girl? She winds up selling out Bing for Hollywood, and she's on that fake stage set of the inn waiting to marry Fred. Watching her, you know *she* knows she's thrown away her happiness. Then she starts singing White Christmas and hits the chimes with Bing's pipe. That's how she knows he's come back for her—the pipe. Remember?"

He nodded, stirring from his silence at last. "Sure, I know that one. I haven't seen it in years."

"Well, let's hurry up and finish. It starts at eight."

When it came time to clear away the plates, however, I noticed Charlie had barely touched that second helping.

We were just into the Easter bonnet routine when the phone rang. I picked up and then held it away in surprise.

"It's for you," I said.

"Must be the hospital," he said, rising. "I left this number." He took the phone.

"Yes? Uh huh. Sure. No, that's okay. Really. It's okay. I'm coming in right now. Okay. See you in a few minutes." He hung up, fished a card out of his wallet, and started dialling.

"Who're you calling?" I asked.

"A cab," he said. "I've got to—" He stopped and spoke into the receiver. "Hello? I'd like a cab, please. Yes. I'm at . . . " He looked back at me.

"Twenty-eight forty-five Hawthorn Drive," I said.

He repeated the address, gave my phone number, and hung up.

"You have to go?" I asked.

He nodded. "Yes. I'm sorry. They're shorthanded in the ER and I really can't say no."

"Oh," I said. I wished he looked more unhappy about the situation, but if anything he appeared relieved. "You didn't have to call a cab, you know. I would have driven you."

"Thanks, but I didn't want you to have to dig your car out. Plus, you'd miss your movie," he said.

"I wouldn't have minded," I said.

For a moment we stood there.

"I'll call you," he said.

I nodded. "Okay."

He stepped closer and kissed me. "I'll see you later, all right?" Then he moved toward the door to put on his boots.

"Fine," I said. For a moment I watched him. "Oh—what about your new number? All I have is your old one for the house on Rosehill."

"Sure. Do you have a pen?"

I handed him a pad and a ballpoint. He scratched out a number and then handed them back.

"That's the extension for Fairchild's lab. I'm there most of the day."

I watched him get into his coat.

"Charlie—" I said.

He had just fitted the bottom of his jacket zipper. When I said his name he stopped and waited, his hand on the metal tab.

"You could come back here, you know," I said. "Tonight, when you're done."

He looked at me and then away. "I can't," he said. "I'll probably be up all night. And Fairchild's expecting me in the lab tomorrow." With a quick movement he zippered his jacket.

I nodded.

The glare of headlights swung through the windows, followed by a short blast of a car horn.

"That was quick," Charlie said. He put his hand on the door. "I'll see you, then. Okay?"

"Bye," I said. "Don't work too hard."

He gave me a small smile. "Look who's talking," he said, and was gone.

T he next morning I awoke to the sound of steady dripping from the gutters. The snow was still there, although it had lost its puff. I went to the window and tried to find my angel. There was only a faint hollow where the wings had been.

A snowplow rumbled by, making another pass down the street. It didn't look like there'd be any problem driving to the office. Whoopee, I thought.

Within the hour I was climbing the stairs to the third floor of Russell, my overstuffed leather satchel weighing down my every step. I had a fleeting fantasy that it was my fate to climb these stairs, Sisyphus-like, for eternity.

Now that really *would* be hell, I thought.

When I got to the third floor I found the halls as deserted the day after Christmas as they had been the day before. I figured most folks were home observing the usual post-holiday rituals, such as eating turkey sandwiches and gathering up crumpled gift wrapping to take out to the trash.

After Charlie and the cheer he'd brought, at least this year I could think of other people's Christmas gatherings without the usual bout of depression. That was an improvement. Now it was only their day after I envied.

I fitted my office door key into the lock and let myself in.

"Hey, Pete," I said to the still-unframed Max poster. Then I threw my purse on the desk and sat down to work.

It's amazing what a person can get done in an absolutely silent environment. As the hours ticked by, every now and again I'd stop and relish the stillness. It was hard to believe that in a little over two weeks these same corridors would be ringing with shouts and bell buzzes and the scuffling of countless shoes. Once the semester began one might as well kiss goodbye any chance of uninterrupted concentration within the confines of one's office. The doors were thick, but not thick enough.

By mid-afternoon I'd drafted various lectures for the first weeks of classes. I was teaching two courses for the spring semester, one on political parties and the other on organizational theory. The last one was a new course for me, which meant I had no previous lectures to fall back on. Both were for undergraduates only.

I had just finished typing up a syllabus for the political parties class when I heard footsteps and then a light rap.

I stared at my closed door, and then hurried to answer.

"Charlie?" I said, and pulled the door open.

"Who's Charlie?" Pam asked.

"Pam! What in the world are you doing here?" I asked. "I thought you were in California."

"I was, and now I'm back," she said, and held out her arms. "Here. Let me give you a Christmas hug."

I allowed her to embrace me and then stepped back. "That was an awfully quick vacation."

"You're telling me! And exhausting. I just got in an hour ago. That's a long flight coming back."

"Here, have a seat," I said. I moved my coat off the chair and then sat back down behind my desk. "So why the rush? I thought you liked spending time with your parents."

"Oh, I do," she said. "But I've got a three-course load this coming semester, all new ones. I wrote some of the lectures the week right after finals, but I'm still a long way from being prepared. I feel like I'm behind on everything."

"What about your book?"

She took a breath. "Don't even ask. I haven't looked at it since . . . well, since the summer, I guess."

I shook my head. "Pam," I said in a warning voice.

She held up a hand. "I know, I know. I've got to finish it soon or else." She turned slightly and gazed out the window. "The snow sure makes everything look pretty, doesn't it?"

"For a while," I said. "Until it starts turning a mushy gray."

She looked back at me and laughed. "That's what I like about you, Lydia. Always so cheerful."

"Right," I said. "Little Miss Sunbeam. That's me."

Keeping me in her sights, she repeated, "So who's Charlie?"

"No one you know."

"Well, obviously. What I'm wondering is how *you* know a Charlie."

I picked up a pen and uncapped it. "Oh, I interviewed him for my new project. He used to be an HFA member."

"And?" she asked.

"And what?"

"Lydia, don't be so mysterious," she said. "Are you dating this guy or what?"

I capped the pen and shrugged. "I think so."

She leaned forward in her excitement. "You think so? Come on. Either you are or you aren't. "

"Then I am," I said. "I guess."

She half-frowned, half-smiled. "You know, I worry about you sometimes. Here you finally meet a guy and you can't tell whether you're dating him or not. This is not a good sign."

I paused, thinking. "Would you like to meet him?"

"Of course!" she said.

"Well, I'm supposed to have Tom and Margaret Shepherd for dinner sometime," I said slowly as the idea unfolded. "Maybe I could put together something for next week."

"You've invited Tom and Margaret for dinner?" she asked, and sat back. "What brought that on?"

It's all Victor's fault, I wanted to say, but decided it was too complicated to explain.

"I'm just being collegial," I said. "Showing my solidarity with the department family. Isn't that what Tom is always exhorting us to do in faculty meetings?"

"I guess," she said in a now-I've-heard-everything tone. "So, when's the party?"

"Let's say a week from Thursday, on the fourth. Are you free?"

"You're kidding, right? Yes, of course I'm free."

"Good."

"Hey, what about New Year's Eve?" she said. "Want to come over to my place and watch the ball fall in Times Square?"

"No, thanks," I said. "I'm hoping I'll be busy."

"Charlie?"

I nodded.

She sighed and stood up. "Well, all I can say is thank God for cats. At least I'll have someone with whiskers to kiss at the stroke of midnight." She picked up her purse. "By the way, have you had a chance to look over Tony's prospectus yet?"

I blinked. "Uh, no. I thought I'd wait—I want to talk to him about something first."

"If it's about Bill Tanner, you don't have to worry. I had a long chat with Tony the day he helped me move my books. He's given up trying to force Tanner to admit to anything. He told me he's going to put all that behind him, now that he's got you to direct his dissertation."

"Well, that's good," I said. I made a mental note to leave a message for Tony in the graduate students' lounge to see me as soon as he got back. What had started out as a loose end was fast turning into a noose, and I wasn't about to let the knot get any tighter.

Pam started for the door, then stopped and looked back. "Oh, and I also had a talk with Meredith Kospach," she added in a low voice. "I told her not to worry about retaking her oral exam. I said she could trust you to take care of her, the way you're taking care of Tony."

"Pam—"

"I know, I know," she said. "You can't make promises. But I didn't want her to have any doubts that you'll see her through this, one way or another." She smiled. "Well, that's it. I'm off. Can I bring anything Thursday night?"

"Nothing, thanks."

"Okay. I'll probably see you before then, anyway. Take it easy, Lydia."

"You too," I said.

With a wave, she turned to walk toward her office.

For a moment I sat there and thought over my dinner party plan. Entertaining the Shepherds wouldn't be so bad if Charlie were there, too. In fact, having a nondepartment person present might force Tom to discuss subjects that had no direct bearing on himself. Listening to him sometimes, you'd think he actually had some standing in the discipline before taking the job of chairman, and that people were now interested in what he had to say for reasons other than he decided everyone's salary.

I picked up the phone.

"We'd be delighted to come for dinner," Margaret said when I explained the reason for my call. "Tom and I will look forward to it."

I doubted that, but Margaret was not one to shirk the obligations of Tom's position. A chairman had his duties—noblesse oblige!—and showing forbearance toward the minnows was one of them.

Regarding Charlie, I went so far as to remove the folded slip of paper with his number from my purse and smooth it open. I fingered it for a moment and then put it away again.

Better to let him call first, I decided. No need to appear unduly anxious, after all.

My stomach grumbled and I glanced at my watch. It was long past lunchtime and I realized I was starving. All I had left to do was run off copies of my syllabus, and then I'd be done for the day. I shuffled together the necessary pages and headed for the Xerox machine.

Karl was in the far corner of the main office, his back to the door, stapling handouts.

I stopped still at the sight of him.

"What did you do?" I asked. "Drive up to Boston, turn around, and drive right back?"

He glanced over at me and then went on stapling. "I didn't go," he said.

"What?"

He spoke loudly and more slowly. "I said, I DIDN'T GO."

"Oh." I watched him slam his palm down hard on the stapler once, then twice. "That's too bad. What about Emily?"

"She won't be back until next week."

"She went by herself?"

He stopped and turned his head slightly in my direction. "Sounds that way, doesn't it?"

"I guess so," I said, frowning. "Look, you don't have to get so—so—"

He threw up his hands and spun around. "So WHAT, Lydia? I don't have to get so WHAT?"

I stepped back. "So *defensive*, Karl. I was only asking."

"Is that what you were doing? Only asking? Well, that's what I was doing. Only ANSWERING."

My impulse was to walk out, but instead I stood there and crossed my arms.

"What the hell is wrong with you?"

"Nothing!" he yelled. "Nothing is wrong with me! If people would just leave me the fuck alone, I'd be fine! All right?"

I nodded. "All right." I turned on one heel and started for the door.

"Lydia—"

I stopped.

"Look, I'm . . . I'm sorry. I didn't mean that."

I turned around to respond, and then didn't. There were hints of tears in Karl's eyes.

"I'm sorry," he repeated. He sagged against the copier. "I don't know what's the matter with me."

I walked over and put a hand on his arm. "You're under a lot of stress. We all are. Everything that's going on in the department these days—it takes its toll, that's all."

He blinked away the wetness. "This crazy profession. You know, I've been thinking. In what other career do you have six years, six lousy years, to prove yourself completely or be kicked out of a place for good? And if you *are* kicked out and you're *real* lucky, you get to start all over somewhere else and go through the whole process again. Can you think of one?"

I shook my head.

"It's really something, isn't it? I mean, look at you!" he said, gesturing. "You're a machine! You've got no husband, no kids, practically no life at all except work, and even so you're looking pretty iffy these days for tenure. It's ridiculous!"

I dropped my hand and shifted my weight from one foot to the other. "I wouldn't say I'm exactly *iffy*, Karl."

"Well, then you're the only one who *isn't* saying it," he said. "Come on, Lydia. Do you really think you're going to write a book in six months? Because that's the deadline you're facing, you know. And even then the manuscript won't see hardcover for at least another six months, assuming you find a publisher on the very first submit. So that makes a year from start to finish, easy. Good, but, given what Shepherd says, maybe not good enough."

"Well, don't you worry about me," I said with some heat. "Worry about yourself first."

"That's what I'm talking about! Hey—don't get mad. I'm saying I couldn't do what you're doing. So if you don't get through, I'm not going to stand a chance, and that's all there is to it."

He hadn't left me in a position to offer much consolation, and I wasn't sure I felt like giving any, anyway. I sighed.

"Look. Just focus on your own work. You've got some great ideas for a project and terrific opportunities for travel and research. Whatever happened to Walter and whatever happens to me, the only thing that will count in the end is *your* work. Write a great book. That's your best defense."

Something approximating a smile crossed his lips.

"Thanks, coach."

"You're welcome," I said. "Now move out of the way. I need to use the copier."

He pushed off and gathered his handouts.

"What are you doing next Thursday night?" I asked.

"Nothing. Why?"

"Would you like to come to my place for dinner?" I glanced up to find him giving me the once-over. I had never seen such a bald and calculating look, at least not from Karl. I went on in a rush. "And Emily, too, of course, if she's back. I have to warn you, though. I've already invited Tom and Margaret Shepherd. Pam's also coming, if that helps."

The look vanished. "Sure," he said. "I'll come."

"And Emily?"

"She won't be back until the next weekend," he said. "What time?"

"Seven," I said, and slipped my pages into the feeder.

He headed for the door. "Okay. Later, Lydia."

I waved and he disappeared. I pressed the big green start button and watched the sweep of intense light spill out along the edges of the copier cover. It occurred to me that Karl had more than tenure on his mind these days.

Probably just a phase, I thought. Typical, really. A starving ego will seek reassurance from any quarter. I shook my head. Karl was right. This *is* a crazy business.

And I waited for my pages to copy so that I could go home.

The first thing I did when I returned to the townhouse, before even taking off my coat, was run to the answering machine. There were no messages.

"Damn!" I threw my coat on the couch and went into the kitchen. From the refrigerator I got out the makings of a ham and cheese sandwich. I was in a carnivorous mood.

I worked in my study well into the evening. Twice I picked up the phone to check for a dial tone. At nine o'clock I switched off my computer, went back into the kitchen, and made myself another sandwich. Then I laid down on the sofa and flicked the TV on to C-Span. Showing that night were reruns of an American Enterprise Institute conference on reforming the budget process. I recognized the pundits—all stock players for this debate—so there was no risk of hearing anything I hadn't already heard before. I stuck a cushion behind my head and settled in.

I awoke the next morning in the same position.

Time to get up, I thought. Take a shower, have breakfast, drive to Russell, walk up those stairs. Do everything you did yesterday all over again. Come on. You can do it.

Not a muscle moved.

Okay, okay, I told myself. How about: take a shower, have breakfast, CALL CHARLIE, and *then* drive to Russell. Can you handle that?

Within five minutes I was naked and wet.

Next I decided coffee qualified as breakfast. Cup in hand, I dug out Charlie's number and called.

It was pretty early, too early to count on his being in. Even so, my heart beat so hard it hurt.

On the third ring the line clicked and a man's voice I didn't recognize answered.

"Doctor Fairchild's lab," he said.

I asked for Charlie.

"Hold on a second." The phone clunked down. In the background I heard barking, then footsteps.

"Hello?"

"Charlie," I said. "It's Lydia."

"Oh, hi," he said. "How're you doing?"

"Fine. Just fine. Yourself?"

"Good, thanks."

There was a pause.

"You've been busy?" I said, and then flushed. What was I doing? Asking him to offer excuses for not calling?

"Yeah, we're just about finished setting up the protocol for a new drug trial. In fact, I really don't have much time to talk right now. Can I call you back?"

"Sure," I said, and then hurried on, afraid to wait. "Actually, I just wanted to ask if you would come for dinner next Thursday night. I've invited my chairman and his wife, and I could really use an extra body at the table."

"Next Thursday? Um, I'm not sure."

My grip on the phone tightened.

"You'd be doing me a big favor," I said.

Again he paused.

"Uh, okay," he said. "What time?"

"At seven," I said.

"Okay. I'll see you Thursday then, all right? I really have to go now."

"Sure, that's fine. Bye, Charlie."

I hung up and stared down at the phone.

Okay, I thought. He's coming. That's the important thing. Of course he's coming *as a favor*, but at least he'll be here.

I went back into the kitchen, poured another cup of coffee, and opened the paper. Congress and the president were gearing up for another tussle, fuelling the careers of political analysts and commentators all across the land.

Not one word about New Year's Eve.

I turned the page and read on.

T he new year received its predictable welcome. Revellers in Time Square cheered the falling ball while the Pam Clarks of the world kissed their cats in vicarious celebration. As for me, I was already asleep, dreaming. I was racing the final leg of a gruelling marathon and had just pulled ahead of the pack. All I had to do was cross the finish line. I saw myself arching toward the tape, my manuscript held above my head in a victory salute.

Just one more step. One more. . . .

I awoke in a cold sweat, turned on my light, and looked at the clock. Five past midnight.

My tenure year had begun.

When Thursday, the day of the dinner party, finally came, it had been more than a week since I'd phoned Charlie at the lab. In all that time he had made no attempt to see me or even talk to me. Perhaps it was true that he was busy. I certainly was. As people trickled back from their holiday vacations my interview schedule filled. Most afternoons I was out running around, while evenings and mornings I spent keying in transcripts. So, even if Charlie had called I might have had trouble squeezing in a date. Or at least that's what I told myself.

Of course there was also the distinct possibility that something between us had gone awry. If there was a problem, I hoped it could be fixed. Indeed, I was counting on a second chance. There was no way I was going back behind the convent walls without a fight.

That morning I cleared the decks and did all the cooking myself. Normally I would have let the gourmet food section of my favorite grocery store handle these delicate preparations, but I doubted I could count on a selection of vegan meals. By nightfall there was nothing left to do except light the candles and select the background music. I decided some Vivaldi would be nice.

Pam was the first to arrive. She entered sporting a new coordinated outfit.

"Do you like it?" she asked. "It was a Christmas treat to myself."

I complimented her choice even though it looked no different from every other suit she owned, right down to the matching scarf.

"Here," she said, and held out a bottle of wine. "I hope red's all right."

"Great, thank you," I said. "Go on in and have a seat by the fire. I'll be right back with some glasses."

While I was uncorking the wine the doorbell rang.

"I'll get it!" Pam called, and in the next moment I heard her exclaim, "Oh! You must be Charlie."

I hurried out just as they were shaking hands.

"Charlie, this is Pam Clark," I said. "She's in the political science department, too."

"Pleasure to meet you." He smiled and gave her a full dose of his beautiful green eyes. Then he turned to me. "Hi."

"Hi!" I swayed forward, hoping he might kiss me, but instead found myself accepting another bottle of wine.

"Oh, good—you brought white," Pam said. "I never know which is better. I brought red."

"Well, to tell you the truth, I never know, either."

I hung up his coat as they drifted toward the couch.

"This is the first time I've seen a fire in Lydia's fireplace," she said. "I always assumed it didn't work."

"Makes you want to break out the marshmallows, doesn't it?" he said.

"Yes! Just like in summer camp," she said, beaming at him. She sank down into a cushion and he took a nearby chair. "When I was a kid I used to go to a Y camp in the upper peninsula of Michigan. I forget all the songs. It's the black fly bites I remember."

Charlie nodded. "I did my time in a camp in West Virginia, where the poison ivy vines grew as thick as your arm."

"Oh, we had acres of the stuff, too. Plus, there were snakes, if you can believe that. Nothing poisonous, but no one ever wanted to go swimming. We were convinced half the sticks floating in the lake had heads."

He laughed. I stood behind the couch, my hand on my hip. I had never known Pam to be especially funny.

"Would you like some wine?" I asked. "You have your choice of white or red."

"White," Pam said, just as Charlie said, "Red." They both burst out laughing.

I left them and returned to the kitchen. By the time I came back with their drinks, they had moved on to the tricks of campfire cooking.

"Remember buried potatoes?" she asked. "You'd wrap them in tinfoil, dig a hole in hot ashes, and cover them up for hours and hours on end."

"Yeah," he said. He glanced up and saw me holding out the glasses. "Oh, thank you." He turned back to Pam as she took her wine, and went on. "And there were always one or two you'd forget and find a couple of days later. They'd be like rocks—totally metamorphosed into solid lumps of carbon."

The doorbell rang again.

I went to answer it, and found Karl on the threshold. "Welcome," I said.

"Happy New Year," he said, and handed me yet another bottle of wine.

"Thank you. Come on in and I'll introduce you," I said. I hung up his coat and then led the way. "Charlie Whittier, I'd like you to meet Karl Willis. Karl, this is my friend Charlie."

"Really?" Karl said. He sounded nothing short of shocked to find me in possession of a male friend. "I don't think I've ever seen you around the campus. Are you on the faculty?"

"No. I'm a med student. Are you in Lydia's department, too?" Charlie asked.

Karl nodded. "That's right."

There was another chime of the doorbell.

"That'll be Margaret and Tom," I said, and went back to open the door. "Come in! Welcome," I said.

"Brrrrr, it's cold out there!" Margaret said. She hurried inside, Tom on her heels. She wore a mid-length dark fur coat. "Hello, Lydia. It's wonderful to see you. May I give you this?" she said, slipping out of the coat with exaggerated care. "It's my Christmas present from Tom. Sable. Isn't it too beautiful for words?"

"I'll hang it right up," I said, and hastened to get the thing in the closet and out of sight before Charlie noticed. "Let me take your coat, too, Tom."

"Thank you," he said, shedding it. Then he walked toward the others, rubbing his hands. "Well, well, well. I recognize two of the guests. Hello, Pam, Karl." He peered over his bifocals. "And who might you be, sir?" he drawled.

"I'm Charlie Whittier," Charlie said, shaking hands.

"Tom Shepherd. Nice to make your acquaintance. And this is my wife, Margaret."

Margaret appeared at his side and smiled. "You're a friend of Lydia's?"

"Yes." His gaze slid over to me and then back to the fire, hands clasped behind his back. Anyone waiting for further elaboration had better not have been holding his breath.

I pulled up another chair and gestured. "Please, everybody— have a seat. Margaret, what may I get you to drink?"

"A glass of white wine, please."

"Fine. Tom, Karl?"

"Red," they both said in near chorus.

Pam and Charlie exchanged an amused look. I felt a rush of irritation. *I* hadn't received so much as a smile from Charlie.

"Well, make yourselves at home, everyone," I said with forced heartiness. "I'll be right back."

By the time I'd served the drinks, my guests were well into a lively discussion and took little notice as I eased into the remaining chair.

Margaret was laughing. "Tom likes to think we're rustics," she said. "He refuses to set the thermostat any higher than it has to be to keep the water pipes from freezing."

"Now, Margaret, you're exaggerating just a bit," he said. "Remember, that big old farmhouse of ours was built in the days when they didn't have any central heating at all."

"How old is it?" Charlie asked.

"The place was built over two hundred years ago," Tom said. "By pioneers."

"He makes it sound so romantic," Margaret said, "but you should hear what he says when his feet hit the cold floor first thing on a winter morning." She took a sip of wine and then glanced at Karl. "You know, I just realized. Where's Emily? Isn't she here?"

"No," Karl answered. "She's in Boston. Visiting her folks."

"Oh. Well, good for her. We certainly enjoyed our visit with the children for the holidays." She paused and turned to Charlie. "Are you faculty, too?"

He'd been staring at the fire and looked up, slightly startled. "No. I'm a medical student. Sort of."

"Charlie finished one year of med school and then took some time off last fall," I explained. "He's reenrolled for the coming semester."

"Really?" Tom said. "I have a squash partner at the medical school. David Fairchild. Know him?"

"Sure," Charlie said. "I work in his lab."

"He's a good man," Tom said.

Pam looked at Charlie. "What sort of work are you doing for him?"

"Doctor Fairchild is studying the effects of a particular drug on damaged heart muscle," he said.

"You ever have trouble finding volunteers for testing?" Karl asked.

"Not exactly." Charlie set his glass on the coffee table. "We're using animal models."

Karl snorted. "Makes them sound like airplane kits. What are they, white rats?"

"No." He folded his hands. "Dogs."

"Dogs!" Pam said. "How sad. Are they from the Albemarle Animal Shelter?"

"No, no. There's a law against that now."

"Where do you get them from, then?" Karl asked.

He shifted slightly. "These are greyhounds, retired racers from Florida. Doctor Fairchild likes them because they're used to being handled and are very docile."

"Oh!" Pam said. She frowned and looked away.

"Sounds like interesting and rewarding work," Tom said. "David's a fine physician. You're lucky to be assisting him."

Charlie didn't answer. He reached for his drink.

"You know, David and I have had a regular Wednesday game for the past ten years," Tom went on, looking around at the rest of us. "Isn't that something? What about you, Karl? Are you still playing tennis?"

Karl shook his head. "Too cold outside now."

"You should join the Fox Tail Inn Sports Club," Margaret said. "They have several indoor courts."

He grimaced. "I'm sure they do. They'd better, for what they charge for a membership."

"Say, what about Strasbourg?" I said. "Have you made any more plans?"

And the conversation took another turn, which was good. I didn't want to talk about the docile greyhounds, and from the look of Charlie, neither did he.

The pumpkin soup was a great success, and I'd just served the main course when Pam asked, "So, Lydia, how are the interviews going?"

Tom arched his brows. "Interviews?"

If Pam had been closer, I would have kicked her. Instead I smiled at Tom. "Research for my current project," I said.

"What sort of project?" Margaret asked.

I glanced at Pam with the same smile fixed on my lips. She gazed back with a cheerful, interested expression.

"I'm doing a case study of a local interest group."

"And what sort of group might that be?" Tom said.

"An animal rights group," I said.

"Really?" Margaret said. "There's an animal rights group in Albemarle? How dreadful."

I shot a look at Charlie. He concentrated on cutting his food.

"Have you uncovered anything interesting?" Tom said.

It was a casual question, but coming as it did from my chairman, I hesitated before answering. I felt the muscles at the back of my neck tighten.

"Well, yes, I have," I said. "Initially I intended to do a straight analysis of how an interest group organizes itself, but lately I've come upon an unexpected twist."

Even Karl started to pay attention. "What's that?" he asked.

"All this week I've been doing interviews with members of the other left-wing groups in town. When I worked on *Bringing in the Green* I found there was a lot of crossover between various liberal causes. For instance, it wasn't at all unusual to find an environmentalist who was also a feminist—someone who'd be out protesting offshore drilling one day and then attending a pro-choice rally the next. I'm sure today that's still the case. But that's not true when it comes to this particular movement. Nobody else seems to want to have anything to do with the animal rights crowd."

"But why?" Pam asked.

"Oh, I hear all sorts of reasons," I said. "The African Americans, Jews, and feminists are insulted by the parallels animal rights people draw between their group experiences and the plight of the animals. They say being compared to monkeys and dogs is degrading and trivializes slavery, antisemitism, and sexism."

"And they're absolutely right," Margaret put in.

"What about the environmentalists?" Karl asked. "What's their beef?, if you'll excuse the expression."

"They're more concerned with the preservation of habitats," I said. "They want to ensure the protection of species, not of every single being within that species. And they aren't just interested in living things; they also advocate the preservation of rivers and rock formations."

"Are those all the relevant groups you could find?" Tom asked.

"No," I said. "I've also been talking to the gay rights people in town. They say they could never oppose the use of animals in medical lab testing because of their importance in AIDS research." I shrugged. "Even the vegetarians I've spoken with are split on whether people should abstain from meat for health or ethical reasons. In any case, they show no inclination to climb on the animal rights bandwagon, either."

"I'd say on the whole this group has mighty few allies," Tom said, and took another bite of dinner.

Margaret chewed and nodded.

I went on. "Meanwhile, the animal rights people feel deserted. They don't see how environmentalists or human rights activists can separate themselves from the issue of animal rights. From their perspective, they're all resisting oppression and should therefore be united."

"And what do you think?" Pam asked. "Are they right?"

I leaned forward, elbows on the table. "Look. The way I see it, the other activists don't have much of a choice. You've heard the arguments people make against animal rights. It always comes down to the same question: Would you put the life of a guinea pig before the life of your child?" I sat back. "The animal rights people are the only activists who can be accused of pegging human welfare consistently in second place. That's not a very popular position. So why should other movements want to be tarred with their brush?"

"Why indeed?" Margaret muttered.

There was a pause. Then Pam turned to Charlie.

"Well, what do *you* think?" She smiled at the rest of us. "Charlie used to belong to the animal rights group in town. That's how Lydia met him."

Beneath my sweater I felt a bead of sweat race down my side.

"Really?" Margaret said, blinking. "You were an animal rights activist?"

Tom frowned. "But I thought you just said you were doing animal research—"

"He did," I interjected. "Charlie is a *former* member. Anyway, getting back to my original point, I've changed my entire approach to focus on this new angle. I can even tell you my book's title: *Orphans of the Left: The Loneliness of Animal Rights Activists.*"

Tom nodded. "Sounds very good, Lydia. Very good."

But Margaret was still staring at Charlie in amazement. "What on earth led you to join?" she asked.

For the first time in the discussion Charlie's eyes left his plate. He levelled a look at her. "Because I believed in the cause."

Tom swallowed a bite and continued to me, "We're really very fortunate to have you in the department, Lydia. It's nice to see a junior professor live up to her potential."

Oh, no, I thought. Here it comes again. The Speech.

"We have high expectations of everyone we hire, of course, but after the terrible disappointment Walter Kravitz turned out to be—"

Charlie's look swivelled to Tom. "Did you say Walter Kravitz? I read his book. It was great." He paused, thinking, and put down his fork. "You know, I was sort of hoping he'd be here tonight."

Karl made a sound like a choking cough and reached for his water glass. "Not much chance of that," he managed to get out.

Charlie frowned. "Why? What did he do?"

Tom sat up straight. "In this instance one would have to say it's what he *failed* to do. He didn't show sufficient evidence of scholarly merit."

Charlie turned to me, his face blank with wonder.

"He came up for tenure this fall and was denied," I said.

"He was denied?" he said. "But that's crazy! His book—"

"Wasn't quite *great* enough," Margaret said. The words positively tripped out. She leaned toward Pam. "Could you pass the rolls, please?"

"Is that right." Charlie folded his arms. "You read the book, did you?"

She laughed and broke her roll in half. "Of course not. His colleagues did, and that was their opinion. In a tenure review one is judged by one's peers. Pam, could you pass me the butter, too, please? Thank you."

"But you read it," he said to Pam. "What did you think?"

"Well, actually—" She fingered the stem of her glass as her eyes skipped from Karl to me. "Actually, I haven't read it. Assistant professors don't count in something like this. We aren't allowed to vote on tenure until we have it ourselves."

Charlie followed her gaze around the table and then shrugged. "Well," he said to Tom, "I guess it's a draw—I liked it and you didn't."

Tom pursed his lips. "Well, that's not exactly so," he said. He cut another bite of food. "I haven't read it, either." For a moment no one spoke.

"*You* haven't read it?" Charlie said.

"You see, that's the way it works in our department," Pam said. "There's a subcommittee for each person up for tenure, and the people in it are the ones who do all the reading."

Charlie stared. "And how many people are in a subcommittee?"

"That depends," she said. "In this case I heard three."

Tom stiffened. "I'm surprised you heard anything at all," he said. "The tenure process is supposed to be conducted strictly in confidence."

Pam looked down at her plate.

But Charlie was not as easily silenced. "You mean three people out of a department of—of—"

"Thirty-five," Karl said.

"—thirty-five decided whether this guy got tenure?" Charlie's voice had gone up a decimal or two. "Don't you think that's a little unfair?"

Tom smoothed his napkin across his lips. "No. I think it's quite fair. And the subcommittee never decides the issue, not officially. It makes a recommendation, which the department may or may not accept. If it does, and the decision is negative, the review process essentially ends there—unless the person under consideration decides to appeal."

"You have to understand," Margaret said. "The political science department is full of very busy productive people—people who don't have time to stop and read a book, at least one that's not in their field." She smiled at him. "You aren't quite far enough along in your studies to understand, but you'll learn. Sometimes you just have to rely on the judgment of others." And she bit into her roll.

Charlie picked up his silverware and bent over his plate. "I don't really think you're in much of a position to lecture me on using good judgment," he said in a low voice.

She stopped chewing. "Excuse me? I'm sorry. I didn't quite catch what you said."

He glared at her. "I said, I don't see killing animals for the sake of personal vanity as a sign of such terrific judgment."

She put down her roll and arched back. "What in the world are you talking about?"

"Your fur coat," Charlie said, flushing. He jabbed a finger into the tablecloth. "Those creatures died just to satisfy your frivolous vanity. How can you walk around wearing such a thing?"

"Now, hold on one minute, young man," Tom roared.

"No, YOU hold on," Charlie said. "What kind of chairman are you, anyway, not reading some guy's book when his whole career depends on it?"

"How dare you criticize me!" Margaret said. "That coat's the only thing I have that keeps me warm."

Charlie made a face. "Yeah, right. Sure. We really have arctic winters down here in Virginia."

"Ha!" Tom said. "As if you weren't just as dependent as the rest of us on animal byproducts." He gave a superior smile. "Take this meal, for instance." He poked through the layered noodles with a fork, prompting everyone else to do the same.

There was a pause.

"What *is* this?" Margaret asked.

I cleared my throat. "Spinach lasagna."

Karl grinned. "Meatless."

Tom put down his fork, as if the serving on his plate had become a conspiracy against him.

"Now, look," I said. "What we have here is simply an honest difference of opinion."

"I'm afraid it's a little bit more than that," Margaret said, rising.

Tom threw down his napkin. "No need to show us the way out," he said.

"No, wait!" I said, getting up. I followed them to the door. "Please. Don't go."

"My coat, please, Tom," Margaret said, as he helped her into it. She paused and, looking over at Charlie, wrapped it around her tight. Then she turned and Tom opened the door. "Goodbye, Lydia."

"Can't we—"

I was cut off by the slam.

I stood there, and then returned to the table. I sank into a chair and put a hand over my eyes.

Charlie leaned toward me. "Lydia, I'm sorry."

Karl clapped. "That was really a piece of work, Charlie. You managed to insult them simultaneously for different reasons. Very impressive."

"Hey, listen! I said I was sorry. But if you'd read this book you'd know—"

I dropped my hand. "I've read it, Charlie. It's good, but I wouldn't nominate it for a Pulitzer Prize, all right?"

He stared at me. "You read it? Then why didn't you say something?"

"Because Pam is right. In this department, it doesn't matter what I think. Besides, this is—was—a dinner party, not a committee meeting."

He fiddled with the fringe of the tablecloth. "I'm sorry," he said again.

"Forget it," I said. "They wouldn't have liked dessert anyway. It's meatless, too." I got up and started collecting plates. "Who's up for a piece of apple pie?"

"Me," Pam said.

"Me, too," Karl echoed.

"Uh, none for me, thanks," Charlie said. He pushed back his chair. "I think I'd better go."

I stopped and stood there, gripping the dirty dishes.

"Oh, don't leave, Charlie," Pam said. "Have some pie."

He kept his head down. "I think I'd better." Then he flashed me a glance. "I'll call you, okay?"

I nodded. "Sure."

"Okay. Bye, everyone." He gave a small wave, found his coat, and went out the door.

"Here, let me help," Pam said quietly.

"No, no—please, just sit," I said, and hurried toward the kitchen. "I'll be right back with the pie."

I hoped I'd turned fast enough. With my hands full, I had no chance to wipe away the tears before they fell.

Two weeks later I made my way down the hall toward Pam's office, dodging students as I went. They were back in force, a hurrying, harried herd, each with the new semester's course schedules in hand. Classes had only just begun, and so had the students' quest for ones they could get into. Preregistration existed but didn't really count for much, given that most undergraduates were bumped out of their selections because of rampant overenrollment.

Looking at the harassed expressions all around, I knew exactly what to expect the next day in my first class. From the students there would be handwringing and gnashing of teeth. But the list of who had priority was always the same: graduating seniors first, majors second, simply interested parties last. The cutoff usually hit somewhere within the majors, and the rest had to scramble to get those precious credits somewhere else. There were always complaints and sometimes even tears. But the cutoff remained final.

I crossed against the flow to reach Pam's door and knocked. "Come in!" she yelled.

I opened the door and poked my head inside. "Busy?"

"Lydia—what a nice surprise." She was at her desk, holding the phone receiver against her chest. "I thought you were another student. Have a seat. I'll be off in one second."

I closed the door and sat down.

"I'm sorry, Carol, but I'm already ten students over the limit. Yes, I know. Really, I understand—"

I didn't often visit Pam in her office, and I gave a quick look around. On the wall behind me was a poster of a castle on a hillside with GERMANY printed underneath. On the facing wall hung a framed black and white photograph of a sky streaked with wisps of cirrus clouds. Along the bottom border in flowing script it read: Hope is possibility with wings.

No doubt Pam meant it to be an inspiration to the students. Personally I preferred the ruins of the Hapsburgs to such saccharine sentiments, but then that was me.

As for Pam's desk, it was cluttered with papers and books and small framed photographs of her family, including several of her cat.

"Listen, why don't you come in and we'll talk about it, all right?" Pam said into the phone. "This afternoon is fine. See you then." And she hung up with a sigh.

"Another supplicant?" I asked.

"One of many, I'm afraid," she said. "I don't know what to do. I can't let *all* of them in."

"Hold a lottery," I said. "That's what I do."

"What a great suggestion! Thanks." She smiled. "So tell me, what's up with you?"

"Not much. Been getting lots of work done, that's all."

"Great." She paused. "Heard anything from Charlie?"

I shook my head. "No. Not a word." I forced a laugh. "That dinner party must have set some kind of record for desertions. You know, I haven't spoken with Tom yet, either, since that night. I called Margaret to apologize the next day, and she seemed all right. But you never know."

"Oh, I'm sure Tom's forgotten all about it," she said.

"I hope so." I roused from my thoughts and sat back. "When's your first class?"

"Tomorrow morning," she said. "And you?"

"Same. Did you manage to get a head start on your lectures?"

"Well. . . ." She moved a picture closer to another. "Not exactly."

I frowned. "Pam, that's why you came back early from vacation, remember?"

"I know, I know. It's just that Tom asked me to take care of a few things."

"Like what?"

She moved another picture. "Oh, *things*. Like writing up a new schedule for the graduate students to cover the computer lab. And reorganizing the department library—you wouldn't believe the mess it's in. Oh, and the speakers program, too. Someone had to start getting together a list of names."

I stared at her. "Tom asked you to do all that?"

"Well, yes. We talked about it that night at your house. I guess you must have been in the kitchen."

"I guess so." I sat forward and grabbed her hand as it reached to rearrange another picture. "Pam, listen to me. You're committing professional suicide, do you understand that?" I said, giving her a little shake. "Your own work must come first. You don't have much time! You're up for renewal in two years."

"I know, I know. It's just that Tom's asked me to do these things, and it's hard to say no to the chairman."

I released her hand. "No, it's not. Remember, by the time you come up for tenure someone else will be chair of the department, and whoever it is isn't going to care about all the brownie points you scored with Tom."

She looked down at her desk. "I don't do it for points," she said. "I do it for the students."

"Oh, come on!" I said. "That's an even *worse* reason. Look, I'm telling you—you've got to start watching out for yourself. If you don't, no one else will, I can promise you that."

"But the students—"

"You've got to put them to one side, too. Now, I'm not saying you have to turn your back on them, but you've got to set limits. You can only extend yourself so much. You don't have time to be listening to all their problems."

"Some of these kids, though, they need someone to talk to."

"Then tell them to go to Student Health," I said. "The school has professional psychologists who are paid to listen to them. God knows we aren't."

She took a deep breath and sank back against her chair. "I don't know, Lydia," she said, shaking her head. "I just don't know if I can be that tough."

"Look, do you want to get tenure or don't you?" I asked.

"Yes. I guess so."

"You *guess* so?"

"I've been thinking," she said. "Maybe I don't belong here. Maybe I should be teaching in a college. I don't know if I'm cut out for a research university."

I was stunned. For a moment I didn't know what to say.

"You'd actually quit your job here to go teach in a college?" I asked.

"I've thought about it, yes," she said.

"Whoa. Give yourself some time. You've only been at Patrick Henry one semester."

"I know. Don't worry, I haven't done anything yet. I've just been thinking about it, that's all."

"Well, let me give you some very good advice. Don't tell anyone else, especially any of the guys. Those hyenas would have a feast, and you'd be dinner."

She laughed. "The guys aren't that bad."

"When it comes to culling the herd, yes, they are."

There was a knock at the door.

"Who is it?" Pam called.

A young man with a knapsack slung over his shoulder peered in. "Professor Clark? Can I talk to you?"

"Sure. Can you just wait outside? I'll be through in a minute."

The door closed and she looked back at me with a small smile.

"Thanks, Lydia," she said.

"For what? I haven't done anything."

"For what you're *trying* to do." She tilted her head. "Are you really all right? About Charlie, I mean."

"Sure," I said, and got up. "It's not like we were ever really dating or anything. In fact, I think the description 'one night stand' might even glorify the relationship."

She winced. "I'm sorry."

The phone rang.

"Remember what I told you," I said. "*Set limits.*"

"I'll remember," she said, and reached for the phone. "Hello?" She smiled and waved as I opened the door to leave. Out in the hall a line had formed, the kid with the knapsack staking out first place.

"She'll be just a minute," I told him.

Down the corridor, near the department office, I caught sight of Danny, Felix, Karl, and Victor. Danny motioned me over with a big excited gesture.

"What's going on?" I asked.

"Don't you know?" he asked. A shock of black hair had fallen across his brow. "Can't you tell?"

I looked at the others. "What?"

Victor blinked at me. "Danny thinks the vote on his renewal is today."

"I don't think—I know!" he said, and pulled on my sleeve. "Haven't you noticed? All the fulls are here. I've been watching them come in all morning."

From his office Danny had a view of the whale parking lot, too.

"Dressed up like prom dates," he went on. "Every living one of them. What else could it be?"

Felix gave a half-smile. "It's like Kremlin-watching during the Cold War."

"Yeah," Karl said. "I can't wait to see who gets airbrushed out of the picture." He nudged Danny. "Maybe it'll be you."

Danny reared back. "Hey! That's not funny."

"Oh, come on, Danny," Karl said. "You know you're going to get renewed. I'm just kidding."

He reached up to his ear. "What do you think? Should I take my earring out?"

Felix crossed his arms and turned to me. "He wears that thing for two years and he thinks maybe *today* it'll tick someone off?"

He undid the back and palmed the thin gold-wire ring. "There," he said. "Mr. Respectable."

Just then the office door opened and Quincy Burnbeck stepped out, a sheaf of mail in his hand. He looked up at the group of us and nodded.

We nodded back and didn't say anything until he had walked well past.

"Well, at least Quincy's gotten a load of the new you," I said. "I'm sure you made quite an impression."

"It's all subliminal," Danny said. "You wait and see."

Felix laughed. "Look—let me give Gwen a call. If today's the day, we ought to have a party."

"You're not talking about having it tonight, are you?" Victor said. "I need a little more notice to land a babysitter."

"Okay," Felix said. "Let's make it this Friday, then." He pointed a finger at Danny. "And if you're wrong, and they're not meeting on you today, then we're all coming over to *your* house."

"It's a deal," Danny said.

"Good. Now I need to run," Karl said. "I've got a class in five minutes."

"Me, too," Victor said. "Good luck, Danny."

And the group broke up, wishing the latest minnow-in-the-docket well.

I continued on into the main office. A knot of students pressed against the counter in front of Roberta's desk, all trying to talk to her at once. I heard her repeating, "You'll have to go to the class tomorrow and ask the professor. Ask the professor. Yes, I understand that you need the class to graduate, but you're going to have to *ask the professor*."

I slunk to the mail slots and grabbed the small pile of memos and letters that sat in my cubbyhole. Then I slipped out the door before Roberta could sic any of those desperados on *me*.

I skimmed through the mail as I headed back to my office. There was the usual plethora of ragged notepaper with scrawled pleas for admittance into one class or the other—a warmup for the coming operatic lamentations of the morrow. Mixed in among them was a note from Amy, reminding me of the HFA meeting the next night. Then I stopped and held up a memo from Bill Tanner. As the head of the Financial Aid Committee he was calling a meeting, to be held at the end of the week, on Friday. At last! My best shot at winning over Moby Dick had arrived. It wasn't going to be easy, I thought, given how he felt about me working with Meredith Kospach.

"Hi, Professor Martin."

I glanced up to find Tony Donatello in front of my door.

"Hi, Tony," I said, my thoughts scrambling. "It's nice to see you. Did you have a good break?"

"Yes, I did," he said. "I just got back today. I—uh—got your note." He held up a folded piece of paper. "You wanted to see me?"

There it was—the note, written weeks ago. At the time, it seemed I had figured out exactly how to break the news to Tony. But now all I could remember was the last part, beginning with, I'm so very sorry. . . .

"That's right. Come on in," I said, and motioned him toward the chair as I sat behind my desk. "So." I paused, leaned forward, and folded my hands. "Were you home for the holidays?"

"Yes, I was in New York, with my mom and dad. I didn't think I'd get up there—I didn't want to, really, when I thought I was going to drop out of school. But then when you called me up out of the blue like that and said you'd be my first reader. . . . It ended up being a really good Christmas after all."

"That's nice." Involuntarily I reached up and straightened the collar of my blouse.

There was another pause.

"Were you with your family?" he asked.

"No, I couldn't make it home this year," I said.

"Oh. Well, I hope you had a good time, anyway."

"I did. Thank you."

More silence. Tony's leg started to jiggle.

"Um, did you have a chance to look at my prospectus?" he asked.

"Yes," I said. "I have it right here."

"Any changes you want, it'll be no problem," he said. "Really."

"Look, Tony—" I blurted, "there's something I must tell you. I—I can't—I mean, I don't think—"

The leg stopped. I caught the glimpse of a shimmer at the edge of Tony's dark eyes.

He said nothing. He sat very still, waiting.

I rushed on. "I just don't think that I'm qualified to handle this polling data with you. You need someone else, someone who knows this stuff inside and out. That's why I *really* do think you should work with—"

My lips got ready to say the name, the name that would put an end to my relationship with Tony once and for all: the name. . . .

"Ruby Collins."

Tony blinked. "Ruby Collins?"

"Yes." I blinked back at him. What was I saying? "She and I were roommates in graduate school. She's on the faculty at Georgetown University now. She has her own polling center and does a lot of work on voting behavior. If she's willing, she'd be a great person to have as the outside reader on your dissertation. Then you could go up there and use her data banks to run your survey."

His whole face seem to light up. "That would be fantastic! Do you think she'll do it?"

"I don't know," I said. "We haven't spoken for a while. Let me call her and give it a shot."

"Professor Martin, thank you! Thank you!" He laughed. "For a minute there, I thought. . . . I was *afraid* you were going to say you changed your mind."

"Well, you have to admit, Tony, I'm not exactly the best person to direct this dissertation."

"Yes, you are, Professor Martin." He beamed at me. "Yes, you are."

Dumb, I thought as I drove home that evening. Dumb, dumb, dumb, dumb, dumb. Why didn't I just tell him? Why? All I had to do was say two little words: Bill Tanner.

Not Ruby Collins.

Oh, when I'd called her after Tony left she'd been delighted to hear from me. All those nights we'd sat up late in our graduate student apartment, quizzing each other for exams and gossiping about our professors—she hadn't forgotten.

Of course I'll be the outside reader, she said. Of course he'd be welcome to come up and use our data banks.

But don't you have a polling center of your own? she'd asked. And don't you have Bill Tanner? Isn't nonvoting one of his specialties?

Tanner's too busy, I'd said. You know how it is.

Of course she bought the excuse. She knew all about busy whales, her department having plenty of its own.

When I got home there were several messages on my machine. They were all from students, save the last. That one was from Danny.

"Lydia? I got it! I've been renewed! Isn't that great?"

I nodded.

"See, I *knew* my number was up. Man, what a relief. Anyway, it's over, at least until tenure time. Some consolation, huh? But I'm not going to start worrying about that *now*." He laughed. "Hey, I just wanted you to know the good news. See you Friday night, if not before, okay?" And he clicked off.

Danny, old pal, I thought, it's no good denying it. You *are* worrying about tenure already. And you might as well get used to it, because it's only going to get worse.

I opened the refrigerator and surveyed my dinner prospects. Looked like a good night for popcorn.

That night I forced myself off the sofa and into bed to sleep, but didn't have much luck. I kept thinking how, with school back in session, I wasn't going to have much time for my book. Sure, I'd worked hard over the break, but I still had a long long way to go. I debated whether I should contact publishers at this early stage of the game to see if I could wrangle a contract out of someone, and then decided it wouldn't do me any good. No one was going to sign on to publish an unfinished manuscript from an assistant professor. I'd have to finish the thing first and hope for the best.

I rolled over. The barley necklace from Hathor still hung from my bedpost, and in the darkness I reached out and fingered its beads. Amy's note said the HFA meeting was going to be held at Hathor's house, not Kathy's. I hadn't seen Kathy since that day in the health food store. I wondered how she was getting along without Charlie.

I rolled over the other way, and then threw off my covers. If I was awake, I might as well do something useful, like draft some new lectures.

The thought was enough to make me grope for the blankets and crawl back beneath them. Maybe just lying there wasn't so bad.

In a few more minutes I was asleep.

At school the next morning I downed two cups of coffee to clear my head. I was meeting my classes for the first time that day— political parties at eleven o'clock and the organizational theory course in the afternoon—and it was important to be on my toes. After calling the roll I didn't intend to stand around talking about the course requirements and then let the students out early, as some professors did. No. I meant to deliver a full-fledged lecture in each course. There was too much ground to cover to waste such time.

At five minutes to eleven I was hurrying out the door when I ran into Meredith Kospach.

"Meredith!" I said, and got another grip on my notes. "Good to see you."

"Hello, Professor Martin." Her voice was subdued, hardly audible over the babble of passing students. She looked different. Her face had lost its rosy roundness, and behind the large glasses her eyes were huge. She planted herself in front of me. "Can I talk to you?"

"Sure—but not right now, okay?" I said. "I've got a class. Can you come by later?"

"I just wanted to ask you something."

"All right. Quickly, then."

The words came out in a rush. "When I retake my oral exam, can you let me do it without Professor Tanner?"

"Um, I don't think so, Meredith." I glanced around. "If he wants to be present, he will be. That's his prerogative."

"But couldn't we schedule it for when we know he's going to be away? He travels so much. Couldn't we do that?"

I was about to shake my head and then didn't. She was blinking hard, just as she had that day of the exam, right before she started to cry.

"Look," I said. "I'll see what I can do, all right? Now I really have to run. I'm late already."

She stepped back. "Okay. Sorry."

"You can call me later—" And I hurried off.

At the end of class I performed the usual ritual of signing Add/Drop forms for a long line of students. As I scribbled away, my thoughts wandered to Meredith. Clearly the break had done her spirits little good, and the sooner she retook that oral exam the better. I remembered telling Pam after the debacle that I'd ask Tom Shepherd to be present the next time. It was still a good idea—and definitely easier than trying to cut Tanner out.

On my way back from class I stopped by the main office. The gaggle of students in front of Roberta's desk hadn't gotten any smaller. I peered over the top and asked, "Any chance I could see Professor Shepherd?"

Before she could answer, Shepherd's door swung open.

"Lydia?" he said. "Come right in. I've been meaning to have a word with you, too."

"Oh?" I swallowed. "You know, I'm really sorry about the other night," I said, following him inside. "I hope Margaret told you I called."

"She did. We've forgotten all about it." He gave me a fatherly smile as he sat behind his broad desk. "Please, have a seat."

I sat down on the edge of the chair and clasped my hands.

He took off his glasses and laid them on the desktop. "Now. What did you need to see me about?"

"I just wanted to ask if it would be possible for you to sit in on an oral exam. One of my graduate students needs to retake hers and I'd like very much for you to be there."

"Oh? Who's the student?"

"Meredith Kospach. If there's some day next week that suits you, that would be fine."

"Meredith has to retake her oral exam? That's a surprise."

"Yes, well, I'm afraid last time she ran into a little trouble with one of the examiners. I thought it might be good to have you there for her second try."

"Who were her examiners?"

"Victor Garshin, Pam Clark, Bill Tanner, and myself."

"And she had the difficulty with . . . ?"

"Bill," I said.

"Really?" He sat back and gave me an appraising look. "Well. I'm afraid I don't see why you need me. Professor Tanner is certainly qualified to assess a student's competence in the field of American government."

I undid my hands and grasped the arms of the chair. "To tell you the truth, Tom, I think there's something going on—with Bill, I mean. I'm not sure he's dealing with Meredith entirely in good faith."

This time Tom rocked forward and the eyebrows shot down into a frown. "Oh?"

I nodded.

"That's a very serious charge, Lydia. What makes you say such a thing?"

"I-I just have this feeling," I said. "When Bill first found out that Meredith had asked me to direct her dissertation, he seemed upset. I think he might be hurt that she chose me over him."

"Hurt?" His lips curved slightly. "Is that what you think? That he's jealous?"

"Not *that* exactly, but—"

"Really, I doubt very much that Professor Tanner feels one way or another about you being the first reader. Whatever reservations he may have about Meredith are entirely justified, I'm sure, and I'm not going to do anything that suggests I think otherwise."

My cheeks burned with a hot flush. "Then you won't sit in?"

He shook his head. "No."

"All right." I reached down for my purse.

"If you could stay just a moment, Lydia, I also have something I need to discuss."

"Yes, of course," I said, straightening.

He toyed with his glasses. "I had a chat with David Fairchild after our game the other day." He glanced at me, wearing a ghost of a smile. "He's a little worried about this new book of yours, Lydia. To be honest, when you spoke of it the other night I never considered the possible consequences."

I stared at him. "What consequences?"

"To the medical school. Your study could well draw undue attention to the research being done here, inadvertently casting Patrick Henry University in an unfavorable light."

"But I don't mention the medical school's research at all," I said. "I know very little about it, in fact."

"Yes, but the people you're interviewing from this animal rights group will inevitably bring it up. David told me they staged a protest recently at the hospital—apparently it even made the local evening news. The last thing he needs is for those fanatics to gain *more* publicity at his expense."

"But I'm not concerned with Doctor Fairchild's work. My book is about interest groups, not animal experimentation."

He shook his head. "Whether you realize it or not, you're playing with fire. It would be much much better if you chose some other group for your case study."

I took a deep breath. "Tom, you aren't telling me I *have* to abandon my project, are you?"

"No, certainly not. But I *am* suggesting it." The smile was gone. "Strongly."

I looked away, trying to get a grip on my thoughts. "But I just don't see how I could possibly begin again. I've already put in so much work. . . . " My voice trailed off.

He sat back. "I have a lot of confidence in you, Lydia. I'm sure you could easily turn your hand to another topic." He picked up a paper from his desk. "Now, if you'll excuse me, I have a meeting with the dean."

I rose and almost stumbled in my confusion. At the door I turned.

"Bye—" I said.

He nodded without looking up.

There was no mistaking the message. I was dismissed.

I went through the motions of teaching my next class, and stood afterwards at the lectern mechanically signing the Add/Drop forms. Then I started back for my office.

Can a chairman *do* that? I asked myself. Can a chairman tell me what I should and should not research?

No, came the resounding response. I have the right to pursue whatever course of study I choose. That's what academic freedom is all about.

Of course . . . no one's obliged to grant me tenure for it.

The beginnings of a headache pulsed in my temples.

I can't start over, I thought. I don't have the extra time or ideas. But if my chairman is against me, what are my chances of getting through?

I pictured Tom and David Fairchild discussing me after a hard game of squash. Was this how academic careers were made and unmade, over drinks of Perrier at a sports club?

The headache was gaining on me. I decided I needed to talk to someone. Who in the department could I ask for help? It would have to be someone capable of offering genuine protection—a full, like Shepherd.

I thought of Quincy Burnbeck. He'd always been cordial to me. I'd never had anything remotely resembling a personal conversation with him, but that didn't mean I couldn't try.

At his office door I stopped, took a deep breath, and knocked. No answer. I knocked again.

The door of the office next to his opened and Felix's head appeared.

"Oh," he said. "I thought it was my door. Sorry."

Before he could disappear back inside I stopped him. "Do you have a second?" I asked.

"Sure." He waited for me to enter and then closed the door. "It's hard to catch Quincy in his office. He works mostly at home."

"I didn't know," I said.

"Go ahead and have a seat." He sat down at his desk and tugged at the cuffs of his immaculately white shirt. "What's up?"

I thought for a moment. How much did I really want to tell Felix? As little as possible, I decided.

"I'm just curious," I said. "What do you think of Quincy?"

He laughed. "What do you mean, what do I think of him? He's the senior guy in my area. I love him. Next question."

"No, no, I mean, what do you think he'd do if one of us— one of the assistants—had a problem with another senior person in the department? Would he listen?"

Felix gave me a steady look. I expected him to ask for details, but he didn't.

"Let me tell you a story," he said instead. "It was my first year teaching here, and Quincy had a graduate student who was about to get his Ph.D. Quincy was really excited about this kid, and thought the dissertation was the best scholarship he'd ever seen from a student. So Quincy asked me to sit in on the dissertation defense. He also asked one of his good friends from the law school, another professor of constitutional law. He included him as a favor, because he thought the whole performance was going to be something really wonderful."

He paused. "So the day of the defense came, and we gathered in the Green Room of the Great Hall—you know, the most historic and beautiful setting in Mr. Henry's university. And the kid is glowing. You could just see that he was *ready*, and even eager, to begin the defense. But before Quincy could open the meeting, his law school friend asked for a moment to speak with the other professors, alone. So the student leaves the room and the buddy tells Quincy that he disagrees fundamentally with the main premise of the dissertation's argument."

"You've got to be kidding!" I said. "And he waited until the last minute to say something?"

"Yes. Quincy had sent a draft copy over to him only that morning," Felix said calmly. "Remember, this guy was just supposed to be a visitor paying a courtesy call. He wasn't on the examining committee."

"So what happened?"

"Quincy called the student back in and told him there wasn't going to be a defense."

"*What?*"

He nodded. "He said he had to rewrite the dissertation. From beginning to end."

"But it was *his* student!"

"The kid was absolutely devastated. For weeks he went around showing anyone who'd look the comments Quincy had written on his draft, saying what a brilliant piece of work it was. At one point he even threatened to sue. The last I heard, he'd left the program altogether."

I sat there, unable to say a word.

"Right afterward I asked Quincy why he'd done that. Do you know what he told me?"

I shook my head.

"He said, Collegiality comes first. Now." He sat back. "Have I answered your question?"

I stayed and worked in my office until early evening, when I had to leave for the meeting at Hathor's. By the time I gathered my things to go, night had long since fallen. Looking out the window I could see that not many of the whales' cars remained. It was the dinner hour, after all. For myself, I didn't mind missing it. My appetite was gone.

Out in the hallway I paused to lock my office door. I turned to leave and then stopped. From far down the darkened corridor there came footsteps. They were neither fast nor slow, not loud or soft, just footsteps coming steadily closer and closer.

I couldn't move. I stood there, waiting, rooted to the spot. A figure took shape through the gloom. I caught sight of a bowed head, then slumped shoulders beneath a long winter coat. It was a man. He carried only a briefcase, but he appeared to labor under a far greater and heavier burden.

He walked by me and nodded without looking up.

"Good night, Lydia," he said.

"Good night, Walter," I said, and watched until he disappeared into the shadows once again.

N o full moon spilled light into the sky that evening as I stepped up to Hathor's house. I had brought neither barley nor wine, and when Hathor opened the door there were no flat drums or sistrums to be heard, just the ordinary sounds of people chatting in the living room. Hathor was dressed like every-one else, in jeans and a sweater, and her thick hair fell loose in a tumble down to her waist.

Before letting me in, her glance raked me from head to toe. Her nostrils dilated slightly. But I had taken all precautions in my dress and diet that day. There was not a shred or whiff of animal on me.

"You may enter," she said, and stepped aside.

"Professor Martin!" Amy said beneath the lamplight. Over the vacation she'd added a small nose ring to her accessories. "I was hoping you'd come."

"Hi, Amy," I said, and took a seat beside her on the couch. "How was your vacation?"

"Pretty good," she said.

I looked around. "Wow," I said. "There's quite a crowd here tonight."

"Yeah, we always get a big turnout at the beginning of the semester," she said. "Isn't it neat?"

In the far corner I spotted Kathy sitting crosslegged on the floor, talking to a young man. Her hair was pulled back into a ponytail, and as she spoke she brushed her bangs out of her eyes. I thought she looked much younger without her television makeup. It was a moment before she saw me, and then she gave me only the briefest nod. Her face colored with a dark flush.

She knows, I thought. She knows about me and Charlie.

Hathor lit another cone of incense and placed it on the table. Its musky scent did well enough to mask the pungent undertones of Mother in the air. Then she sat on the floor in the center of the living room.

"Okay," she said loudly. "Let's start. Kathy?"

Kathy shifted her position and everyone turned to her.

"First, I want to welcome all our newcomers and say how happy we are to have you here with us tonight. Humanity For Animals depends on the participation of people like you, people dedicated to carrying out the principles of justice for every living being. For those of you who come for the first time, I hope that this gathering will be the beginning of a lifelong association."

Everyone looked around, smiling. There were about a dozen students in all.

"Also," she went on, "I just want to let you know that we have with us tonight Professor Martin. She teaches in the political science department at the university and is here as an observer. She's writing a study of our group, and we hope that her research will draw much needed attention to our cause."

For a moment they all turned their smiles to me, except Hathor and Kathy. Kathy had looked away, while Hathor gazed at me with sharp unblinking eyes.

Hathor still doesn't trust me, I thought. She suspects I'm going to do exactly what I intend to do, which is blow Mother's cover. But why did she show me that blasted cow in the first place?

Mentally I gave myself a shake. Kathy had moved on to describe some of HFA's ongoing projects: volunteering in the animal shelter, distributing animal rights leaflets at health food stores, writing informational articles for the student newspaper.

"We need all the help we can get," she said.

I sat back and listened as people signed on for one thing or another. A few even offered some suggestions of their own. Amy and Kathy were enthusiastic but Hathor said nothing, appearing thoroughly unimpressed. It was understandable. No matter what they said, odds were that less than half of the new recruits would be back for the next meeting.

That made no difference to me, of course. I wanted to interview them simply for showing up even once. Amy passed around a clipboard to write down names and phone numbers. I would have to wait until after the meeting to copy the list.

Hathor said to Kathy, "Tell them about the debate."

"Amy's been ironing out the details. Amy?"

"Okay, here's the deal," Amy said to the group. "Next Thursday night we've got this speaker coming down from D.C., from the national headquarters of Humanity For Animals. He's going to be part of a debate that we're sponsoring. And I just got the call early yesterday from the Speaker's Committee giving us permission to hold it at the medical school."

"Which is fantastic," Kathy said. "We're hoping to spotlight the animal experimentation they do there."

"Who's the HFA guy going to debate?" someone asked.

Amy grinned. "That's the *really* good part. David Fairchild."

"What?" I said, turning to look at her. "Fairchild's going to be part of the debate?"

"Yeah," Amy said. "Isn't that terrific?"

"Who's Fairchild?" another student asked.

"One of the better known vivisectionists at Patrick Henry University Hospital," Kathy said. "We demonstrated against him and his research last fall."

"Amy marked him," Hathor said, satisfaction in her voice. "She gave him a taste of his own medicine."

"I sure did," Amy said. "You know, I still have ten hours of community service to work off from that."

"Sounds like you already *did* the community a service," someone responded.

"We need help distributing the posters," Kathy said. She asked Hathor, "Have you got them ready?"

"Yes, they're right here," she said, and lifted a thick stack of cut posterboard.

"I'll take some," the woman sitting nearest to her said.

"Me, too."

Then everyone stretched out a hand.

As Hathor distributed the pile Amy leaned over to me and said, "Can I talk to you for a second after the meeting? I've got a favor I need to ask you."

"Sure," I said.

"Okay," Kathy said. "That about covers it for tonight. Next meeting is on February twentieth. Amy, Hathor, or I will call you to tell you where. And don't forget next Thursday night, eight o'clock, at the medical school. The debate's going to be a good one, so don't miss it. Thanks for coming."

The room filled with a loud murmur as the meeting broke up.

"Can I copy that list of names?" I asked Amy.

"Sure!" she said, and handed over the clipboard. "Why don't you take it home with you? You can give it back to me Thursday night."

"Thanks." I tucked it in my satchel. "Now. What's this favor you mentioned?"

"Oh, yeah." She slipped off her shoes, crossed her legs beneath her, and settled into the cushions. "It's about Tyler."

"Tyler the dog?" I frowned. "Is something wrong with him? I mean aside from his overstimulated salivary glands."

"No, he's fine. It's really about my parents, I guess. You know, I took him home with me over the break."

"I remember you said that was the plan," I said.

"Yeah, well, they didn't exactly hit it off with him."

I smiled. "What? They didn't appreciate having their ears cleaned free of charge?"

She squirmed. "No. It wasn't that." She returned a wave from Kathy, who was on her way out the door. I tried to wave, too, but she was already gone.

I turned back to Amy. "Well, what was it then? Did he eat someone's favorite slipper?"

"No!" She made a face. "My parents have these stupid oriental rugs. The way they go on and on about them, you'd think they should be hanging in a museum instead of lying on their floor."

"Uh huh," I said.

"All he did was walk on them! What's he going to do, walk *around* them? He's a dog!"

I folded my arms. "Amy, why are you telling me this? You don't expect me to have any special tips on training dogs to tiptoe around rugs, do you?"

"No." She gazed at me through her spiked blonde bangs. "It's just that I've been accepted into that monk's school—you know, the one I told you about in Italy."

I nodded.

"And my parents—well, they're sort of excited about it, too. They think it could be a really good experience."

I nodded. Whatever hesitation may have existed before, the nose ring had surely obliterated.

"It's just that, well, they say they won't take Tyler. So I was wondering—"

I stopped nodding and started shaking my head. "No."

"Oh, please, Professor Martin! Otherwise I'll have to give him away."

"Sounds like a good idea," I said.

"But I *can't* do that. Please! It would only be for a few months."

"NO," I said. "I'm sorry, but it's out of the question."

"You *know* how much Tyler likes you."

"Sure he does." I stood up and gave her a stern look. "If I were you I'd try working on my parents some more. You'll have better luck with them than you will with me."

"Just think about it, okay? Promise?"

"Amy—"

"Look, we can talk about it again later. I'm not leaving until after the semester's over, and that's months and months away."

"Then you'll have lots of time to find someone else," I said, and put on my coat. "I'll see you at the debate."

"Okay," she said. So far nothing I'd said had dimmed the eager light in her eyes. "I'll save you a seat next to me up front."

"I'm not accepting bribes," I warned her.

Her smile was angelic. "I *want* to save you a seat. As a friend."

"Uh huh, right. See you Thursday, then—" I turned for the door and found Hathor there, watching me. Her face was impassive. "Bye, Hathor."

"Until Thursday," she said.

And I crossed the threshold into the cold.

Two days passed, and it was Friday. The first meeting of the Financial Aid Committee was set for three o'clock that afternoon. Since I had no other obligations—no classes to meet or office hours to hold—I chose to work at home. It wasn't for the luxury of drinking my own coffee, nor was it to avoid students banging on my door, though these were definite advantages. I stayed away from Russell because I wanted to stay away from Tom Shepherd. I had decided that, come what may, I was going to finish my project. I hadn't abandoned the Roll Over Rule; I'd just run out of room.

I timed my arrival on the third floor for ten to three, and caught up with Danny as he came out of his office. He was part of the committee, too.

"Congratulations on your renewal," I said. "Thanks for leaving me that message."

"It was a huge relief," he said. We started walking for Tanner's office. "You're coming tonight, aren't you? To the party at Felix's?"

"Of course!" I said. "I wouldn't miss your celebration. Hey, where's the earring? Don't tell me you lost it."

"Nah. I just thought I'd give it a rest for a while. You know."

Sure, I thought. I know. You got scared, and it was only over your renewal. Gave you a taste of what's in store at tenure time, so now you've decided maybe an earring isn't such a smart idea after all. I know all about it.

Tanner's door was open. He was there at his desk, talking on the phone. He motioned us inside, and we stepped in, closing the door behind us.

"Okay, we're all set for the fifteenth, then," he said into the receiver. "You'll send me those tickets. Okay. See you in Helsinki." He hung up, glanced at his watch, and then sat forward. The ice-blue eyes skipped from Danny to me. "Lydia, Danny, how are you?"

"Fine," we said in chorus.

"Good," he said briskly, and rubbed his hands together. "We're going to have to hurry this meeting along. I must leave in a few minutes."

Danny and I looked at each other.

Tanner motioned to three stacks of manilla folders on his desk.

"I assume you've had a chance to look through all the graduate student files."

"Yes," we said, nodding.

"Good. Well, here's how I've divided them. The ones in this file definitely get money from the department, this group does not, and these students in the middle stack are the borderline cases."

Danny and I looked at each other again and then at Tanner.

His return gaze was ever so light and cold. "This is just to save us all some time. As the department's graduate student advisor I'm obviously the best qualified to judge which of our graduate students are the most deserving, and which have failed to make good progress. Please, take a look for yourselves. I'm sure you'll agree."

Danny reached for the first pile, the group guaranteed money, and I picked up the middle stack, the borderline crowd.

"These look great," Danny said, thumbing through the names on the folder tabs.

I, on the other hand, looked at the name on the top folder of my stack and froze.

"Meredith Kospach," I read aloud.

"Yes," Tanner said.

I looked up at him. "But she has one of the best records of any graduate student in the department. How can there be any question of giving her money for next year?"

"Making good progress is every bit as important as getting high marks," Tanner said. "And after that dismal performance in her oral exam. . . . Well, who knows when she'll be able to get to work on her dissertation?"

"But I'm rescheduling another exam, probably for next week," I said. "Then she can start right away."

He picked up a pencil. Its tip was needle sharp. "I'm afraid you're far more sanguine about Ms. Kospach's prospects than I am. In fact, I would advise against rescheduling her exam so quickly. I imagine Ms. Kospach needs a great deal more time to prepare. Perhaps by spring she'll be ready for another go."

"Spring! She doesn't need that much time!"

A small smile curved the corners of his mouth. "I say she does."

It took a moment for me to realize that what I had just heard was not a suggestion.

"Bill, please," I said, trying to keep my tone friendly. "Can't we work something out? If we make her wait until the spring it'll put her back a whole semester."

"Some things just can't be helped," he said. "Look. We'll see how she does once she retakes the exam, and then we'll decide whether the department will support her next year. Fair enough?"

It wasn't fair at all, but there was nothing I could do about it. Meredith was going to be left hanging out to dry for three or four months whether I liked it or not. For an answer I said nothing. I put the folders back on the desk.

Meanwhile, Danny was going through the third pile, the group that would get no financial aid from the department at all.

"These look okay, too," he said with a nervous quiver, and moved to return them to their place.

"May I see?" I asked, taking them. My heart began to pound very hard as I stopped halfway through the stack.

"Tony Donatello? We aren't going to give him *any* money?" I looked up at Tanner.

"Tony," he said, lingering on the name. "Yes, that's correct."

I opened his file and glanced through the sheets inside. "But his coursework has been extremely good—"

"*Progress*, Lydia. *Progress*. You must keep in mind that grades alone aren't enough."

"But he *is* making progress," I said.

"Oh?" Tanner tapped the eraser end of the pencil against the desk top. "I don't quite see the evidence of that. On the contrary, I understand that he's failed to find anyone on the faculty who will consent to direct his doctoral thesis. In and of itself that raises many questions, about his character as well as his scholarly abilities."

I felt a rush of hot blood. "That's not true," I said. "He has a first reader. Me."

"Really?" The eraser stopped tapping as I saw the blue eyes gleam. "*You're* directing his dissertation?"

I nodded.

"I see." The small smile was gone. "Well, that really doesn't change the situation." He reached over and took the folders out of my grip.

I watched as he neatened the stack and arranged them as they were before. Beside me Danny sat very still, clutching the armrests.

Beware the whale.

"Why not?" The words sounded far away, though they came from my very own lips. "If Tony has someone to work with, shouldn't that make a difference?"

He paused and his glance narrowed, drawing a new bead.

"No, not in this case," he said. "I happen to know that Tony has applied for outside money, grants from private foundations. If he gets one, he won't need help from the department."

"But I'll bet any number of students in that first stack there have also applied for outside money," I said, gesturing toward the pile designated for financial support. "All the good students try for grants."

"In this instance," Tanner said, "I'm relying on my own judgment."

The daggers were drawn now, out in full view.

"I just wish you'd reconsider, that's all," I said, my voice weakening.

His lips tightened. "I may be reconsidering many things," he said.

It was then I knew. I'd crossed the line, gone over the edge. Tanner was going to swallow me whole.

The meeting was over. I walked out of his office shaking. Danny took off down the hall practically running. In no time at all everyone would hear the news: Lydia Martin, minnow extraordinaire, had just served herself up on a platter.

Sushi, anyone?

W hen I arrived that night at Felix's party, my colleagues greeted me with something approaching surprise. I guess they assumed I'd rather stay home to lick my wounds than parade them in public. They were right. I *would* have preferred to stay home, but then the only way to prevent everyone from talking about me was to show up. So I did.

Felix and Gwen lived in an old Federalist house in the historic downtown district. It had big boxy rooms with lots of lintels and wainscoting. That evening the living room was full of assistant professors, many from other departments. They had gathered together, ready and eager to celebrate even this smallest rite of passage. It was an excessive display, really, and out of kilter with the order of things, since renewal was only a prelude to the greater battle to come.

Danny, the minnow-of-honor, stood by the fireplace, talking to Karl. I caught his eye and waved. He waved back, and then went on talking to Karl. Clearly he didn't want his fun spoiled with any rehashing of the day's events.

And why should he? I asked myself. Why shouldn't he keep a healthy distance, metaphorical and otherwise? In that meeting of the Financial Aid Committee he had glimpsed as well as I the fate that awaited me. It didn't matter that I'd written *Bringing in the*

Green. It didn't matter that I was hard at work on another project. When tenure time arrived, those things would count only if they were allowed to count. One might just as easily choose to dwell on the intangibles instead, with questions about the quality of my scholarship and my likelihood to contribute to the discipline—not to mention my collegiality and service to the department. And the department would rely heavily, as it always had, on the senior scholar in the field to make that assessment.

No, there was no doubt that, come Judgment Day, it would be Tanner who would hold me in the balance.

And find me not quite weighty enough.

Victor and Felix came up to form a circle around Danny. Gwen brought him a glass of wine and gave him a hug.

"We're so happy for you," she said.

"Thanks," he said. "It's great to have this part over with."

"I remember what a relief it was when Felix got through," she said, a warm smile crossing her broad face. "Remember, honey?"

"Oh, God," Julia groaned from a nearby couch. Then she tilted her head to down what was left of her wine, her hair falling away in a black cascade.

"Don't mind her," Victor said to Gwen. He adjusted his glasses. "She doesn't like to think about my renewal because for once I proved her predictions wrong."

"Excuse me," she said, and rose, empty glass in hand. She paused, leaning against the sofa's back to steady herself. "Care to make a prediction about where I'm going?" she said to Victor, wagging the glass at him.

"That's too easy," he said to her. "Why don't you ask me something hard, like why you enjoy embarrassing me in front of my friends?"

She let her glance swing across the group and then burst out with a laugh.

All at once Karl took a step and turned to address the room. "Hey, listen up!" he said in a loud voice. "Everybody get a refill. I want to make a toast."

"Wait, wait!" Pam said as she emerged from the kitchen carrying a platter of hors d'oeuvres. "I have to get my wine."

"What about you, Lydia?" Felix said. "Something to drink?"

"Just a beer, if you have one."

In another minute everyone raised a glass in salute to Danny.

"Here's to the first guy to advance under the new rules," Karl said.

"Thanks," Danny said, and everyone drank. He turned to Victor. "And here's to the next guy to get tenure under them, too," he said. "Bet you can't wait to move up to the major leagues where the big boys play." He raised his glass, and then caught himself in time to swing it in my direction. "And you, too, Lydia."

Again the glasses went up, this time amid an embarrassed exchange of glances. Oh, yes—you, too, Lydia, the silent looks said. *Sure.*

Toasts over, the conversation settled back into pockets. I wandered to the picture window. Outside, a three-quarter moon was on the rise.

"Pretty, isn't it?"

I turned. Emily was sitting in a chair back in the corner, all alone.

"My goodness, I haven't seen you in ages," I said. "How are you?"

"Fine." She held a glass of orange juice. "Actually, I'm feeling a little tired."

She *looked* tired. Her face was paper white.

"Are you all right?" I asked.

"Yes. Just tired, that's all." She sipped her juice and then looked up at me. "How's your life these days?"

"Busy," I said, which was as close as I could come to saying "disastrous" without making a full confession. Hadn't Karl told her the latest?

She gazed back at the moon. "Seems so far away, doesn't it? Another world."

"Emily, how about something to eat?" She looked almost ethereal, like a white shadow with a puff of red hair. "Some crackers and cheese?"

"Hi!" Pam said, joining us. "Emily, how was Boston?"

"It was fine," she said, still looking at the moon.

"Hey, have you decided anything about Strasbourg?" she asked. "Do you know if you're going yet?"

Emily blinked and looked down at her glass. Then she rose. "Excuse me," she said, and walked toward the crowd.

Pam looked at me. "Did I say something wrong?" she asked. I shrugged.

"Listen, everybody!" Emily said, holding up her orange juice. "Everybody, I have an announcement to make!"

The voices in the room died.

"Shhhh—listen up!" someone called out.

She looked at Karl and lowered the glass. "I have an announcement to make," she repeated. Then her voice faltered. "I'm— I'm pregnant."

Everyone gazed from her to Karl. A few murmurs went up of How wonderful! That's great!, and then were cut off, seeing the expression on Karl's face.

There was no mistaking his horror.

For a moment no one moved. Then Julia did an odd thing. She set down her glass and walked over to Karl. She stood a hair's breath away, staring right into his eyes. Then she spoke.

"Bastard!" she said. "You goddamn liar!"

With the flat of her hand she smacked him hard across the face. Then she pushed her way to the hall, wrenched her coat off its hanger in the closet, and walked out without even bothering to put it on.

Karl covered his cheek. Already you could see a dark red mark forming.

Emily frowned. "Karl . . . ?"

He didn't answer. He went to the couch, sat down, and put his head in his hands.

Victor stood over him, blinking so hard he couldn't see.

"*You*," he said.

Karl didn't even look up.

Victor turned and strode out, too, leaving the door wide open behind him.

A cold, cold chill swept in.

There was a pause, completely still and quiet, and then all at once people went searching for their coats and scarves.

I hurried forward.

"Emily?" I said. She still stared at Karl. "Emily, do you want me to take you home?"

She shook her head.

Pam came up. She had my coat. Hers was already on.

I left, following the others as they rushed down the walk-way to their cars. When I got to my Civic, I slid in and started the engine. It needed a moment to warm up. When I finally pulled away, my lights picked out Emily and Karl making their way down the walk. They went step by step, not hurrying anywhere.

When Monday rolled around, the talk in Russell Hall was not of me but of Julia and Karl. I suppose I should have been happy that their affair had displaced me from the departmental spotlight. I should even have been titillated myself, given that I was not immune to tabloid-esque fascination with the mess others make of their lives. But in truth I was none of those things. In this particular drama the players were too close and the damage too clear for me to feel anything but sorry.

Walking back from class that morning, I didn't see any sign of Karl or Victor. What's going to happen now? I wondered. What about Strasbourg, the baby, Victor and Julia's kids?

For a moment I'd forgotten about my own situation—at least until I collected my mail. In my slot was another memo from Tanner. It stated that the work of the Financial Aid Committee was complete, and that letters had gone out to the graduate students indicating the level of financial support they would receive.

The memo closed with: "The amounts reflect the decisions of the committee taken on January 22."

I crumpled the sheet of paper in my hands and threw it in the trash.

Then I stepped into the graduate student lounge and put out the word that I wanted to see Meredith and Tony as soon as possible. I left notes in their mailboxes and then, when I got back to my office, sent them E-mail messages.

Tony found me less than a half an hour later. I sat him down and closed the door.

"Professor Martin?" he said, taking in my expression. "Is something wrong?"

Within five minutes of learning he would receive no support the next year, he was up and out, striding down the corridor. I picked up the phone and called Roberta.

"Tony Donatello's on his way to see Professor Shepherd," I told her. "Please try and stall him until I get there."

"Will do," she said.

Then I hurried after him.

By the time I reached the office, however, it was too late. Tom Shepherd's door was open, and Tony stood just inside.

"But you aren't *listening!*" he yelled. "Tanner wants me out of the program because I'm on to him. I know what he is! He's a liar and a thief! He stole my paper and now he wants to run me out!"

"I'm going to ask you just *one more time* to leave, Mr. Donatello," came Shepherd's voice. "Go somewhere and cool off. And then make your appeal through the usual channels."

"But it's so goddamn obvious what he's doing!" Tony shouted. "You can't let him get away with it! You've *got* to believe me!"

"I don't have to do anything," Shepherd said. "Now you've taken up enough of my time. LEAVE."

Tony stood there, breathing hard. Then he jabbed a finger in the air. "You're all the same, all of you! You don't care about anyone but yourselves!"

Then he turned on his heel and ran out of the office.

"Tony!" I called. I caught the door to the hallway before it slammed and looked up and down the corridor. Among the streaming crowds he was nowhere to be seen.

"What was all *that* about?" It was Quincy Burnbeck. He and Hamilton Farrell were in the office picking up their mail.

Hamilton shrugged. "Don't ask me." He paused. "Well, would you look at this. I've received another invitation to speak at the Kennedy School."

I stepped out and let the current of jostling students carry me back down the hall.

It was late afternoon when Meredith finally arrived at my door.

"Hi," she said. "I heard about Tony."

"Come on in and let's talk," I said.

She was bundled up in a ski jacket and scarf, and her large glasses were slightly fogged. When she sat down she pressed her hands together hard.

I moved my chair so that there wasn't a desk between us.

"Meredith, you won't be able to retake your oral exam until the end of the semester. Professor Tanner insists you need the time to prepare."

One of her jaw muscles flinched. I went on.

"In a day or two you'll receive a letter from the department. It will say that your financial aid status is undetermined at this time. Whether or not you get support next year will depend on how well you do on the exam."

Behind the glasses her eyes widened.

"This is absolutely ridiculous," she said in a low voice. "I have the best record of anyone in the program."

I leaned forward and covered her hands with my own. Hers felt icy cold. "Listen, I know this is unfair—"

She snatched her hands away and stood up. "I can't believe it! I've gotten an A in every one of my classes. I've *always* gotten the maximum level of support, and now you're telling me my status is *undetermined?*"

"Meredith—"

"No!" she said loudly. "This just isn't right! I'm telling you, it isn't right!"

"I know," I said.

"Then *do* something about it!" she said. "Tell them!"

I rose. "Meredith, there's nothing I *can* do."

She started to say something and then stopped, choked with frustration. Then she walked out.

I didn't even try to call her back. Instead I gathered my things to go home.

It was enough for one day.

The week rolled inexorably on. I waited to see what other lives it would crush and flatten, but Tuesday and Wednesday went by without incident.

Then came Thursday—the day of the debate.

Flyers announcing the event were everywhere on campus. In big letters they read:

WHOSE LIFE IS IT, ANYWAY?
A Debate On The Use Of Animals In Medical Research

That evening at a quarter to eight I followed the signs to one of the larger auditoriums at the medical school. I was surprised when I arrived to find a throng at the door.

"Excuse me," I said, pushing through. "Excuse me."

I wormed my way to the top of the aisle and had to stop a moment to take in the scene. The place looked more like a concert hall than a classroom, with its rows and rows of fixed seats rising away from the lecture stage at a steep pitch. And it was packed. Sprinkled among the students in the audience was a heavy concentration of doctors as well as other professorial types of the non-medical breed.

"Professor Martin! Professor Martin!"

Way down in the front I caught sight of Amy. She had an arm up, waving at me. Beside her was an empty chair with a coat thrown over it.

I started down the steps, picking my way among the students who had staked out seats there. Below, the local TV station was busy setting up the lights on stage. A blonde woman in a dark blue suit crossed back and forth in front of the camera and gave directions. I stopped to take a good look.

Not Kathy.

"Finally!" Amy said, pulling her coat off the seat. "I was starting to get worried. You wouldn't believe the people I've fought off to save this place."

"Thanks," I said, settling in. Everyone in the first two rows wore huge buttons that read: VIVISECTIONIST = MURDERER. "You must have come awfully early to get all these seats."

"We were here when the doors opened. Look, there's Hathor helping the TV people. She told me she was bound and determined they weren't going to screw up the shot."

As I watched, Hathor ripped off a piece of duct tape and used it to plaster a cable to the floor. Her hair was pulled back in a thick braid, the way it had been when I first saw her. Automatically I uncrossed my legs and tucked my leather pumps out of sight beneath the seat.

"Where's Kathy?" I asked, looking around. "I thought she'd be the one covering this."

"Don't know," Amy said. "Hey, isn't the turnout great?"

"She should be here." I twisted around to scan the noisy crowd behind us. Actually, I was really hoping to spot Charlie— would he smile or look away?—but I couldn't find him, either.

Instead, a different yet equally familiar face sprang out at me, just a few rows back. Having seen me first, Tom Shepherd was ready. He gave me a slow nod, and kept his expression grave. I swallowed and nodded back. To his left sat Dean Munsey, the final executor of my fate.

I faced forward and sat up straight. Still, I could feel them at my back. They had come in support of Fairchild, their beleaguered colleague. And they had found me with pride of place in the cheerleading section for animal rights.

That's it, I thought. Game over.

"Look!" Amy said. "Here they come."

David Fairchild strode out from one side of the stage, and a tall middle-aged man came from the other. They took up positions in front of separate podiums. Then a young woman crossed over to the lectern that stood between them.

At once the loud murmuring in the hall quieted.

"Who's the moderator?" I whispered to Amy.

"Someone from the University Speaker's Committee," she said.

As the woman leaned forward into her microphone, the TV camera's small red light blinked on.

"On behalf of the Speaker's Committee at Patrick Henry University, I'd like to welcome all of you to the third program in our series on Dilemmas at Century's End. Certainly the subject before us this evening poses challenging questions for the future: Is the accordance of rights to animals the next logical step in the evolution of human ethics? Or is the animal rights movement a misguided cause whose ultimate effect will be to sabotage human progress?

"Tonight we address these questions through a debate over the use of animals in medical research. We are fortunate to have with us two eminent speakers in the field. On my right is Doctor David Fairchild of Patrick Henry University, a renowned cardiologist who has done extensive laboratory research in the development of new drugs."

A solid round of applause went up. Doctor Fairchild rested his hands on the podium and smiled. I hadn't seen him but that one time in the emergency room, and I realized my memory had not been true to life. His white hair still posed a striking contrast to his youthful physique, but he was shorter than I recalled, and of a slighter build.

The woman waited for the noise to die down before she went on. "To my left is Doctor William Howe, spokesperson for the organization Humanity For Animals and currently on the staff of the Dolores Wilfred Foundation, which funds research into alternative methods of medical research."

There was more clapping—loudly from the front rows and more evenly distributed from the rest of the audience. Dr. Howe gave only the briefest acknowledgment and then took a folded paper from his breast pocket. His microphone picked up and amplified the crackle as he smoothed it open on the podium's tilted surface.

"The rules of the debate are as follows," the woman said. "Doctor Fairchild will speak for fifteen minutes, and then Doctor Howe will speak for fifteen minutes. They will then take your questions, which you may pose to either or both speakers. Doctor Fairchild will go first. Doctor Fairchild?"

"Thank you," he said. At once a young man in blue jeans from the TV crew leapt up to adjust his microphone. "And thank *you!*" Fairchild said to him. Laughter rippled through the hall.

Amy checked her watch against the clock on the wall.

Fairchild began. "I'm pleased to be here tonight to talk with you about a matter that is, I think, of enormous concern to us all." He spoke in a deep, calm voice—just the sort you like to hear over the intercom during a bumpy airplane ride. "Throughout history there have been numerous challenges to science. The attacks have been mustered mostly under the banner of religion, and have sought to subordinate empirical knowledge to doctrines born of fear and superstition. But we have come a long way. No scientist today is forced, as Galileo was, to recant that the earth goes 'round the sun. Indeed, in modern times there is no inherent contradiction in being a religious scientist. Yet even as belief and reason have joined together, there has arisen a new threat to progress, one just as pernicious as the challenges of old. It is called the animal rights movement."

He stopped for a moment and shifted his weight.

"In this century, more than any other, we've reaped the fruit of medical progress. Life expectancy in the United States has increased from forty-seven years in nineteen hundred to seventy-five today. Diseases such as typhoid, tuberculosis, whooping cough, scarlet fever, and diphtheria no longer ravage our children. Vaccines, developed first in animals, are largely responsible for these victories. The advances we've made in the war on other illnesses, such as diabetes, AIDS, and cancer, have all come through animal experimentation, and our eventual success depends on continuing this research.

"Yet the animal rights movement ignores these facts. Instead, it makes simplistic appeals to our compassion and sympathy. It decries the suffering of helpless creatures at the hands of evil scientists. It places before us photographs of laboratory procedures and says we have no right to harm other beings for our own sake. It says we are all equal: the ant, the elephant, the child. When human beings tyrannize their weaker brethren, it says, we sin."

He paused and let his gaze wander over the crowd. There were a few coughs, but otherwise the hall was silent.

"Yes, sin. It's an old-fashioned word for what is presented as such a new-fashioned wrong. But don't let the proponents of animal rights fool you. This movement is nothing more than a throwback to old-time religion, *real* old time, when people knocked on wood to appease the tree-dwelling spirits and worshipped God in the shape of a cat or a pig."

I thought of Mother and scanned the nearby rows for Hathor, but didn't see her.

"In advocating rights for animals, these people are not asking that we give other creatures the respect and kindness that is their due *as animals*. Instead, the people in this movement wish to bestow upon beasts the equivalent of *human* rights. They anthropomorphize animals, attributing to them human feelings and personalities. They put animals on the same moral level as humans; in some cases, even above.

"But I tell you we are *not* the same as rats and dogs. We are not even the same as apes, our closest animal relative. There is an unbreachable qualitative difference between humanity and the animal kingdom, and to deny it is to allow sentiment to fly in the face of reality. It is we who construct moral codes, not the beasts, and it is we alone who are bound by them."

He stopped and looked down for a moment, furrowing his brow.

"In my laboratory I test drugs on animals, preliminary to their use in humans. It is an absolutely essential step. I derive no pleasure from using animals in this way, and I do everything possible to minimize their pain and discomfort. I defend my use of them in these trials because, though I deem a dog's life to be valuable, I consider it to be less valuable than human life.

"Now, those in the animal rights movement wish to put a stop to further progress in medicine. They say nothing can justify the profession's exploitation of animals. But I will wager that there isn't a single parent in this room who would not sacrifice a white rat, if it would save the life of his or her child.

"I believe our moral code directs us to treat animals with respect. I do not, however, believe that animals have rights. Human beings are the only ones with rights, given that we are the only species for whom ethical conduct has any meaning. It is just one of the many unique characteristics that sets us above and apart from the elephant and the ant."

Again he paused. His glance swept the room.

"In your lives, I'm sure each of you strives in your own way to serve others to the best of your ability. For me, as a physician, I have chosen to pursue scientific research for the sake of human welfare. The use of laboratory animals is a necessary part of this research, and I believe its practice should be honored, not condemned. I thank you all very much," he said, and took a step back.

Sudden applause boomed through the lecture hall and remained steady for a good minute.

Well spoken, I thought, and glanced at Amy. She didn't clap. She didn't even look at Fairchild. Again she checked her watch against the clock over the stage.

"Thank you, Doctor Fairchild," the young woman said when the noise tapered off. She turned to the other podium. "Doctor Howe?"

Dr. Howe had listened to Fairchild with his weight balanced back on his heels and his hands in his pockets. Now he leaned forward and perched an elbow on the lectern's edge, as if he were about to have a confidential chat.

"Well, well, well," he said, and smiled, showing deep creases in his long narrow cheeks. "To hear this good doctor tell it, there's precious little we humans have in common with the animals. Yet he admits to making free use of them in his laboratory as our surrogates—stand-ins, if you will, for the likes of you and me. Doesn't that make you wonder, even a little bit?"

There was a titter. He tilted his head slightly and looked out over the crowd.

"Alas, some of you in the medical community do not wonder. You're beyond that sort of thing. You've been trained, not only in how to conduct your operations and examinations, but also in how to think. And all your training tells you that animal experimentation is necessary to good science.

"But I'm here tonight to tell you that it is quite the opposite. It is, in fact, *bad* science"—he rapped his knuckles on the podium for emphasis—"and the evidence is there for all to see."

From the front rows came brief but enthusiastic clapping.

He straightened. "Let's examine a few assumptions. First, the improvement in life expectancy in this country has not been due to animal research, contrary to what has been stated here tonight. We owe that debt to advances in nutrition, hygiene, sanitation, and better working conditions. For example, by the time an effective drug treatment for TB was introduced in this country in 1947, the number of deaths had already dropped to one sixth of what it had been at the turn of the century. And in Britain, the records show that almost ninety percent of childhood diseases had been eradicated *before* the distribution of antibiotics and vaccines.

"Second, progress in the battle against the major modern killers—heart disease, cancer, and stroke—depends not on animal experimentation but on preventative measures. A report by the U.S. Centers for Disease Control states that lifestyle and environment are responsible for seventy percent of early deaths. This means that if we would stop smoking, eat sensibly, engage in moderate exercise, and curb excessive drinking, we would do more to wipe out the diseases killing us today than any other medical breakthrough."

He turned to a new page of his notes and stopped for a moment to study it.

"I'd like now to make a third point. Earlier I said it was odd that Doctor Fairchild used animals as human surrogates while at the same time emphasizing the differences between us and them. Quite a few of you chuckled at my remark, no doubt because you thought I'd confused physical similarities with ontological differences. But I tell you it is the Doctor Fairchilds of this world who have confused the issue, seeing differences where there are similarities, and similarities where none can be said to exist."

Dr. Fairchild shared with the audience a knowing smile and shake of his head.

Dr. Howe continued. "The Anti-Vivisection Society estimates that upwards of fifty million animals a year are used in experiments by businesses, universities, and federal institutions. That's a lot. But it has yet to be proven that data from animal testing is any more accurate at predicting how a drug will act in humans than a flip of a coin. The differences that exist from species to species are simply too great to allow for reliance on animal models."

He gestured with an open hand. "For instance, aspirin is helpful to humans, toxic to cats, and has no effect on horses. Mice and dogs don't need vitamin C, but guinea pigs and humans do. However, penicillin is poisonous to these same guinea pigs and lifesaving to us. Time and again certain drugs have passed animal trials only to prove harmful to humans—as was the case with thalidomide. And other therapies that were almost discarded because of their effects on other species have turned out to be beneficial to our own.

"In fact, the only research methods that yield results that are relevant to people are those that rely, in some fashion, *on people*. I'm speaking here of work with human tissue *in vitro*—whether from living volunteers, biopsies, or from autopsies—as well as general population studies."

He gazed up to the farthest rows and then focused on those of us in front. The TV lights cast several shadows behind him.

"So much for the supposed similarities between ourselves and the beasts, to use Doctor Fairchild's term. Now what about the supposed differences?"

Again he leaned on the podium.

"In her introduction the moderator asked whether the recognition of animal rights was the next logical step in the evolution of human ethics. I say it is not only logical, but inevitable. We measure our spiritual and intellectual development by how well we have confronted and overcome prejudice. We judge as enlightened a person who is free of sexism, racism, or religious discrimination. Such a person looks upon the world with a vision unclouded by any sense of his or her inherent superiority."

He put his lips right up to the microphone and said in a low voice, "So should it also be when we judge our place among the animals."

He paused, and then went on. "We as a species are unique; this is true. But it is also true that every other species is also unique." He glanced over at Fairchild and then back to the audience. "Even, my friends, the elephant and the ant. Oh, we humans have certain undeniable advantages—this is true, too—that make us the most powerful of all animals. But does the possession of that power grant us the right to enslave other creatures, to torture and mutilate them for our curiosity, or to cage them for our entertainment? The moral foundation of civilized law has been the belief that it is necessary and right to protect the weak from the strong. It is only our prejudice that prevents us from identifying the plight of the animals with that of the weakest among ourselves."

He shook his head. "Doctor Fairchild said that I would claim he is guilty of sin. This is not so. He is guilty of ignorance. He is blind, and it is his education that has blinkered him. But this does not have to be. If we open ourselves to the truth, we will see: All animals have the same moral rights."

He pushed his weight from the podium and stood at his full height. "Leonardo Da Vinci, one of the greatest scientists who ever lived, once said, 'The time will come when men such as I will look upon the murder of animals as they now look upon the murder of human beings.' Perhaps with the help of those of you here tonight, that time will be now."

Another vigorous round of applause burst forth. I shot a peek over my shoulder. Shepherd and Munsey sat with their arms crossed. I quickly turned back around.

Amy was one of the last to stop clapping.

"Thank you," the moderator said, nodding to each of the speakers. "Now we'll open the discussion to the audience. Who would like to ask the first question?"

A dozen hands went up.

"Go ahead," the moderator said to a student in the third row. "And please stand, if you would."

"Hold it! Stop!" A young man stepped quickly down the aisle, waving an arm. "Doctor Fairchild, Doctor Fairchild!"

"Excuse me!" the moderator said loudly. "You'll have to wait your turn!"

"That's one of my assistants," Dr. Fairchild told her, and hurried to the edge of the stage. "What is it, John?"

"Something terrible's happened!" he cried, and pulled up before him, breathing heavily. "It's the lab. Doctor Fairchild, all the dogs are missing!"

"All of them? *All* of them? Who was supposed to be covering tonight?"

John took a gulp of air. "Charlie," he said. "Charlie Whittier." He trembled violently as he held up a piece of paper. "He wrote you this note."

Dr. Fairchild gripped it with both hands as he read. When he looked up, two red spots had formed above his cheekbones.

"If I find out you've had a part in this," he said to Dr. Howe, "I'll have you arrested. This is eco-terrorism."

Dr. Howe frowned. "Sir, I have no idea what you're talking about."

The television camera swivelled to catch Fairchild as he strode out of the hall. A wave of loud murmuring rose up in his wake.

My thoughts skipped to a rapid surmise. It should have been Kathy with the television crew, but it wasn't. Hathor had disappeared as soon as the debate began. And Charlie had never showed.

I turned to Amy. She sat back, her eyes off the clock, and smiled a little smile all to herself.

25

made it home with only a minute to spare before the local ten o'clock news. When I switched on the TV the last strains of the dramatic theme music were just dying away. Then there was the young anchorwoman sitting behind her desk, clutching her newscopy.

"We have a breaking story over at Patrick Henry University Hospital," she announced, staring wide-eyed into the camera. "We're going live with an exclusive report from Channel Three ActionNews reporter Lynn Grady. Lynn?"

The blonde woman in blue who had been at the debate appeared, filling the screen. She was standing outside with the brightly lit hospital as a backdrop.

"Megan, the scene at Patrick Henry University Hospital tonight is one of confusion and anger," she said, her breath white in the freezing air. "While a debate over animal rights drew a standing-room-only crowd at the medical school, someone broke into the research wing of the hospital and took a group of laboratory dogs. The staff here is simply reeling from the shock. I just spoke to one of the physicians involved with a project in this lab, and he said, 'A lot of research and hard work vanished with those dogs. Whoever did this should be punished to the fullest extent of the law.' When I asked one of the members of the audience for a reaction, however, I received this response." She read from her notepad. "'It was an act of liberation, the first step towards abolishing barbarism in the name of science.'"

The picture switched to the anchorwoman. "Thank you, Lynn. We'll be getting back to you later in the broadcast." She shifted to face a different camera from another angle. "Shortly after nine o'clock a videotape was delivered to this station, purportedly made by the persons who claim to be responsible for the break-in. We are now going to play the tape in full, and it will run for several minutes. Here it is, a Channel Three exclusive on this rapidly unfolding story."

She stared down at her monitor and waited. After a pause she disappeared and there was Charlie, brushing back his lock of hair.

"My name is Charles Whittier," he said, "and I'm a medical student at Patrick Henry University. I'm speaking to you from inside Doctor David Fairchild's research lab at the university hospital. When I leave here tonight I'm taking the lab dogs with me to a place where no one will ever find them, and I'm making this tape to explain why. A lot of people will be giving their own reasons for what I've done. I want to make sure anyone who cares to listen can hear mine.

"First, for those of you who've never seen the inside of a dog lab, let me show you around." He stepped back and the camera followed him. "This is one of our operating tables," he said. "See these metal clasps here? They bind the dogs' legs. And these belts keep their torsos strapped in. Not that the dogs ever struggle, really. They're always under some kind of anesthesia during the procedures."

He unrolled a long narrow strip of graph paper and smoothed it flat on the table. There was a closeup of parallel black spiky lines running the length of the page.

"See this? This is an EKG reading of Silver's heartbeat. She's one of our greyhounds—a retired racer. Right through this part Silver's pulse scoots along just fine, until we get to here." And his finger pointed to a sharp dropoff. "This is where we stopped the heart. See how the line stays flat? Okay. Nothing, nothing, nothing, and then zap! We jumpstart the heart and the pulse picks up again—a little ragged from muscle damage, but a pulse nonetheless." Charlie looked up. "From this point on, Silver's the perfect canine model, ready for drugs, a pacemaker, more surgery—anything."

He rolled the graph paper back up and then leaned against the table.

"Only, Silver's days as a lab dog are over. She's about to start a new life in a home where she'll be loved and cared for, just as she deserves to be. Let me tell you why.

"Tomorrow Silver was due to begin testing a new heart drug. The only problem is that the drug isn't really new. It's a medication that's already been proven safe for humans, but now a different drug company wants to market it under its own label. When I asked Doctor Fairchild why we were repeating this trial— and needlessly sacrificing the lives of these dogs—he told me that it happens all the time. The testing of already proven drugs is simply business as usual."

He looked down for a moment, and then back. "Why did Doctor Fairchild want to do the testing? Maybe because he has a longstanding relationship with this pharmaceutical company—it's been the source of a lot of research money for the lab. I might add that it also sends a number of the cardiologists in the department to conferences all over the world each year. Doctor Fairchild, for instance, just came back from an all-expense-paid trip to Stockholm."

"Charlie, remember, we haven't got much time."

I sat up. It was Kathy's voice, from off-camera. She was the person filming.

"We still have Silver to worry about," she said.

"Okay," he said, and pushed off from the table. "Let's see if she's ready yet." He walked to a line of cages against the far wall. They were all empty save one. In it was a sleek silverhaired greyhound. Close up, you could see quivers rippling across her flanks as she cowered against the back of the cage. Her chest was shaved. Down the pink flesh ran a long incision, crisscrossed with stitches.

The wire door to her cage was wide open.

"It's all right, Silver. Take it easy, girl," Charlie said, and held out a hand to her. She tried to move back even farther. The tip of her long thin tongue hung out the side of her mouth as she panted. Her eyes were so wide, they were ringed with white.

"I'm not going to hurt you. Not this time. Don't you want to come with us? The other dogs are out there, waiting for you."

Still she crouched.

He withdrew his hand and straightened. "I don't know, Kath. We're going to have to give her a couple more minutes, I think."

"Okay, but we really can't stay here much longer."

Charlie stuck his hands in his pockets and looked back into the camera.

"Anyway, that's why I'm taking the dogs—because of business as usual. A guy named Walter Kravitz once wrote, 'When tyrants speak, they make believe. When truth speaks, it makes belief.' Well, Doctor Fairchild and doctors like him want us all to think that they are the only ones who can decide when it's appropriate to take an animal's life. But doctors are just like everyone else. Their judgment isn't always clinical—not when they're competing for government grants or justifying university expenditures. The oversight boards, such as they are, aren't much help. They go along with business as usual, too. There has got to be more public access to the work of the labs. So I say, raise the curtain. Let the truth speak for itself."

He paused and took a deep breath. "Well, that's it, then. I know some people will think I threw away my medical degree for nothing, but they're wrong. I've discovered that if you just keep playing along to get along, eventually you lose the very thing you set out to win—your own place in the world. I'm not going to let that happen, not to me." He looked past the camera and said to Kathy, "Okay, that's it."

"I want to keep filming until we're out of here," she said.

"Okay," he said, and looked back at Silver. "Do you think we should just take her in her cage?"

"Let's try something else first." The camera swerved from Charlie to the dog. "Let's leave and see if she follows."

"Do you think that'll work?"

"It's the only thing left to do."

The TV screen blurred and then refocused.

"We'll wait right here," she said, and the camera turned back to pan the room. All at once there was a closeup shot of the cage and of a long grey nose sniffing at the opening. Then the whole dog came into view as slowly Silver got to her feet and crept forward.

"It's working!" Charlie said.

"Shhh! Here she comes."

Silver cleared the cage. For a moment she stood on the tile floor, shivering, her whip tail pressed between her legs.

"Here, girl," Charlie said softly. "Come on, Silver."

She hesitated and then stepped forward, head low. Again Charlie reached out to her—Kathy moved the camera so that his hand was all you could see. For a moment there was no sound save for the click of Silver's nails against the tile. Then there she was, her snout smack up against the lens. Slowly she turned to sniff Charlie's fingers. There was a pause before, very gently, she licked them.

The picture went to black.

The doorbell rang.

I got up to answer just as Megan reappeared at the anchordesk.

"The police have reason to believe that the person who assisted Mr. Whittier in making this tape may be Channel Three reporter Kathy Durban," she said. "At the moment the police are looking for her as a possible witness. If anyone among our viewers has any information about her whereabouts, or those of Charles Whittier, you are asked to contact the Albemarle Police Department immediately."

I opened the door to find two police officers, a man and a woman, complete with holstered guns and creaking leather jackets.

"Yes?" I said.

"Are you Lydia Martin?" the man asked.

"Yes, that's me."

"May we come in and speak with you for a moment?"

I held the door wide. "Sure." I gestured to the couch. "Have a seat."

They perched on the edge of the cushions. I turned off the TV and then sat down in a facing chair.

"What do you wish to talk to me about?" I asked.

"You were at the debate at the medical school tonight?" the woman asked.

I nodded.

"So you know about the missing dogs."

"Yes. I was in the audience when Doctor Fairchild's assistant rushed in with the news. Plus, there's just been a report on TV."

The man shifted his weight. "Professor Martin, we understand Charles Whittier is a friend of yours."

I paused. "May I ask who told you that?"

The woman said, "Doctor Fairchild mentioned it."

"I see," I said. "Well, yes, I know Charlie. I know Kathy Durban, too. I met them both during my research on the local Humanity For Animals group."

"Then do you have any idea where they might have gone with these animals?"

"No," I said. "I haven't the faintest notion."

The woman gave me a steady look. "Did you have any knowledge that they were going to take those dogs?"

"No," I said. "None whatsoever."

She looked at her partner and then they stood up.

"Well, thank you for your time, Professor Martin," the man said. "If you hear anything from either one of them, please let us know."

"All right," I said, and led them to the door. "Good night, officers."

They left. Outside I caught a glimpse of the police car as it pulled away.

Well, that was a first, I thought. I've just been questioned by the police. Won't Mom and Dad be proud.

Before I turned away there was a knock.

"Who now?" I muttered, and opened it.

"Frances!"

"Hello, Lydia," she said. Little wisps of her short gray hair stuck straight up. "I saw that police car—"

"Oh, there's nothing wrong," I said. "They just wanted to ask me about—somebody."

"Well, I must have fallen asleep. I've been sitting up, waiting for you."

"Look, you'd better come on in," I said. "You don't even have a coat on." And I closed the door behind her. "Did you say you were waiting for me?"

She nodded and held out a flat package. "This is for you. Charlie asked me to give it to you as soon as you got home."

"Charlie?" I took the package and held it for a moment. "When did he give this to you?"

"He came by around six."

"Charlie. Charlie Whittier gave you this package to give to me?"

"Yes. Lydia, are you all right?"

I realized I was still staring at the brown paper-wrapped object in my hands. I looked up. "Did Charlie say anything else?"

"No. Well, wait a minute. Yes. He said, Tell her it's hers to use in whatever way she wants." She yawned. "I hope you don't mind if I go home now. My bedtime was hours ago."

When she was gone, I carried the package to the couch and then tore it open. Out tumbled a spiral-ring notebook with a creased cardboard cover.

It was Charlie's diary.

I stayed up late into the night, reading on the couch. At some point I fell asleep, though not for long. When I opened my eyes the darkness had only just begun to fade. I put the journal aside and then walked to the window. Everything was very gray and still. I put on a warm coat and mittens and went outside.

I headed for the schoolyard at the end of the block, and crossed its broad playing field. The stars had gone. To the east, through the skeletal trees, the sky was tinged with pink. I took a seat on a bleacher and hunched against the cold.

The diary was a record of Charlie's life over the last year and a half. It began with his enrollment in medical school and covered his decision to drop out and then reenroll. It traced the course of an intense internal struggle. All the key elements for analysis were present and accounted for—motivation, ambivalence, satisfaction, and desire. You couldn't ask for a better portrait, or one more complete.

When I began reading, I had to force myself not to skip to the end. I knew what I should have been most interested in: the reason Charlie abandoned once and for all the straight and narrow for activism, and radical criminal activism to boot. But what I really wanted to discover was what had happened between us. Why had he abandoned *me*? I hoped the journal would offer some clue.

The pink had smeared itself across the horizon, and overhead long strips of clouds lightened. They didn't move.

In the end, you could say I got more than just a clue.

Charlie, it turned out, had indeed written a full account of our relationship, starting with our interview. He'd liked me, and thought my attraction to him was pretty obvious. So after he broke up with Kathy, he had a reasonable expectation that the two of us would hit it off well. After all, I understood his decision to reenroll in the medical program. I'd had to make a few compromises myself along the way. I was practical where Kathy was idealistic, and more flexible and pragmatic than she. He thought I set a good example of how one should deal with the world.

And then he got to know me.

All it took were those two days and a night. Well, there was the dinner party with Tom and Margaret, too, but by then he'd already made up his mind. It was the time we'd spent alone—our Christmas together—that convinced him.

It was funny, really. There I was, busy collecting his dots, when all along he was collecting mine. Only, when he completed the connections and glimpsed the picture I made, he drew back.

Recoiled, actually.

In fact, you'd have to say that the primary reason Charlie re-embraced activism, and Kathy, was me.

So there I was, not only *with* the diary but also *in* it. If I included Charlie in my study he'd be the centerpiece of the book, a showcase of activism seen in all its precious and astonishing details. My only problem was, there was no way to tell Charlie's story without also telling my own.

I pulled my coat closer. The sun was but a red wink on the horizon, and then more. I watched it rise, shivering.

One tear fell. Then another.

It was my call, my decision to make. And I didn't know what to do.

T he first phone call came that morning at about eight
o'clock.

"Professor Lydia Martin?" a man asked. "This is Ken
Shetterly with the *Albemarle Register*. I would like to talk to you
about the break-in at the university research lab last night. You're
an expert on animal rights groups, I've been told, and have actually been studying the people involved in this particular incident."

And so it began.

By the end of the day I'd been interviewed by the local
papers and radio stations, and had appeared in a two-minute spot
with Megan on Channel Three. A couple of the Richmond papers
had even called.

Then a fluke occurred. I call it a fluke because every day
things happen all over this country, word of which never travels
past its own backyard. But once in a while something catches—a
story breaks, gets picked up by the wires, and before you know it,
it's *national* news.

That's what happened with the dog lab break-in.

My phone kept ringing. On the other end were the *New
York Times*, the *Washington Post*, *Time*, *Newsweek*. CBS, NBC, ABC,
and CNN all sent reporters to interview me. Over and over again
the networks broadcast clips from Charlie and Kathy's video. People

just couldn't seem to get enough of the gentle wounded Silver and her renegade rescuers.

The frenzy lasted about a week before it finally died down. I was in my office when I got one last call. This time it was an editor from The Free Press on the line.

The Free Press is one of those rare publishers whose books have popular appeal as well as standing in the academic world. The editor had heard mention on the news of my work-in-progress, and she wondered if, when my case study was complete, The Free Press could have a look.

Of course! I said, and tried to keep total amazement out of my voice.

My fling as a media maven stood in sharp contrast to the lowly position I now occupied within the department. Shepherd spoke to me as little as possible, and then only in the most cold and formal tones. For his part, Tanner couldn't bring himself to utter a word to me at all. When we happened to pass in the hall he didn't bother to look away, but instead gave me his fishiest stare.

For the next few months I closed myself in my study at home, emerging only to teach my classes and scour the library shelves. Naps took the place of sleep, and even they were fitful. Whenever I closed my eyes I saw the trucker's equivalent of the white line: my computer screen. Stacks of transcripts piled up on my window sills, blocking out the light. Then came the first rough draft of text, then the second, then the third. When I'd revised for the fourth time I sensed the emergence of a distinct entity at last.

By the end of May I had a completed manuscript, an astonishing feat by any measure of speed. My haste was misleading, however. When I'd begun, another publication was supposed to be my life preserver. But now it was just as likely this particular book put me dead in the water. No, I rushed instead to meet my destiny because it was, at least, of my own making and choosing. What other minnow had ever been able to claim as much?

I sent it off to The Free Press and waited.

The editor called a week later. She was briskly business-like.

"I've already spoken with our editor-in-chief. We'd like to fast-track it."

"Fast-track it?" I asked.

"The book will be out by September," she said.

My advance copy of *Orphans of the Left* arrived at the end of August, just as the new academic year had begun. When I got the package I didn't even wait to return to my office, but stood right there by the department mailboxes and tore off the wrapping. The book's title was in big black letters against a pale gray background. And below it was my name.

Pam came through the door, and when she saw me she cried, "Oh, Lydia—let's see!" She took the book in her hands and held it at arm's length. "It looks wonderful. They did a great job with the colors. When can I read it?"

"You can have that one, if you want," I said.

"Thanks!" She hugged me. "I can't believe it happened so soon! Congratulations, Lydia. I'm going to go home and read this right now."

The next day she appeared in my office, the book in hand.

"Well?" I said from my desk. "Have a seat and tell me. What did you think?"

She didn't sit down. She looked at me without a trace of a smile.

"Lydia," she said quietly. "Did you really mean to write that? About what Charlie thought of you, I mean."

"Yes," I said.

"But, why?"

"Because it's true."

"But it's not." She frowned down at the book. "This isn't you. It isn't. You're a *good* person." She looked back at me. "You know, Tony Donatello called last week to tell me he had been awarded a fellowship from the Patrick Henry Foundation. And he said he owed it all to you."

I shrugged. "So I wrote him a letter of recommendation during that week I was all over the news. Big deal. Someone just finally paid him a little attention for a change."

"Thanks to you," Pam said. "And what about Meredith?"

"Oh, come on, Pam," I said, grimacing. "That was months ago, already. Stop."

"No, I will not stop. If you hadn't packed that exam with every assistant professor under the sun, Tanner would have pulled the same stunt again. I know it."

"Meredith handled herself beautifully," I said. "And she got her usual level of support, just as I knew she would. After all, she *was* prepared—for absolutely anything."

"But there were even assistants from the religion department, for God's sake," Pam said.

I laughed. "It was something, wasn't it? The look on Tanner's face when he walked in. . . . "

We both laughed.

Then she held out the book. "I was wondering. Would you autograph it for me?"

I took it, opened to the title page, and wrote: "To Pam, my best friend." And then I returned it.

"Oh!" she said, reading, and her eyes began to well.

"Pam, don't you dare!" I warned her. "Or I'm taking it back."

My book did not create the same sensation as the lab break-in. Its debut, however, did attract more notice than usual, probably because the epic of Silver, Kathy, and Charlie still got people talking. As a result, the reviews came out almost immediately, appearing not only in trade journals but in the Sunday book sections of the big papers as well.

When I read them I was relieved, and then excited. There were phrases like, "A truly original approach," "Martin's analysis shines," and (my favorite), "Hold on to your hats—this is one academic case study that is guaranteed to surprise you."

My phone started ringing again.

This time, though, I wasn't being asked to leap from one sound bite to another. People were inviting me to give a lecture or participate in a conference. They wanted me to talk about my work, and especially what they kept calling my "unique perspective."

"How did it feel," Brian Lamb asked me during the *Booknotes* interview on C-Span, "when you found *you* were the one who tipped the scales for Charles Whittier?"

It was the question everyone loved to ask.

In October I got a postcard with a picture of cows grazing in a field. On the back were the words: Mother thanks you.

I knew what it meant. The book had made no mention of her.

It was the only time I ever heard from Charlie.

At the end of the month, Victor learned he'd been approved by the department for tenure. Word was, however, that he'd limped through on a split vote, which meant the dean's committee would make the final decision. I felt sorry for him—he had another four-month wait, easy. But as he told everyone later, he didn't really have time to worry, not since Julia had given him full custody of the kids.

I don't know why the whales separated my case from Victor's. Usually everyone up for tenure was considered at the same time. Probably Shepherd hoped to heighten the tension, and prolong my suffering as long as possible.

The delay, it turned out, was a tactical mistake.

Two weeks later I received the announcement. *Orphans of the Left* had won the university's Phi Beta Kappa award for the best book of the year.

So here I am, standing in the hall outside my office door. Roberta just called to say the department has concluded its vote on my tenure, and that Tom Shepherd is on his way.

I told Pam no parties tonight, no matter what the decision. Instead we're going out to dinner—Pam, Emily, and me. Karl is staying home with the baby. And Tyler will have to settle for whatever treats he can wheedle from the doggy bag later.

Yes, there—I've spotted Shepherd now. He's turned the corner and is striding closer, big big smile, and hand outstretched, ready to greet me, one whale to another.

I suppose that's the difference between a whale and a minnow. One refuses to remember he was ever anything else, and the other is never allowed to forget.

I take his hand amid a profusion of congratulations, and then pause. Inside I feel a flutter.

Ah. I know what that is.

It's the minnow in me.